OF SORROWS

BY

STEPHANIE HUDSON

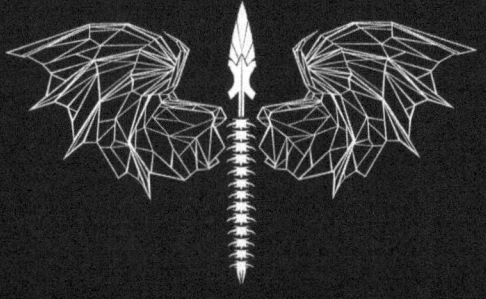

Map of Sorrows
The Transfusion Saga #5
Copyright © 2020 Stephanie Hudson
Published by Hudson Indie Ink
www.hudsonindieink.com

This book is licensed for your personal enjoyment only.
This book may not be re-sold or given away to other people. If you would like to share this book with another person, please purchase an additional copy for each recipient. If you're reading this book and did not purchase it, or it wasn't purchased for your use only, then please return to your favourite book retailer and purchase your own copy. Thank you for respecting the hard work of this author.
All rights reserved.
This is a work of fiction. Names, characters, places, brands, media, and incidents are either the product of the authors imagination or are used fictitiously. The author acknowledges the trademark status and trademark owners of various products referred to in this work of fiction, which have been used without permission. The publication/use of these trademarks is not authorised, associated with, or sponsored by the trademark owners.
Map of Sorrows/Stephanie Hudson – 2nd ed.
ISBN-13 - 978-1-913769-40-6

I would like to dedicate this book to all who are suffering in our world's time of crisis, through both hardships and times of loss. I would also like to thank all of those who are selflessly working hard to help others, whether this be working the front line in hospitals by way of doctors and nurses and all other hospital staff involved in trying to save lives. It is to the care givers, the truck drivers, the forces and other key workers that are all working tirelessly together in order to ensure our wellbeing during this pandemic. To those who are self-isolating and struggling with it, know that you are not alone and that together we stand as a symbol of the true beauty of humanity at its best.

We stay at home to save lives and because of that, you should be proud.
On a personal note, I would also like to thank and show my appreciation for our wonderful NHS and all its staff.

My heart is with you all during this time.

WARNING

This book contains explicit sexual content, some graphic language and a highly additive dominate Vampire King.

This book has been written by an UK Author with a mad sense of humour. Which means the following story contains a mixture of Northern English slang, dialect, regional colloquialisms and other quirky spellings that have been intentionally included to make the story and dialogue more realistic for modern day characters.

Thanks for reading x

PROLOGUE

CRASH BOOM BANG

"Seriously, what are the odds of twice in one fucking week!" I complained the second I heard the new song come over the car's expensive stereo making me tense my grip on the steering wheel as the words started to ring true just like the song had done before it…

My Papa told me to stay out of trouble,
"When you've found your man, make sure he's for real!".
I've learned that nothing really lasts forever
I sleep with the scars I wear that won't heal.
They won't heal
Cos every time I seem to fall in love
Crash! Boom! Bang!
I find the heart but then I hit the wall
Crash! Boom! Bang!
That's the call, that's the game and the pain stays the same.

"Thanks for nothing, Roxette!" I grumbled as I took yet

another road that led me even further away from what I had foolishly believed was my fate.

Well, now I knew.

Now I knew.

I knew, that just like that plane could have ended my life, it was in fact everything after it that was one big…

Crash, Boom Bang.

CHAPTER ONE

CRASH

"Seriously Pip, Crash Boom Bang by Roxette?" I asked the second she popped her head through the door, phone in hand with its speakers blaring.

"What, I thought it was appropriate for our current situation but wait, I've got another one that's perfectly nose divingly perfect..." she said pausing for a second before tapping her phone a few times and shouting,

"Eureka!" After which an upbeat tune filled the cockpit which I recognised as a song called 'Crash' by The Primitives and with lyrics like,

> *Here you go, way too fast*
> *Don't slow down, you gonna crash*
> *You should watch, watch your step*
> *Don't look out, gonna break your neck,*

I let my head fall back against the headrest, turned to Lucius and muttered,

"There is still time for me to crash this plane on purpose if you're still up for that vacation in Hell?"

"Keep hold of that thought until Abba is her next choice," Lucius muttered back making Pip squeal,

"Oh, good thinking, SOS coming right up!"

"I am blaming that one on you," I said before continuing in an effort to save us, and not plummeting to death this time,

"Aunty Pip, you know I adore you, but right now what I am about to say I say with all the love in the world…"

"Yeah, Petal pants?"

"Get your ass back in the cabin, buckle up and do me a favour, no more songs about crashing or calling for help… yeah?" I said before Lucius could say the same thing only including a threat, two fucks and a hammered fist into the console just for shits and giggles.

"Gotatcha, my girl whose momma is my beastie boob buddy!" she said before saluting me and then with another tap on her phone to the next song on her list, she left to the sound of 'Flying without wings' by Westlife. This made me shake my head before hitting myself with the flight plan.

"Did that help?" Lucius asked as my forehead was still against the clipboard.

"Why, do you want a go next?" I mumbled making him laugh.

"Well, she is still playing music, so the chances are high… no pun intended," was his funny reply.

"Yeah, but at least it's no longer got 'crash' in the title, so I will take it as if she now has confidence in my ability to fly and therefore, I am counting it as a win," I told him putting the flight plan back down and stretching out my arms to ward off the stiffness.

"Well, you did shoot another fucking pilot, so I guess you need at least one," Lucius replied making me stop mid-stretch and grant him a look that said it all, even if the growl that followed didn't.

"Yes, you've already mentioned that and like I said earlier, unless you wanted to see this bird crashed and in pieces amongst the streets of Stuttgart, then I believe I had no choice this time…oh, and you're welcome by the way," I said in a snippy tone that he clearly didn't take seriously, not if the chuckle that followed was anything to go by.

"Well, my 65 million dollar wallet certainly thanks you, but as for my heart, well then it thanks you more for keeping yourself safe and not the fucking plane that could crash and burn as long as you remain unharmed." This was such a sweet reply I couldn't help but give him a soft and warm look in return before telling him,

"You know, I think that statement is like opening a door for a girl on steroids and now renders all other chivalrous acts obsolete, as I doubt many could compete with the 65 million dollar price tag reference, seeing as I know you're good for it," I told him making him wink at me in return before saying,

"That may be the case but you can still expect me to open the door for you all the same." At this I blew a kiss at him in an over dramatic fashion making him give me his typical, 'My girlfriend is cute' look. It was sweet that he thought this, even after he had seen what I did to the pilot, not to mention the state the other two were in. Although, in my defense, there were no piano stool related injuries, strangulation with lamp cords or fatal pencil stab wounds to speak of.

However, this didn't stop Lucius commenting shortly after I had quickly regained control of the plane, annoyance most definitely being first on his list of emotions.

TEN HOURS EARLIER

"Fuck! Amelia, what did you do!?" Lucius shouted after I had shot the guy in the head. But then I had to give it to him, as seeing me with a gun in hand and an ice bucket on the now dead pilot's head was the last thing he would have expected to see. But then again, this was me we were talking about, so who knew what he expected to see when walking in here. So, I told him in a rush of words,

"I took care of a problem, now quick, get him out of the seat!" Lucius didn't wait for more of an explanation, not especially seeing as the plane was taking a steady nosedive in what was definitely the wrong direction. The second he grabbed him and started dragging him through the door I ignored the blood splatter and climbed in the dead man's place, quickly letting my flight training take over.

"Now get the other guy out of here and then take a seat!" I ordered the second he made it back.

"I can't believe you shot another fucking pilot!" he complained on a grunt as this time taking the less 'fresh' dead guy under the arms ready to drag him out of the seat. So, I looked back to the front window, took the controls and told him,

"Oh, don't worry…*This one, I know how to fly.*"

Lucius gave a me wide eyed look that had he been the type to panic, it would have been classed as getting close to that point. Instead, he did as I asked and got the guy out of the seat, dragging him to where he had dumped the pilot outside the cockpit somewhere.

"Holy shit! Well, that's one way to stop a bloody mess from getting on the controls!" Pip said as she watched the bloody ice bucket roll from the guy's head and back into the cockpit. All after first whistling through her missing tooth.

"Get your ass back there and strap in!" I said as the plane wasn't yet under control and we were still losing altitude.

"Jeez, the last pilot wasn't that bossy," Pip replied making me shoot her a look over my shoulder after she was forced to grab onto the two seats so she wouldn't fall forward.

"No, he wasn't, in fact for someone trying to kill us all, he was just a super swell guy really," I said as I reached up, flipping switches overhead before pulling on the throttle lever, controlling the flow rate of air to the cylinders, trying to slow our ass down so as not to rip the fucking plane apart!

"Point taken, I think I am gonna go sit my ass back down and strap in." I jerked my head to the side like you normally would when someone agreed with your plane sized good point and replied dryly,

"Good plan that, Pip."

After that Lucius came back inside the cockpit and asked in a strained tone,

"What can I do?!"

"Sit your ass down, Vampy, this is going to get a little Mary," I said pulling back on the yoke and straining against the controls as the big bitch fought back! Lucius climbed into the seat next to me and asked,

"Mary?"

"Hairy," I replied in a strained tone, making him mutter,

"Fuck."

"Yeah that too, now when I tell you, click all those switches down one after the other…"

"I am not sure I am…"

"Now!" I shouted ignoring him as the tiny objects on the Earth below us started to grow bigger far too quickly for my liking.

"What exactly are our chances here?" Lucius asked me, so I told him,

"Well, assuming we have enough space between us and the ground to pull up before we can make out livestock in fields, and also depending if we don't get into a catastrophic failure in the form of our wings or tail section tearing off the fuselage from the aerodynamic force…pretty good I think." Of course, my confidence in the 'pretty good' part of that statement would have been a lot better had the altitude indicator warning light shut up and stop screaming at me.

"Now grab the yoke and pull up with me!" I told him, making him frown,

"Yoke? What the fuck is a…"

"The control wheel, this thingy!" I said shaking my arms to indicate what I'd had a death grip on ever since shooting the fucking pilot!

"Oh right!" Lucius said pulling on the controls with me making me grit my teeth as I silently begged for the plane's nose to start lifting and finally level out.

"Now what?" he asked, and I laughed nervously before telling him,

"Well, I would say pray to the Gods to send down an army of golden ass Angels to pick this shit up like Superman, but something tells me they would be too busy to pick up the call." Lucius scoffed and said,

"Then I suggest we fuck that idea and instead I pray my girlfriend just saves the fucking day again."

"Hey, you just called me your girlfriend!" I shouted excitedly, grinning at him.

"I did and unless you want it to be the last time you ever hear it, then may I suggest we get back to more important shit, like flying the fucking plane!" he snapped making me smirk at him and say,

"Oh, but you say the most romantic things, Sweetie." His response was to groan in exasperation before telling me,

"Yeah, then remind me later to celebrate our survival by putting you over my knee, Sugar." I laughed and said,

"Well, after being in this seat for hours, then I will need it just to wake my ass up again."

"Then depending on the basis of our survival, I will class it as a win, win," he replied making me giggle. Then Lucius glanced down over his shoulder as the bloody ice bucket rolled towards his seat, even as we both continued to maneuver the plane back to the right altitude he still had to say,

"Well, I have to give it to you, Pet, you're certainly resourceful." In turn, I couldn't help but wink at him before replying,

"You bet your ass I am, Handsome, now strap in and watch just how resourceful I can get!" I said before going back to flying the plane and as a bonus, impressing the hell out of my boyfriend when finally the bloody plane started to play ball and level out.

Well, I thought I had impressed him but that was until he commented drily,

"I am not sure whether to be turned on or terrified at that statement."

My look said it all.

But even after I had safely taken back control of the plane and was finally able to engage the autopilot, Lucius' faith in me to do much more than not kill us all was obviously limited. I knew this when he started listing airports in Germany where I could land his expensive 65 million dollar toy.

This was when I informed him that I had no intention of landing it until we were in Portland International as we intended, something he obviously didn't agree with.

"Uh, didn't you hear the bit about my ass going numb. We are not landing in Frankfurt, Lucius, we are landing in Portland as planned, now flick that switch with the flashing light would you," I told him but seeing as he was still processing what I just said, the light continued to blink at me.

"Come again?" he finally said and seeing as I was getting impatient, I leaned across the centre where the throttle control was and flicked off the switch myself. Then I told him,

"Did Adam roar too loudly in your ear... I said we are landing in Portland."

"We are not," he stated as if he was the one running this show which considering I was the only one who knew how to fly this thing, he *so wasn't*. Which was why I folded my arms, gave him a pointed look and told him,

"Okay, so for starters, Frankfort airport is not expecting us and without stating it's an emergency and giving reasons for needing to suddenly change our flight plan in about two minutes time, then I really don't want to have to radio their air traffic control and tell them the reasons I am landing..."

"Amelia be..." I quickly cut him off,

"Reasons like I put an ice bucket over the pilot's head and shot him because he wanted to land us in Stuttgart where there was an armed ambush waiting to take me hostage *yet again*..."

"You may have a point there," he agreed with a shrug.

"Good, then we are landing in Portland as planned," I said but then he said my name in that warning way of his making me continue,

"Amelia."

"Look, we are in a Gulfstream G550, which means this bird is capable of flying 6,750 nautical miles. Now, according to the flight plan it is only 4694 of those miles from Munich to Portland with a flight time of just over ten hours," I told him but he still didn't look convinced, something that was confirmed when he said,

"Yes, ten hours for you to fly a fucking plane that could have been tampered with!" Okay, so I knew that he was only worried about me but it was time for him to trust my judgement for once, even if I had given him more than enough reasons to question it in the past.

"Okay look, the only thing I was worried about is if they had disconnected the IDGs but seeing as they haven't forced duel generator failure, which would have meant flying on batteries and emergency power only, then I don't see any reason we need to land."

"Fuck me, but how do you know all this shit?" he said shaking his handsome blonde head a little as if he couldn't get his head around the fact that I, well...*knew this shit.* So, I shrugged my shoulders and told him,

"I didn't much like being a passenger and used to get restless, so spent most of my time playing co-pilot and learning all I could...shame I didn't think to do the same in my Dad's helicopter, eh?" Lucius shot me a look side on and commented drily,

"Indeed."

"So, you see, there is nothing to worry about, the gauges all look good, fuel looks good, altitude is back to being what it should and nothing looks to have been tampered with. So, my guess is that we have a better shot at no more shit happening if we just get to Portland like we planned instead of landing at another airport close by like the bad guys might assume we would...besides, it's like I said, I have technically flown this exact plane a few times now as my dad has one."

"But of course he does," Lucius muttered sarcastically, something I chose to ignore as I continued to convince him,

"So, you see, there is nothing to panic about...I have it all under control."

"With you in my life, then all I seem to do these days is fucking panic," he said rubbing the back of his neck and making me frown, before snapping back,

"Gee thanks."

"Amelia, that's not..."

"No, no, honestly, thanks because I have to say, all your confidence in me is making it so much easier to fly this fucking plane!" I snapped, making Lucius release a deep sigh and run a hand through his hair before swearing under his breath.

*"Fuck sake...*I didn't mean that, not how you took it anyway," he told me, making me flick on the right switches and set the controls so it was back on autopilot, doing so now so I could fold my arms and grant him a look that silently told him he needed to explain it.

"Alright, look at it this way, before you walked into my life how many things do you think ever gave me need for the emotion?" he asked, and I decided to give the question thought. I mean yes, I could kind of see things from his side as he didn't strike me as the type of man or powerful being that would panic about anything. But then, in that way, he was very much like all the other Kings. The only thing that ever gave them need to panic was the thought of losing the one thing they had waited all their lives for...

Their Chosen Ones.

Which meant that Lucius was no different and considering the raw deal he'd had so far with my life at risk at every turn, then I wasn't exactly making this any easier on him. Which is why I said,

"Okay, so I will admit, you have a point, as I doubt before I came along you had many reasons for panic but come on, you must realise by now that I can hold my own."

"Oh, don't I fucking know it, Sweetheart, and by now every merc in the whole of Germany knows it too, but that isn't exactly what I am getting at here," he told me and I couldn't help but smirk, especially remembering what the stewardess bitch in the cabin had said when pointing a gun at me, about hearing what I was capable of.

"Just because I know you can handle yourself it doesn't mean seeing you being held at gunpoint is a sight I relish," he added making me reach out and put my hand on his forearm to give him a squeeze before saying,

"I know and if it helps, then right now I am thinking of signing myself up for army bootcamp, or basically anywhere they trained Rambo, James Bond and John McClane, because it's like the movie title says, that guy's hard to kill…like, did you know he once used a motorbike to take down a helicopter? Now, unfortunately, as the way things stand then it is looking like the term 'highly likely' will most probably become my life's new moto." Lucius' lips twitched in amusement and I carried on,

"Which means that bringing down helicopters with bikes will be the type of shit that is definitely going to come in handy to know…hence my need to leave shortly for badass camp." After I said this Lucius burst out laughing before leaning over the centre, snagging me behind the neck and pulling me to him for a kiss over the controls.

Hence the end of our conversation and my easing of Lucius' doubts. But shortly after this it was time for my own, and unlike Lucius', it had nothing to do with flying the plane and the reason why was simple…

Afterlife was our final destination.

CHAPTER TWO

LANDING OF THE GUARDS

"Tell me you have done this before?" was Lucius' strained question as I leant over and yanked at the straps of his belts, tightening them after first doing my own. I then ignored his question and looked over my shoulder to shout to Pip and Adam, who was back to normal after his Hulk out,

"Buckle up, guys, this isn't going to be smooth!"

"Amelia?" I laughed nervously as a way of answering Lucius' questioning tone after he said my name and decided it was best not to get into the details right in that moment. So, instead, I ran through the checklist of stuff I had memorized after communicating with traffic control that I was coming in and confirming which runway was assigned to us ready for me on approach. Then, once we were ten miles away from Portland international, I started to line up with the runway once I was 3000 feet above the ground.

"Please tell me you know what you are doing here, Sweetheart?" Lucius asked, obviously getting concerned the closer to the ground we got, and I had to admit, it was the most anxious I had ever seen him. His fists were gripping the armrests for dear life and his body was held rigid against the back of the seat. It almost made me want to reach over and pat him on the shoulder to tell him everything would be fine. Well, that was if I wasn't slightly occupied in trying once again not to kill us all upon landing.

"I'll answer that question once we have landed, yeah?" I said as I adjusted the speed that was appropriate for our weight and configuration of the aircraft and started to sound out what I was doing as I was doing it,

"Landing gear down. Flaps set." Then I used the controls to get the plane into position, pitch rolling left and right and using the pedals to aim the plane to the end of the runway I could see coming closer. Then, when I was only 50 feet from the ground, I slowed the rate of our descent pulling back on the yoke slowly, moving it more and more to bring up the nose, so we landed on the back wheels first.

"Here we go!" I said so everyone could brace for the bumpy landing I was anticipating. But there was no time to take it all in as the second we did, bouncing in our seats, I was pulling the throttle all the way back so as not to generate any additional thrust. After this I relieved the pressure on the control so it gently lowered the nose of the plane allowing it to touch down onto the front wheels. Then I applied the reverse thrust to aid the slowing down of the plane whilst using the rudder pedals to keep the plane straight on the runway. After this I applied the toe breaks that were on top of the rudder pedals carefully balanced between the two. This combination slowed us down enough for me to taxi the plane into the designated spot near a private hanger, where I could already see cars waiting.

After this I was finally able to turn off the engines and the second I did, every muscle in my body seemed to deflate. Then I turned my head to Lucius as he too looked side on at me.

"So, in answer to your question if I have ever done this before, well, yeah I have now," I said after we had all breathed a sigh of relief. Oh, and not forgetting the party music I could now hear coming from Pip's phone in the background.

But of course, it was Gloria Gaynor's 'I will survive'.

Lucius growled and I didn't know if this was due to the song playing or my answer. Either way he looked at me with his hands still holding onto the armrests as if they were the source of the plane's power and had prevented us from exploding upon impact.

"Tell me you are joking…*please,*" Lucius said, stressing the please in that sentence in a strained tone that told me he was in all likelihood asking the Gods for patience.

"Well, let's just say when you see me drinking later tonight, then I will be doing so whilst silently congratulating myself, so make of that what you will, Handsome," I said with a wink before unbuckling my belts and getting out of the seat that I wasn't exactly sorry to leave. Don't get me wrong, I loved flying it. But after ten hours of inwardly praying that I wouldn't suddenly forget absolutely everything… including my name, from stress related amnesia (if there was such a thing) and therefore causing us to plummet to our deaths somewhere into the North Atlantic Ocean, then to say that I was a little tired was an understatement. In truth, my nerves were fried!

But Lucius must have seen this, as the second I was up and out of my seat he was too and faster than I was, being how he was able to grab a hold of me as my legs nearly gave way. Which was why I quickly found myself being pulled in for a hug, holding me to him so I couldn't fall. And I had to say the comfort I found in his arms in that moment was staggering. Then he hooked a crooked finger under my chin to raise my face so he could grant me a passionate kiss, this after first telling me in such a tender tone,

"Gods, Amelia...I am so fucking proud of you." The kiss that followed started off as sweet as the words of praise he'd just bestowed on me but in no time at all it became heated and near desperate. With Lucius tugging at my clothes and me doing the same, it was a passionate moment and one that only grew with our need for each other. It was as if the moment we had reached our destination and the threat was completely over, was when the reality hit us both of all the things that could have gone wrong. Of all the possible ways my life could have been taken from him yet again and our lives would have been ripped apart. Because he would have survived the crash, seeing as he had wings of his own, but his worry had been for me...the only human on board he cared for.

Meaning it was no wonder that we only came back down to the ground our plane now sat on when we heard the cat calls coming from Pip who was standing in the doorway watching us with a great big, toothy grin...one that was now unfortunately missing one of those pearly whites. A war wound that happened after being hit in the face with the bottle of champagne and was something once discovered, she swore enough that it would have made a pirate blush. Even Adam found himself trying to control his emotions, but this was something that thankfully, Pip decided to help him with in the best way she knew how. Which meant staying firmly in the cockpit for both me and Lucius, trying to ignore the screams of pleasure from the back of the plane for a large portion of the journey.

As for the two bruised and bleeding passengers, who currently resembled broken airplane theme dolls, ones hogtied on the floor, well I wasn't sure if they were forced to endure the Pip and Adam X-rated sex show or not. However, when I had managed to slip out of my pilot's seat long enough for a few quick trips to the toilet, they had been unconscious each time. Thank the Gods for autopilot that was all I could say, as each time I went Lucius shot a panicked look at all the hundreds of switches and navigational screens in front of him. Which, in response, I not only found cute as Hell but also took the opportunity to tease him about it by patting him on the shoulder and telling him,

"Don't worry, just shout me if the plane starts to shake or alarms start blaring." His response was to just growl and mutter under his breath,

"Pilot and a comedian."

Naturally, I walked away chuckling.

But now, he was framing my face after our kiss and bending slightly so he could catch my eyes. Because my face now said it all, how I wished in that moment we could have stepped away from reality and run away from the immediate future that was about an hour's drive away from becoming real.

"You're worried?" he asked and I couldn't help but nod.

"Why?"

"Is that a joke or did you forget where we are going?" I replied making him give me a pointed look in return.

"It will all be fine, even better if you would agree to finally telling your parents about us," he said making me wince at the thought.

"Oh yeah, homecoming with the added twist of an attempted murder would make it all just peachy," I replied sarcastically, stepping back and folding my arms over my chest despite Lucius' unconvinced chuckle.

"You think I am joking?" I challenged making him smirk.

"Not at all."

"Then what do you find funny, the part where my dad turns into a bad ass demon and tries to chop your head off with his trademark twin blades that slide right out of his arms or the part where my mum is screaming blue murder and threatening to kill you both if you don't stop fighting?" I asked in a tone that said it all.

"That won't happen," Lucius said with his knowing grin still sat in place. As if this was all very amusing to him and my internal freak out could have been about why there were no teal coloured jelly beans in the world, for all he cared!

"No? What makes you so sure?" I asked in a disbelieving tone.

"Because even despite the physical difficulty he would have in doing so seeing as we are evenly matched, put simply, he knows he can't kill me as he is forbidden to do so," he replied making the biggest point of all without even saying the words, so I did it for him,

"You mean because you sired my mother?" This was said in a small voice I couldn't help, as it was just another reason I was dreading this meeting. I tried to look away from him, but this was something he didn't allow for long as I felt him once again take hold of my chin and force my face back to his.

"Because I sired an entire race and he is responsible for all supernatural life, not just those he cares for, just as I am to my own kind and to kill me would be the cause of genocide…that is why," he told me and I nodded, seeing as I knew this already but still, having it as a safety net didn't sit right with me. Because at the core of it all I was still a daughter that didn't want to disappoint her parents as most daughters and sons didn't.

I wanted just once for that slice of normality. That basic scene of a girl bringing home her boyfriend to meet the parents for the first time and everything being totally amicable. Not the clash of weapons over the dinner table as I announced our relationship to my parents. I could even see my uncles Vincent and Zagan being the ones to pass my dad the extra steak knives! Gods, but it was going to be a disaster!

"You don't understand...it's not going to be that simple," I told him after stepping back yet again.

"It also doesn't have to be as difficult as you believe and besides, just how long do you intend to keep it from them, until after there has been a wedding?" he asked making me react instantly,

"Why, do you know someone who is getting married?" Yet again I received another pointed look from him and if he had worn glasses, then it was one where he would have been looking over them at me in that expectant way.

"You know what I mean," he said making my heart pound in my chest because I did know what he was saying and deep down I was almost wishing he would just get down on one knee already and ask me. Even though that was crazy in itself as we hadn't exactly been dating long, even if I was the only one who was using the term, seeing as the mighty Lucius didn't date! Although, he had referred to me as his girlfriend earlier, so there was hope yet.

"So, you want to get married now?" I asked making him suddenly look uncomfortable and rub the back of his neck with a hand before saying quickly,

"Now is hardly the time to discuss this, Amelia." His awkward answer made me end up laughing at the same time reminding him,

"You brought it up."

"I know what you are doing," he said narrowing his eyes down at me and I unfolded my arms and shrugged my shoulders,

"I don't know what you mean."

"You're stalling, Sweetheart and it won't work," he said, now being the one to fold his arms and without a doubt it was more intimidating when he did it, making his arms bulge and the material around them tighten. Lucius could most certainly intimidate you with his tall frame and muscular upper body, just like my dad could with the sheer size of him.

"Fine, I am, but really do you blame me!?" I snapped making him now relax his arms and grant me a soft look that told me he didn't.

"Besides, me and my dad aren't exactly on speaking terms, not since I found out he owns my building, planted a load of spies in it and basically made me believe I was in control of my own life when I wasn't...so no, I am not exactly looking forward to this, or the endless lectures that will follow my return," I told him because it was true, I hadn't spoken to my dad since I hung-up on him that day I left, and I knew that he had been trying to speak to me since.

Lucius gave me a strained look, one that was mixed with something else I couldn't detect, making me question...*did he know something about it?*

"Amelia, I..."

"Hey sexy Pipets, are we ready to bounce 'cause there seems to be quite a bit of a welcome party outside and unless they are all dancing to the same beat, then there is also a bit of side stepping and impatient shuffling involved," Pip said, choosing that moment to pop her head in and inform us of this. Therefore, I couldn't help but roll my eyes at the thought of how my parents were going to react to the news of the hijack attempt. Especially if a car of armed guards was the reaction to everything else that had gone on. But then I followed Pip out of the cockpit door and saw for myself the six blacked out SUVs that were waiting for us that looked armoured and built with machine gun fire in mind.

"Gods, it's a bloody armoured convoy," I muttered pinching the bridge of my nose and closing my eyes against the sight.

"Erm, do you really blame the big King man, I mean this is you we are talking about and no offence but lately that kinda got you the name 'Queen shit hit the fan' and trust me, you do not want to see the royal flag for that house name …eeww is all I am saying?" I wrinkled my nose at Pip's comment and decided to shoot Lucius a death glare when he scoffed in agreement.

"So, you all think this is necessary, I mean there are armed guards for bloody hell's sake!?" I snapped and one by one they all answered,

"Yes."

"Yup dilly."

"Fuck, yes."

I groaned in return and rolled my eyes, before turning to Lucius and Pip saying,

"You two I expected this from but Uncle Adam, are you really turning traitor on me?" I said looking to the only one who answered a simple yes. He shrugged his shoulders, with his torn sweater now hanging loose on him after his near change into his beast and slipping on one side from the action. This before he pushed his glasses further up his nose and said,

"We still love you, Little Bean." I released a deep sigh before telling them all,

"Right, well let's get this shit over with then." Pip clapped her hands and said,

"Yey, reunion time!" I shot her a look and she stopped clapping, scowled and said in a deep voice,

"I mean shit we gotta get done time." I nodded once, then silently allowed Lucius to lead me from the plane and down the steps towards the blacked out convoy of cars my dad had obviously sent for us. Oh, and the army of his guards, one which included his head of security. A giant who was currently getting out of the first car the second he saw me coming down the steps.

Which also meant that before Lucius could stop me, I had set off running shouting his name…

"Uncle Ragnar!"

CHAPTER THREE

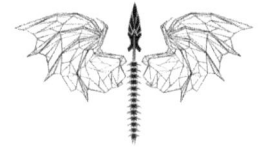

VAMPIRES AND VIKINGS

I shouted his name the second before throwing myself in the giant's arms with mine barely making it halfway around his colossal frame.

"Ah, min øjesten," he said in return, which was a Danish term meaning 'My Darling' or 'my sunshine'. But for Ragnar, who was the famous once Viking King, it also meant something more. It was a variation of 'lille øjesten' a term his son, Sigurd, had once given my mother, which means 'little apple'. Something my mum had told me once was meant in a sisterly, affectionate way after they had spent some time together when searching for my dad.

Now, as usual, I was hazy on the details as no-one ever really spoke about the past when I was around. But I had grown up with Ragnar as my bodyguard, being that he was also resurrected upon his death when being thrown into a pit of snakes by the King of Northumbria. But the part of history that hadn't been written was that Ragnar never sailed to England with the view to conquer it, but it was in fact done so out of revenge after English scouts had killed his wife and taken his daughter who was later murdered by that same King.

It was a devastating part of his past and a horrendous death that signified the end of his human life. But that was when one mortal door closed, and the door to my father's world opened up to him. This was because Ragnar was actually a descendant of the God of War, Odin. Which was why my father requested he have his body reclaimed and his soul returned with the added demonic side granted to him, becoming the first of the Norse Devourers to reside on Earth.

Meaning that even when he was human he was still considered a beast of a man for his time but now, well now with the added demon inside of him, he was gargantuan. He stood at six foot seven and was so big, he looked to have the bone mass double that of a normal human man. His arms alone were bigger than my head at the bicep and his limbs were long and meaty, being very much in proportion with his height. Even his shoulders were large enough that I could have probably sat on one quite comfortably without any part of my ass overhanging. I'd most certainly had more than enough space sat up there when I was a child as it was where I nagged to be most of the time he was watching me.

But it was his face that most would have considered disturbing as his skin was hard, weathered and marred with what many would have considered to be scarred with the pocks, as it was pitted from the many snake bites he had received during his final agonising minutes as a human. His hair had been cut in a way that added to the intimidation which was buzzed to his skull each side of a square cut mohawk down the centre. This showed off a large scar on the side of his head, showcased proudly and one I never knew the story behind, as when I asked as a child, *like children often do*, he always told me,

'Tis but for another day little one, when you are grown.' Now the way he said it, with a glint of amusement in his eyes, well it always made me wonder if it had anything to do with the woman in his life. I didn't really remember much growing up about the way they met, but I did know it was when I was in my first year of school as I was the cause, seeing as she was my teacher.

Her name was Tyra Benson and she was a sweet, kind and generous curvy lady who still looked to be in her late forties due to the circumstances that brought her into Ragnar's life. She was also one hell of a cook, no pun intended and could bake cakes as if they had been blessed by the sugar Gods!

But, despite Ragnar's aggressive looking presence, it was his hazel coloured eyes that were kind and had flecks of olive green like lightening attacking the pupil. His full lips were currently framed by a full beard that was more red than the dark blonde on his head and one that had been groomed to almost looking stylish. He was also wearing his typical 'guard' attire that consisted of black trousers, black shirt, that looked close to tearing should he flex a muscle and big boots, as I doubted they made dress shoes in his size.

However, to me it never mattered how he looked, as he could have been dressed as the bringer of doom or a death dealer for all I cared, because growing up with him in my life, he was always like one big Viking teddy bear. One I would jump on his back and demand we ride into battle as if he was my very own Norse beast at the gates of Hell. Of course, at that time he had a long-plaited Mohawk instead of it being cropped square as it was now. And I had a feeling this had been so I had something to wrap my little fists around as I held on when he was down on all fours roaring around the room with me on his back.

Of course, I had also seen him in his Demon form and,

like I'd explained, after seeing those you loved in their demonic sides, then nothing really phased me. In fact, when my parents weren't around I would simply pester him into growing his horns just so we could play our games and make them more realistic. Often telling him, if I was going to ride into battle and storm through the gates of Hell, then I needed to look the part. And seeing that this logic at the time had come from a four year old me wearing an overly big medieval helmet, with a plastic axe he had bought me for my birthday in hand, then let's just say it was near impossible for him to say no to me.

But then, even I had to admit it to myself, I had become the master manipulator at a young age, being able to wrap these powerful beings around my little finger, my dad very much included in that list. Saying that, I wasn't exactly a bad kid either, just more mischievous and curious than anything else. I was always asking questions and eager to learn more and more of the world my dad ruled. And to be honest, I even remembered a time when I had been indulged with the ways of his world. But then it was as though something just happened one day and it all stopped. I had often wondered what made it all change and what had occurred in my parents' life that made them take a different path with me?

"You are looking well, baby apple," Ragnar said which had been his other nickname for me growing up, as it was a take on what he called my mother. I laughed and punched him in the shoulder, after saying,

"Hey, less of the baby, Fenry, didn't you hear, I'm a badass now." He burst out laughing which was a deep and throaty noise that wasn't your typical amused sound. Of course, my 'Fenry' nickname for him was from the Norse beast Fenrir he used to pretend to be, who was a monstrous wolf. This I had combined with one of my stuffed toys I used to carry around with me called Henry and was bought for me as a baby from my 'human' grandmother, nanna Joyce.

"Yes, I have had many a time to hear of your escapades in the form of your father's rage," he told me making me wince.

"I guess he's been a nightmare to live with recently," I replied in a dire tone as I could just imagine what those around him had had to endure, as let's just say that my father wasn't exactly known for his patience and was very much known for his famous temper.

"He has struggled, little one, of that everyone is sure of and he is more than eager to see you, well… as are we all." I swallowed hard and looked down at my feet feeling guilty that I had ignored the feelings of those who cared for me. Because my father would have heard most of what had happened these last few weeks, if not from Lucius then from those loyal to him that would have had their ears to Munich city streets. After all, he was King and Munich may have been under Lucius' rule but that did not mean that my father had his back turned against it. Which meant that the dread about going home merely tripled.

"Vampire." I looked up the second I heard Ragnar's irritated greeting as Lucius approached with Adam at his back and Ragnar's eyes narrowed the second he saw how close Lucius chose to stop and stand next to me. Meaning I, in turn, panicked and took a step away from him, putting distance between us so as to keep up the appearance we were nothing more than acquaintances brought together due to the circumstances we found ourselves in. And in doing so I didn't dare brave a look back at Lucius as I could feel his annoyance and disapproval at the space I had put between us.

"Viking," was Lucius' own short and clipped greeting and it was one that felt like a taster for things to come. Because there were those who were naturally loyal to my father. Meaning that due to the past bad blood between Lucius and their King, then even decades later it was one that still left a sour taste in the mouths of many, no matter how many years had passed. Which was why, even before setting a foot inside Afterlife, it felt like the battle lines were already drawn and this was his world against my own. A world that felt more to have claimed me through birthright alone rather than embraced me as one of their own.

But, as for Lucius, well he had made it his mission to not only include me in his world, but to fully immerse me in it. Meaning that for the first time in my life I had felt a part of something other than the human life I had felt no other option to embrace as my own.

Which meant that I couldn't help but feel as if I was betraying him by taking that first step away from him, but really…what else could I do? I had to keep up that fake act of indifference so no-one discovered the truth. Because despite what Lucius thought, now was most definitely not the time to announce our relationship to my world…one that barely ever felt like my own.

Because Lucius' world now felt like my own. Being one he had tried to tie me to, instead of keeping those roots at a distance like my father had. No, he had fully entwined me and taken me into the fold, including me the way I always should have been. In fact, being with Lucius had been the first time I had felt a part of the Supernatural world and less…*human.*

But now I was back here and with that came the instant feeling of segregation I knew would follow the moment I was home. Because no matter how much I knew my parents loved me and only wanted what was best, they believed that it meant protecting me came above all else. They didn't yet trust that I could do that job on my own, even when up against their kind.

"There are two on board that need to be dealt with," Lucius

informed Ragnar, snapping me out of my thoughts and making Ragnar grumble a threatening sound before he barked out,

"Dealt with how?"

"Well, seeing that they tried to hijack the fucking plane at gun point, I think you can guess how." At this information Ragnar's eyes narrowed evermore dangerously this time and were now directed at the plane before he released a deadly growl, one definitely deeper and more gravelly than most other demons.

"The King will want to question them himself," he replied and I inwardly shivered at the thought and I almost felt sorry for them, as my father's wrath was no joke. My mother even let spill once that he had nearly snapped the neck of one of his people just for bumping into her once, in the VIP section of the club. She admitted the guy had been an asshole about it too but still, he hadn't deserved to die…well, not at that point, she had added cryptically, not really giving me much more after that. But to say that my dad was a bit protective and possessive over my mum was a Hell sized understatement!

"He will also want you to get rid of the dead pilot she shot," Lucius replied making me gasp. I mean Gods, couldn't he have said it a little better!

"That is not amusing, Vampire," Ragnar said obviously thinking it was a joke and Lucius sneered back before telling him,

"No and it wasn't at the time, but fortunately, Amelia seems to be an excellent student and one we are all lucky enough to benefit from seeing as she flew the fucking plane. Now, are we done reminiscing here or is there any other shit you wish to discuss before we can get the fuck on with our journey, for naturally Amelia is tired and I would like to get her home before she passes out from exhaustion?" Now this really got Ragnar's attention as I swear it looked as if he had swallowed a palm sized bug as he even coughed twice before words followed,

"Is this true, min øjesten?"

"Are you questioning me, Devourer? I was fucking there! Now move aside so I can get her in the fucking car!" Lucius snapped making me shoot him a disbelieving look and snap,

"Lucius!" He ignored this, as did my guard Ragnar, as he just stepped up to him and growled down at Lucius, making him rumble a threat,

"Careful, Vampire, your place above me expired long ago." Lucius stood up to the threat without fear and replied,

"And yours expired as a King even longer, so unless someone gave you a fucking kingdom to rule and I am stood in it, don't speak to me about fucking rank!" I rolled my eyes at this and snapped,

"Seriously, can the both of you just give it a rest! Ragnar, please, Lucius is right, it's been a long and draining flight...*for both of us*, and I just want to get on the road and go home." Ragnar finally moved his death gaze from Lucius who was clearly not backing down, despite the size difference and was holding his ground. But to be honest, I wasn't surprised seeing as even with the extra bulk and height, Ragnar wouldn't have had much hope of beating him...not with Lucius' power and like he said, *rank*. But then again it wasn't in a Devourer's nature to back down from anything, as was the way with most of my father's men that had a place at his council table.

But this wasn't my father commanding him to back down, this was me asking him to.

"As you wish, little one, you are in the middle car. Vampire, you are up front with your people," Ragnar said, nodding to Adam and conceding by taking a step back at my request. I nodded and moved a step towards the car he indicated when suddenly a hand grabbed my arm and held me still before Lucius stated firmly,

"Where Amelia goes, I go." I sucked in a breath and I swear if this first five minutes was any indication as to how the rest of this time here was going to go, then basically…I was well and truly fucked! Because Lucius wasn't really helping me in what I was trying to achieve but then maybe that was his plan all along?

Ragnar snarled at the sight of Lucius' hand gripping onto my arm before he forced out a single one worded question,

"Why?"

"Because I was the one charged with protecting her and I will continue to do so until I see fit that her protection is no longer needed, just as I have been doing since London, so I suggest you not question my motives again!" Lucius snapped back before placing a hand at the small of my back and leading me to the vehicle of his choice, which was behind the first. Then Lucius growled at the first body in his way,

"Get the fuck out of my way before I do so of my own accord, an action I promise you will not like when I sever your head from your shoulders!" Lucius threatened and the guard first looked over to Ragnar who was his boss. I looked back and gave him a pleading look not to cause anymore friction, making his gaze soften before he nodded to the guard, silently telling him to let us through. I breathed a sigh of relief before mouthing a thank you at him.

"Amelia." Lucius said my name in a way that he wanted me to do something, so I looked back to see that now he had the door open ready for me. So, I got inside refusing to accept his help when stepping up onto the foot stand, because I was near boiling over in my anger at how he had behaved when there had been no need. And from the looks of the frown he was now

sporting I would say he was getting the idea too because he looked about as happy with the exchange as I did.

"My second will drive, Adam and Pip will ride with us," Lucius commanded the moment it looked like one of the guards was about to get into the driving seat. Once again the guard first looked to the one he considered in charge before Ragnar conceded once more and agreed with a nod, allowing him to take a step back and Adam take his place behind the wheel.

I looked towards the plane to see Pip bouncing down the few steps from inside now holding up a dinted bloody ice bucket whilst shouting,

"Can't forget my souvenir!" This made me groan aloud whilst Adam just shook his head as if he never really knew what to do with his wife other than love her unconditionally.

And as for me, I turned to Lucius the moment the door closed and said the first thing that came to mind,

"What the Hell was that?!" And his response came just as easily, and it was one that gave me zero hope that we were ever going to pull off this charade of friendship when he said...

"Proving my right to claim what is mine."

Yep...I was so screwed.

CHAPTER FOUR

HOME WAYWARD BOUND

Watching the world go by was not the relaxing statement most people tended to make, as I had been doing it now for forty minutes with my arms folded, silently stewing in annoyance. This was because for the first five minutes of the journey me and Lucius had argued. Thirty seconds into that argument Pip had tried to get involved, being told by all three other passengers in the car to keep out of it.

I felt bad for this as she was only trying to help in her own unique way, but instead she had wisely popped on a pair of headphones that had cat ears attached that lit up and flashed to the beat. But even this was clear that she was trying to make a point as she had been listening to Adele on repeat since we left, favouring songs like 'Remedy', 'Turning Tables', 'I miss you', 'Water under the bridge' and 'Set fire to the rain' the second it started to pour it down outside. All of which you could hear blaring full blast from the small speakers, due to the cutting silence in the car. Meaning we were all unable to get away from it, so finally when 'Hello' came on, I was close to breaking point…and it seemed I wasn't the only one who had hit their limits.

"Amelia." I tensed the second I heard Lucius utter my name and felt his hand at my thigh in another attempt at gaining my attention, something I had shrugged off the other two times. This time, however, I knew we were nearing Afterlife, which meant this would be my last attempt at trying to get him to understand why it was so important to me for him to try and hide our relationship. So, I turned to face him and unfolded my arms that had been crossed for so long they ached.

"Lucius." I said his name in a tone that told him I was still pissed off and challenged in silent question, what he was going to do about it? He gave me a pointed look at the reaction but refrained from commenting on it instead focusing on the problem at hand.

"Can we get past this already?" he asked and I couldn't help but wonder just how many girls in his long lifetime had he said that to? My gut told me not many, if any at all…or was that hope speaking?

"Sure, just tell me that you are going to make a conscious effort to keep this quiet and we will be just peachy again," I told him without losing my 'bitch tone'. Lucius released a frustrated sigh that was the same one he had released forty minutes ago, only it had been added to with a muttered curse under his breath. It was also one I had snapped about hearing in my anger at the time.

"Lucius, we have been through this," I reminded him because we had, a few times in fact, with the first being back in his office before we even left.

"*You* went over this," he reminded me and yes, looking back

I had been the one doing most of the talking at the time, listing I don't know how many reasons why it was for the best.

"I don't understand why this is going to be so difficult for you, I mean you practically spent most of my life pretending I was a leper and didn't exist!" I snapped knowing the second it was out that it was a harsh and unnecessarily cruel thing to say… but hey, I was only human after all. Even Pip and Adam cringed with their shoulders rising even though they were both trying to pretend they weren't even in the same car with us. But it was Lucius' reaction that attacked my guilt, because he actually closed his eyes and tensed for a few seconds before commenting dryly,

"Yes, and how you do seem to enjoy reminding me of the fact and making me pay for past mistakes…*often.*"

"I'm sorry, that was wrong of me to say," I admitted quickly and instead of the verbal acceptance of that apology, he simply squeezed my thigh, one he still had hold of.

"It is difficult because you are mine and every fibre of my being roars this at me. Every single piece of me is consumed by the knowledge. And it is difficult because my demon demands this side of me to take dominance and charge of flaunting this fact freely. Therefore, seeing the Viking embracing what is mine without being allowed to first prove my own claim isn't merely as simple as fighting with your instincts, it is battling a fucking demon that threatens to rise to the surface and take over my soul completely to do the job where he believes I am lacking…*that is why, Amelia,*" he said by emphasising the end of his statement and this time, it was I that was sighing in frustration. Because I was torn as, admittedly, this statement was one I had waited what felt like most of my life to hear, yet right now it was one that didn't exactly help what I was trying to achieve.

"Okay, so put like that, then I understand why this is so

difficult for you but you have to admit, that turning up after everything else my dad has had to deal with these last few weeks and then adding to that by telling him about us isn't exactly fair or in our best interests right now." Lucius' features turned hard and unyielding, which was why I added,

"We need him on our side, yours especially considering he has just offered his loyalty in all this."

"I do recall it is also in his best interests to do so," Lucius interrupted and yes, considering Lucius had Sired my mother, then yeah it was, but that was also beside the point.

"Alright, I will give you that, but still, is it not better to have him on our side by his own desires and not with the feeling that he has no choice and his hand is being forced to do so?" I asked, making Lucius silently gesture with his hand, and holding it out in a way that said, 'perhaps'.

"Then what do you suggest for the time we are there together?" he asked making me hopeful that he was finally coming around. So, I decided to try my best to clinch the deal and did this by unbuckling my seatbelt and despite the two in the front who had been silently listening to this discussion play out, I made my move.

"Amelia, what are you...?" Lucius never finished as it quickly became clear what I was doing, especially when I shifted over to his side and straddled his waist, now sitting in his lap facing him. His hands instantly framed my waist before sliding down to rest at my hips.

"You asked me what I suggest, well I will tell you..." I said before getting closer to his lips but before kissing them, I aimed slightly lower and started peppering my kisses along his stubbled jawline. The moment I heard his satisfied grumble I couldn't help but smile, one he felt against his own skin.

"I suggest... *we get sneaky,*" I told him on a sexual whisper as I continued to kiss him softly and in a teasing way I knew was working thanks to the way his hands tightened on my hips.

"Sneaky huh, well just what did you have in mind?" he asked with his steel grey eyes almost hooded as the sexual thoughts overtook his earlier frustration.

"Oh, I am sure we can get creative and besides, I know all the best dark and hidden spaces in Afterlife, places where no-one would find us…*not for hours and hours.*" I whispered this last part directly into his ear and again his hands tensed before they travelled further down and cupped my ass.

"Mmm, I will admit that this eases the idea of being forbidden to touch you freely somewhat. However, what will you do about the other stipulation I have and just how sneaky are you willing to be I wonder in trying to achieve it, as I warn you now, your answer will depend heavily on my own in accepting your terms," Lucius said making me pull back a little so I could take in his expression and just like always his handsome features near took my breath away.

"And just what stipulation is that?" I asked like he knew I would. But then his bad boy grin appeared, and I knew I was in trouble even before he told me, one that only ended up enhancing his reply,

"That your nights are spent in my bed and nowhere else." At this my eyes widened, and my mouth dropped slightly before I had chance to recover, and I did so with it starting as a stutter.

"But I…you…I can't…I mean, how can we? We will get caught and…"

"Tut, tut, little Pet, you're losing your battle and not convincing me of your 'sneaky skills', but I am willing to make you a deal in return," Lucius said after saving my voice from rising any higher into full blown panic.

"What's that?"

"It's simple, you merely trust in me and my own abilities to steal you away when my need of you becomes too great to bear and you end each day with your body next to mine," he replied with another grin and I had to say that even just talking about sneaking around and doing it behind any closed door we could find was starting to turn me on. Oh, and he knew it, especially when a growl rumbled from his chest as his nostrils flared telling me so.

But then, before I could do or saying anything more, Lucius took hold of my jaw in a demanding grip so he could kiss me without fear of me moving. And I had to say the kiss was most definitely one that spoke of so many emotions, so many thoughts and feelings of what he wanted to do and didn't do. The 'do' part being declaring to the world that I was his and he didn't give a fuck who had a problem with it! What he didn't want to do was hide it from that world, my father included.

And I had to say that as his kiss deepened it became harder and harder to remember the reasons I wanted to hide it and limit the moments like this. But then again, wasn't that his plan, therefore, the second the kiss finished and I opened my eyes, all I saw was a look that said only one thing...*challenge accepted.*

Meaning I now had a Vampire King with a mission in mind and with me in his sights, his weapon of choice was sexual temptation...and Gods, but after that kiss, then it was little wonder I was feeling doomed to fail. Especially the way he made me moan in pleasure the second his fingers slid along my jaw, towards my neck before embedding themselves into my hair as he continued to lock my lips to his. It was also little wonder that when it unfortunately ended, I was close to panting and grinding my hips down against what I felt was a very obvious erection.

Forget doomed...*I was fucked!*

"You know, I would suggest us pulling over and letting you two shag it all out and have one last shinfuckerdigathon, but then I think the serious suits in front would kinda notice," Pip said making me burst out laughing and doing so enough to make Lucius vibrate beneath me as I buried my head in his neck. I then lifted my head up as yet another flaw in my plan hit me and it was sitting in the front seat making sex jokes and thinking that me and Lucius, being a few layers of material away from getting jiggy with it, was the cutest thing ever. I knew this when she said,

"Aww, I do love it when the lovebirds stop fighting and kiss and makeup, don't you, cuddlebutt…? I mean it makes me want to argue with you about some unimportant shit and then pretend we can't fuck as much, but then do it anyway any place we can…Hey wouldn't it be funny if we turned up at the same dark corner and found these two…"

"No," Lucius said interrupting her whirlwind direction change mid-sentence, doing so in a stern enough tone to make Pip retract her head from in between the seats. I suppressed a giggle and Adam received a dirty look from his wife for chuckling. I then shifted off Lucius' lap after he gave me one last squeeze with one hand still to my ass. Then, once back to my side, I decided it was time to tackle my next hurdle and doing so with what I hoped was with Pip diplomacy.

"So, while we are on the delicate subject matter, you do get this means keeping our secret…well, secret…right, Aunty Pip?" I said after she had finished trying to drill a hole in her husband's head with nothing but her eyes. However, he just hooked the back of her neck, pulled her to him and said,

"Consider this our argument, my Little Bo Pip and as soon as we get back to Afterlife, we can play your game wherever you wish." After this he kissed her own chuckled response right out of her, whilst skilfully still driving, I might add.

"Erm…anyway, just wanted to mention it, you know, so there are no accidental slip ups…*Aunty Pip,*" I said again, emphasising her name so she knew that I was once again mainly aiming this at her.

"Oh, as if I would…" she started to say and then stopped to take in the fact that all three of us were looking at her in exactly the same way. So, she wisely took that as a sign and said,

"Yeah, yeah okay, so I totally would spill the kidneys, but this time I little toe swear that I will try my damn diddly doomest not to do that this time. I am like totally zipped up like that creepy 70's Rainbow show's Zippy has been gutted and its stuffing used for a granny pillow…okay?" I shot a confused look to Adam in the mirror and after he mouthed a quick and silent, 'I have no clue' I looked back to Pip and said in an unsure tone,

"Erm yeah, okay." But I had to say, I didn't think her reply said good things about my future and the attempted boyfriend murdering stress-free life I was aiming for. And one look at Lucius' smirk, one he was doing a shit job of hiding behind a casual hand near his lips and I knew he was thinking the same thing…minus the stress-free murdering bit of course. Because who knew, there I was thinking that his greatest weapon against me in getting what he wanted was sexual persuasion. But now from the looks of things maybe he only needed one thing to achieve his goal and that was a sure (secret blowing) thing named Pip.

Yep, totally fucked.

Which was why I looked back out the window once more with a sigh that said it all. But also knowing that now all words had been said then I was left with nothing else but to go back to watching the world whiz by. Now seeing the sights I had grown up seeing, noting anything that had changed since the last time I was driving in this direction on the way back home. But all the while, with every mile closer we travelled, the more my anxiety started to come through physically. Doing so until I felt Lucius take hold of my hand and pull my fingertips free of my mouth, as I had been nibbling the ends without even realising it.

"It will all be fine, Sweetheart, I promise you," he told me in a caring tone, one that said he knew exactly where my thoughts were. In that moment I could have said so many things, most of which would have argued against such a positive statement. But as we turned onto the last long road that took us to Afterlife, then I found myself with only the ability to nod.

There were just so many different emotions that were running through my mind right then that it was hard to pinpoint just one. Of course, I was naturally looking forward to seeing my parents again, along with the rest of my family. But then, just looking down at mine and Lucius' entwined hands, and I knew just how hard this was going to be for both of us. How, the second I had to separate them, it really meant separating so much more. It felt more like Romeo and Juliet and the houses of Montague and Capulet in conflict. Even if it was true that Lucius and my father were no longer at war with each other. But then, if that was the case, why did it still feel as if I was bringing the enemy home with me? Because in truth, wasn't that really why I was hiding our relationship?

Now I knew it wasn't that I was ashamed, nothing like that. But it was more worry for Lucius and that shame I would feel at the reaction of others against him. As if during this time I was hoping that with his continued presence, that the miraculous would happen and my father would be reminded more of the friendship they once had. That King Dominic Draven would remember when Lucius Septimius had been his loyal right-hand man.

Well, only time would tell and for once I really hoped that the Fates were on my side with that one because the second we turned into the overhanging tunnel of trees, I knew that any second my family home would come into view. Meaning there really was no escaping what came next.

Because there, opening up before me, was Afterlife in all its majestic and Gothic glory and stood outside waiting was its King and Queen,

For now, their Princess was once again…

Home.

CHAPTER FIVE

HOME BITTERSWEET HOME

Taking in the sight of one I had grown up seeing daily hit me in my chest like my own fist had reached in, gripped my own heart and ceased it beating…oh, and wasn't letting go. Afterlife was at its front and first appearance, a huge manor home, one that had been reconstructed hundreds of years ago. In fact, it had actually started off life as an ancient monastery over a thousand years old. One left crumbling and abandoned, nestled out of sight in the Turkish mountains. One my father had commissioned to be rebuilt here, block by block. It had also been redesigned and merged with a grand manor house he also had once owned in Bath, England, deciding to have this to be the front of the building to hide the true nature of what its walls held inside.

At its centre a stunning Temple was built and one directly over a gateway to Heaven and Hell and the many realms in between. This gateway was also powered by a gigantic tree of life, one that looked frozen and fossilised in time. It too was centred in the Afterlife crypt, which essentially was a tomb and resting place for Supernatural life that chose not to be resurrected into a new host.

They were all free to make that decision which, after thousands of years of living, many chose to give up, as was their right to do so, seeing as all creatures on Earth had been granted with the Gods' free will. It also held those that had fallen in battle or those no longer granted life on Earth due to the hundreds of reasons this may be.

But something they all generally had in common, despite the difference in circumstances, was they each wanted to have their hosts laid to rest out of respect for the life once sacrificed to give life to their own souls.

All Supernatural life on Earth first needed a host or a vessel, as it was also known, to reside in, one usually granted by the Gods or Fates to do so. These were often gifted the moment a human soul has passed on and one from Heaven or Hell then took its place. But of course, it would be somewhat suspicious should that dead person suddenly pop up from its resting place and begin life back in the land of the living once more. Which was why, after a time, a demon or angel would start to morph that vessel into one they fit into, personalising it so to speak. It was how my Uncle Vincent and Aunty Sophia, my father's siblings managed to continue looking the same as they always had. However, I had been told that with my father's vessel this was not the case, as his hadn't changed once since the day he took possession of it, still to this day looking like a man in his thirties.

This, many believed, was because he was solely unique in the fact that he was the result of two souls fusing as one, both Angel and Demon and up until Lucius, the first and only one of his kind. It had been the reason he had been chosen to be sent to Earth and rule over all supernatural life that resided there. Something that happened thousands of years ago, an exact age no one but a few knew… and unfortunately, as usual, *I wasn't one of them.*

Of course, I would nag him as a child, asking him of his age but a smirk and teasing answer was all I would receive. Now, as for Lucius, then as far as I knew he hadn't started out as what he was now, for he had been reborn in the Devil's name only. But then something must have happened years after this for him to have become like my father and inherited back the promised Angel part of his soul.

But like most things, I didn't know the details surrounding this and like his hand, it wasn't a subject I had been brave enough to approach. Even though, bitterly, I knew it was most likely something my mother knew the details of.

Speaking of my parents, Adam followed the convoy around the massive open parking space in front of the building and I could see them standing at the grand entrance at the ready to welcome their wayward daughter.

The front of the building looked like the manor house it portrayed to be, which granted wasn't exactly your typical venue for a Gothic nightclub. But with most of the building hidden by the cliff face on one side and the thick forest on the other, then only those who resided there knew just how far back it went. The exterior was built from thick blocks carved from pale stone, with two thirds of the front of it being overtaken by a blanket of thick ivy, creating a curtain of green that looked as if the building was only barely peeking out from underneath.

Tall, arched windows sat framed in the greenery, too high up to allow those on the ground of having any hope seeing through. The grand entrance situated out from the centre of the building with it's imposing stone archway, was framed either side by thick and heavy black gates that were barely seen closed. This was because the massive carved, castle style oak doors were enough to keep anyone out when locked up after closing. Doors that were adorned in heavy hammered iron work and also a carving of our family crest at the centre of both sides, one that no humans knew the true meaning of. It was the same crest that could be found as a theme throughout our home, in both carvings on the walls or decorated on some of the furniture, like that of my parent's twin thrones.

I couldn't help but suck in a deep breath the moment I saw them both and again my heart ached at the sight. My mum looked as beautiful as ever, stood next to my dad and like always being half curled to his side with his arm anchored around her, holding her to him as he always did. She started waving like a crazy woman, the tears glistening in her eyes in both excitement and emotion could be seen from even in the car behind the darkened tinted windows. I felt Lucius squeeze my hand, one still held in his grasp as I uttered under my breath,

"Oh, mum."

Because suddenly I wanted out of this car to go running to her which, the second it finally came to a stop, was precisely what I did. I felt Lucius' fingers slip through mine as he had no choice but to let me go as I opened the door and started running. My mum also slipped through my dad's grasp and did the same until suddenly I found myself in her arms, with tears rolling down my cheeks.

By the Gods, I loved this woman, and my wonderful mother who was now crying right alongside me, whispered,

"My baby girl, my Faith is finally home...God, I have been so worried."

"It's okay, I am fine, mum, honest," I told her in return, trying to ease her emotional outburst which, all things considered, was totally warranted. Even after all this time no longer human and completely part of my dad's world, she was still more human than most and remained so down to her core.

Like the way she would say God instead of Gods, and even

on occasion saying things like, 'oh for Christ sake' like most humans would. She also snorted when she laughed, bit her lip often (something that drove my dad crazy), and was even clumsier than I was! She also rarely ever swore, something that warned you the shit had hit the mother fan whenever she did. And she was also one of the most beautiful people you could ever meet, including that of her soul. But with long waist length blonde hair that lay in natural waves she often reminded most of a Goddess. Especially when worn down, something she didn't do often as it clearly annoyed her, seeing as it would get caught in anything from door handles to spindled tops of chairs.

Her stormy blue eyes were large and framed with thick lashes, like my own, that gave her an eternal innocence that was cute and added to this was when she would wrinkle her nose in annoyance. As for the rest of her, she was five foot four, with a curvy frame and slightly larger bust than mine. She also looked about the same age as me seeing as she was barely twenty-five when she was turned, so to the supernatural world we would have looked more like sisters embracing now, not mother and daughter.

However, to the rest of the human world, she would have looked like a beautiful woman aging well in her early fifties. As for her other many attributes, she was also kind, generous, loyal, had a will of iron and was fiercely protective of all she loved and held dear. Added to this she could be quirky and was known for both her wit and silly humour that I like to think I'd inherited.

Now, as for the man that had been stood next to her, her husband and my father, was without a doubt, an exceptionally good looking man. He stood at the same height as Lucius at six foot four, only with slightly more bulk in the muscle department. Where Lucius reminded me more of a sleek jungle cat, with the body of a natural born fighter with stealth and speed, my father would have been the lion, with the body of a warrior swinging the heaviest of weapons and roaring out his death call as he severed limbs and heads. Both were just as deadly, but Lucius had the calm deadly vibe going for him with the abundance of rippling muscles, whereas my dad had raw brutality.

He was also where I got most of my looks from as I was dark haired like he was, with olive, sun brushed skin, where my mother was golden blonde and as pale as a fresh blanket of snow. But, unlike my own, his eyes were dark, closer to black than brown and ones that sparked with purple fire depending on his mood. Or that of a more subtle, warm purple ring circling the black, when he was touched by a sight, like he was right now.

"Now, what has a mum got to do around here to get her girl to come home more often, because you know I already started baking my chocolate strawberry cake." I grinned huge and said,

"Yep, that will do it!" This made her laugh, but she purposely stopped herself before the snort could arise, making me smirk. Then, she grasped me by the tops of my arms and held me back at arm's length to look at me.

"Oh, just look at you, I swear you get even more beautiful every time I see you." I blushed and tucked my hair behind my ear before muttering,

"Mum." This made her laugh again.

"Well, it's true! Come and just look how beautiful and grown up our girl is!" she shouted back to my dad whom I noticed hadn't yet approached and was for once, looking unsure. Then my mum gave me a hug and whispered,

"Go easy on him, he's been beside himself with worry." Then she pulled back and I looked over her shoulder to see my dad was approaching us, telling her with a smirk when he got there,

"I heard that, little one." She rolled her eyes at me and grumbled,

"Damn supernatural hearing." This made me chuckle as it was the same complaint she had been making since I could remember, which was why I said on a laugh,

"Wow, I am officially home."

"Will you not put a father out of his misery and grant him a hug from his beautiful daughter?" My dad said making me reply in a teasing tone,

"Well, it seems only fair, but make it quick as mum promised cake." He scoffed at the same time pulling me in for a hug, and holding my head to his chest whispering down at me,

"You're a lucky little lady, that it is damn good cake." I laughed once in his hold and wrapped my arms around him, unable to help taking in a deep breath and feeling comforted at the familiar scent of home.

"Thank the Gods you are safe," he said giving me another squeeze as if he had needed this just to believe it was true, that I was in fact *safe.*

"Well, I had help," I told him and looked back to see Lucius was now leaning casually back against the car door, allowing me this time with my parents. I also had to say that in that moment, I would have loved nothing more than to introduce him as my boyfriend.

But they already knew him and that was where the problem lay. Far too many years stood in the way, despite what he thought or the simple fact that he just didn't care. Because he didn't need approval from anyone to claim me, he had made that perfectly clear. I, on the other hand, had people who loved me, people I respected, despite what my father had done and lied about, I still loved him enough to care about his feelings.

So, I was hoping that with time it would ease the blow and one day it may mean that I could have both in my life, not the two sides at war. But then this thought was shattered for the moment as my dad looked over my head at his once enemy and frowned, looking more annoyed than grateful.

"TOOTIE PIE!" Pip suddenly shouted leaping from the car and actually vaulting over the large hood of the SUV to get to my mum, her best friend, quicker. Which had to be said was an impressive sight, seeing as she was little and the SUV was anything but.

"Squeak!" my mum shouted in return bracing herself just in time for Pip to throw herself in her arms,

"Whoa, bloody Hell Pip, you haven't been gone that long!" my mum said laughing.

"But haven't you missed me?!"

"Holy shit, Pip, what happened to your tooth?!" my mum asked in high pitched horror.

"Oh that, just a little mishap we had when the plane was... erm fine, absolutely fine and dandy, I slipped is all, not at all when we were about to crash or from a bottle of wine...nope, nope, nope...did I mention wine?" Pip said, sort of stopping herself after I had released a 'here we go' groan.

"Crash!?" my mum shrieked panicked and my dad looked down at me seeing as I was still in a hug and asked,

"Do I want to know?" Therefore, I looked back up and told him truthfully,

"Think of it more as something you *don't want to know* and more as something you probably should but only after Lucius has had chance to tell you and not whilst you are welcoming your daughter home...yeah?" His face turned stern but he nodded all the same, thankfully granting me my wish.

Adam then exited the car and first nodded to Lucius. This had me wondering if this was done to show his loyalty as Lucius nodded back in silent reply, as if giving him the go ahead before he was free to address my parents.

"My Lord, My Queen," Adam said stepping forward and glanced at his wife who was squishing my mum's cheeks telling her that she was going to raid her personal sweetshop (as yes, she actually had one in her room) and see what sweets fit her gap the best. This was when Adam reminded his wife of royal decorum.

"Pipper, I think you are forgetting yourself...*again,*" he said muttering this last word and making me smile. My Aunty Pip however just rolled her eyes and let go of my mum and rolled her arm around before bowing over it towards my dad and saying,

"Royal boss man and all that other stuffy stuff." Then she turned to my mum and said,

"Royal Boobetty, how's my favourite queenie hanging?" I chuckled along with my mum as Adam just groaned and shook his head at his wife's antics. Then he was clearly about to apologise but my dad beat him to it by raising his hand and saying,

"No need, Adam, for I have told you before that we are after all, used to it by now." This granted him a scathing look from my mother who mouthed silently when Pip wasn't looking,

'Don't say it like that!'

My dad rolled his eyes and my mum mouthed a quick,

'I saw that!' before going back to amusing Pip with her personal preference of a list of sweets she thought would fit best. But one thing I noticed was that Lucius had still remained where he was, just silently taking this all in. Well, that was until my mum took notice and shouted suddenly,

"Luc! You blonde devil you, get your ass over here and let me thank you for keeping our girl safe!" Then I watched as my dad tensed his upper body, with his hands curling to fists as my mum left Pip to go and embrace him, meaning Lucius had no choice but to do the same.

"Little Keira girl, how's the world's biggest trouble maker?" he asked smiling down at her and making her step back from the embrace and punch him in his arm like I had done to Ragnar before telling him,

"Oi, less of the trouble maker and besides, I have taken up knitting, so what do you think?" He laughed at this and said,

"Sounds fucking boring, that's what."

"Hey, be nice or I will make you a bobble hat and scarf to wear whilst you're here," she replied and I had to say watching their easy exchange was anything *but easy.*

"Yeah, good luck with that, blondie," Lucius said in reply as Ragnar approached our group.

"Hey, I am a queen don't you know, that means my rules… besides, Draven just loves the sweater I made him, don't you, honey?" she said looking back at my dad who had now stepped forward making me brace myself for what was coming next.

"That I do," he said at the same time putting his arm around my mum and making a clear statement. She just smiled up at him before turning and walking back to Pip leaving my dad and Lucius to their own meeting. I naturally watched with great interest ignoring the way my mum in turn was watching me. But then Lucius chuckled and said,

"Yeah, like fucking hell you do." I swear I nearly gasped but then I was surprised when my dad actually laughed and held his hand out to Lucius for him to shake.

"And like usual, you must have a death wish if willing to take on the wrath of my wife," my dad replied making Lucius scoff,

"Then I suggest you start to do something more productive with that yarn of hers if it is her wrath you fear," Lucius said making my mouth drop at the sexual act he was implying my dad do to my mum by tying her up with wool. But then again, my dad just laughed and muttered so my mum couldn't hear,

"Starting with that sweater." This time my dad's response made Lucius laugh and I had to say, so far it was going better than I could have imagined…now, if it could only stay this way for the duration then maybe I could get away with telling them at the end of our stay. Say, with my head out the window, shouting it to them as we drove away like the coward I was willing to act in this circumstance.

"Ragnar, feel free to speak," my dad said turning to his head of security as he was clearly waiting on the side-lines ready to speak to his king. Which made me tense yet again as it was time for reality to ruin what I had started to believe was a good thing.

"Did you want the prisoners transported to a cell or an interrogation room?" My dad's frown was once again back in place before he looked firmly back to Lucius.

"I take it this has to do with that thing I don't *want* to know but *should,* Amelia spoke of?" he asked making Lucius take on the same stern facial expression as if the details of their attempted high-jacking came back to his mind.

"It does and like she suggested, it is a *should* that is better explained once the welcoming of your daughter home has been concluded," Lucius replied nodding to me who was watching this conversation and making no attempt at hiding the fact. My dad nodded once, accepting the suggestion and, turning back to Ragnar, told him,

"Then in that case, the interrogation room."

"Yes, my lord." After this response Ragnar then commanded the rest of the convoy to move and as the SUVs drove out of sight around the side of the building where I knew there was an underground garage, my dad turned back to Lucius.

"Keira's right, you kept our girl safe and from what I hear, it wasn't easy, so despite my annoyance at how long it took you to finally get her here, I have to thank you," he said making me suck in a shocked and silent breath at hearing him actually thank Lucius.

"Your thanks are not necessary, for your daughter was in my care and it is my duty. But I confess, I enjoyed hearing it all the same, even if you have been coerced into doing so by your wife," Lucius said making me groan and refrain from smacking my forehead or his for that matter. But then again, my dad shocked me by finding it amusing, telling him,

"Ah, but just wait until you yourself find yourself married and tied to a wife you can't say no to, then it will be I that is mocking you." At this I couldn't help it, but I actually started choking as I swallowed, making my mum smirk at me before commenting in a knowing tone,

"I bet you could use a drink, eh?" My dad looked back at me along with Lucius and whilst holding my gaze Lucius commented boldly,

"Umm, just wait indeed." Needless to say, I swallowed hard as his look said it all…

I could one day be that wife.

"Come on, let's all go inside, it looks like more rain is coming and I have to get my girl some cake," my mum suggested, making Pip clap her hands like an excited child before skipping to Adam and taking his hand so he could lead her inside, now talking about the size of slice she was going to sneak.

"Fae, why don't you show Luc inside whilst I reprimand your father behind everyone's backs for the sweater comment he thinks I didn't hear," my mum said, nodding for me to go to Lucius before giving my dad a pointed look when he chuckled again.

"Erm, okay," I said before nodding to Lucius and saying in an unsure shy tone,

"It's…erm…this way." Lucius smirked down at me as if he

was finding my reaction to him amusing and therefore, he said light-heartedly,

"Yes, I know it is, Pet...*seeing as it's the front door."* He muttered this last part after coming closer, making me growl at him as he passed me. I then watched as my mum walked up to my dad, got right toe to toe with him and raised herself up to say,

"Use that sweater will you...? Tied to a wife eh, one you can't say no to, eh?" My dad looked down at her with a smirk and challenged back,

"Continue this sass, queen of mine and you will find yourself tied to your husband this very night...once again, I might add." This was when I raised my hands over my ears and shouted loud enough so they didn't miss it,

"La, la, la, not listening!" Then I walked inside to the sound of my parents both chuckling. Meanwhile, I shook my head mumbling to myself about how some things never change and wondering how long things would go on like this before the elephant in Afterlife was going to start speaking.

Because as much as I knew my parents had been worried, meaning being reunited with them now wasn't something I was willing to taint by being a ranting bitch, I knew at some point me and my father would be having words. As the reality was that he had still allowed me to believe I had been in control of my life and it had been a lie. So yeah, shit still needed to be said and this time I wasn't simply willing to just let it all be brushed under the supernatural rug along with the salt used to ward off ghosts and demons in make believe land.

But then, with one look back at how happy my mum was, then I just couldn't find myself with the heart to do it in front of her. So, I would just wait and deal with the weight of uncertainty laid heavily against one shoulder, with another named Lucius laid against the other.

Gods and I thought flying a plane for over ten hours was tense!

But now I was safely on the ground that didn't mean that I still couldn't crash and burn. Because one look at Lucius and the wink he gave me told me only one thing…

I was still in for a dangerous ride.

CHAPTER SIX

DEMANDING KISSES CAUGHT

"*Here we go again,*" I muttered to myself the moment I stood facing the imposing double doors that led not only back into the club part of the building but into the VIP area where my father would be sat at the head of his council table next to my mother. Both of whom I knew were waiting for me...*along with another.*

To say that it had been a strange homecoming was a bit of an understatement. One that started the moment I stepped through the doors of Afterlife for the first time in what felt like an age. In fact, what added to that feeling of time was the new person who had crossed its threshold, with my own reflection telling me the truth I knew in my heart...

I wasn't the same Amelia that had left it.

I knew that down to the core of me and it wasn't only down to Lucius and who I now was to him. It was more about self-discovery. It was more about the woman I had finally been given the space to grow into. The feeling of trust and self-belief that yes, I did belong in the world I had been born into. One seated between two kings, a throne my father sat upon and the other belonging to the man destined to seat me beside his own.

I finally stepped through those doors feeling like…

Well, like a Draven.

But once inside I had let my parents overtake me, telling them that I would catch up after first using the bathroom. This had been not only for my bladder's sake, but more for my sanity. I had faced the black glossed framed mirrors and gripped onto the edges of the marble sink bowls after first using them to wash my hands. Then I had asked what felt like my new reflection what I was doing back here and talked myself out of running for the hills and becoming a cave dwelling hermit. One whose hobbies included whittling spoons, twisting my hair into dreadlocks and foraging for shit to eat because there was no way I was killing an animal and dragging its carcass back to BBQ over a handmade pit.

After that I left the bathroom feeling as drained as I looked and continued to walk across the empty space feeling a sense of peace being here once again. Especially when no one else was around. I remembered as a child I used to sneak down here after it had closed and spin around on the dance floor, pretending I was being led around the floor by some handsome prince who had been waiting for me to wake up and realise he was the one.

Therefore, I couldn't help but smile to myself as I started walking through the club and up one of the double staircases that mirrored each other in the large club space either side of a stage area. It truly was an incredible space, with its cathedral ceilings of interlocking carved stone arches and the massive iron chandeliers that hung down from the centres of where the arches met.

Apparently, the interior of the club hadn't changed much, even from when my mum first stepped foot inside it all those years ago. As even after having the seating re-upholstered, they were done in the same blood red velvet so couldn't really be classed as new. Even the wrought iron lamps on the walls were the same, casting a warm glow against the pale stone that looked a lot less weathered than the facade of the building.

As for the club's layout, the large open space was separated into different sections, with the largest clearing being that of the dancefloor situated in front of the raised stage area. The same one framed by the grand dual staircases that swept out into larger steps at the bottom, curving inwards and curling to the edges of the stage. This part had apparently changed, due to some damage years ago, back when I was a teenager. But it was a time when I had been shipped off to the safety of my parents' Scottish castle. And one, even to this day, I still didn't know why or what had been going on. Only that it had happened shortly after I had met Lucius in the flesh for the first time and had found myself saved by him.

I shuddered at the thought of that night and cast the memory from my mind as not one I wanted to deal with, so instead I looked towards the fateful booth. It was one of many that framed the opposite walls of Afterlife. The other wall on the same side as the entrance opposite the stage held the bar area.

It was a piece of artwork in itself with its iron vines covering its frosted glass frontage and piercing it with twisted thorns. These parts were then surrounded by bursts of crimson glass making it look as though the damage caused was bloody. Above the bar was liquor galore, being one of the most well stocked bars I had ever seen, as rows of bottles lined the glass shelves that were also entwined in iron vines.

But like I said, it was that special booth that kept my gaze as it always did. For it was one unlike any other and I couldn't help but think back to my mother's own love story whenever I saw it. It was the one she would always tell and one I knew like the back of my hand. The story of her first time in Afterlife and the first time she believed to have met my father.

She had been sat in that exact booth, having just moved here and out on her first night with her new friend RJ, someone she had met a day or two after first arriving. She told me how nervous she had been, but never more so than when she saw who soon after entered the club.

Dominic Draven.

Walking through the front doors like some masterful king, she had no idea he actually was at the time. Apparently, it had been a yearly tradition for my father to announce the Draven family's arrival in town by walking through the club on the first night, and something that signified the start of the busy season. People would travel from all around just in hopes of getting a glimpse of one of the famous Dravens, as they still did. This was because most had heard the rumours of secrecy surrounding the club.

Of course, according to my mum, this wasn't all that had been rumoured, as his startling and intimidating good looks were well known. And because of it, let's just say every female with a pulse and an attraction to men wanted to get a look at just how handsome he was...disappointment never being on the cards with that one.

I thought back to Wendy's reaction to him and it was one I had been used to experiencing growing up. From teachers, parents, and then later on after hitting my late teens, from friends. But then tall, dark and unbelievably handsome on overload kind of did that to a girl.

And my mum had been no exception.

Especially when he had walked through the club that night with the entourage of his council at his back. But this night, unlike any other, he had stopped dead at her table instead of continuing directly to the staircase that would take him to the VIP.

Now, when I say stopped dead, well, that was precisely what I meant, as he had spotted his Chosen One sat in his very club. Hell, even his council had no clue why their King had just stopped and stared at her brazenly, as the rest of the club stood silently watching on. Something that caused my mother's identity to become a question on everyone's mind...*who was she?*

But back then my mum had been quite different and despite being just as beautiful as she is now, she had been shy and, from her own admission, a little broken. This she explained was due to her past and something that had happened to her that she had been running from. Now she never fully explained what it had been and to be honest, with the sadness in her eyes every time she talked about the past, then it was the reason I had never pushed. The one thing she always did say however was that it had been the reason she had moved to Evergreen Falls, giving me the impression that she had been running from something.

Either way, one thing my dad set out to do and that was make it impossible for her to run from him, as pretty soon she found herself the VIP's new waitress and therefore somewhere he could keep a firm eye on her. And the rest was history and granted, it was one I wasn't entirely sure on after that point. But then, this was my parent's business and not one I felt comfortable prying into. So, I hadn't asked. However, I did know that even after they had got together after this point, it hadn't always stayed that way. Pip had let slip as much. Telling me once that no road to love is smooth and for my mother and father, it wasn't just rough, but at times it was filled with a mountain of obstacles they had to cross and without a fucking donkey in sight.

But like I said, that had been their story and this...

Well, this was mine.

Meaning that I had my own mountains to conquer, starting with the main one I now faced...*one called Afterlife*. So, after my little trip down my parent's memory lane, I took the staircase up to the VIP that was situated on the upper mezzanine level that overlooked the whole club beneath. It was also a space where I had spent most of my nights before bed. A place where my father sat at his council table, hours spent ensuring the rule of his kingdom was as it was meant to be...even if it had been with a baby in his arms whilst feeding me a bottle, or later on when I was being bounced on his lap as I blew raspberries into his cheek at the time.

However, looking at the space as an adult had been quite different than when I had done so as a child. Because back then this had been my 'norm', naively believing this was how it was for most children. This shadowed gothic space with its low lighting and exquisite opulence. Its strange metal artwork on the walls and its ornate and fanciful Absinthe fountains with blown glass green fairies that danced at the top. With its unique mixture of antique carved chairs and metal modern tables that reminded you of the era you lived in, not one set hundreds of years ago in the past.

The floor was the same that also ran throughout most of my home and was a black slate that was usually adorned with thick lush rugs, dark reds and burgundy in the VIP.

As for my father's council table, that was an oval slab of black stone polished to look like black glass and one you could see your reflection in. It sat in the centre of the room on a raised dais that was situated in an area that jutted out over the stage below it and was one that curved outwards in a half moon shape with railings that followed the floor. It was also the point where you could see most of the club, although the same couldn't be said for those below.

Before I knew it, my feet were taking me over to where I'd spent most of my childhood nights, wishing more often than not, that I would have been allowed down below. Ironic really, especially seeing that most of the clubbers down there would have been wishing the very opposite. But being home now was doing strange things to me and before I knew it, I was gripping onto the tall carved back of my dad's throne and closing my eyes trying to block it all out.

In fact, I was so lost in my own escape that I didn't realise I wasn't as alone as I first thought. Meaning the moment I felt a body stepping up behind me, I cried out in fright.

"I lost my guide," Lucius' voice hummed in my ear as he caged me in with his hands gripping the tall wooden spindles that framed my father's throne. I let out a relieved breath, but then tensed the second I remembered where we were. So I sucked in a sharp breath and said,

"I think you remember your way round here." I watched as he gripped the spindles tighter before his face was in my neck and he was breathing me in deep.

"Then I *miss my guide,*" he replied making me smile to myself, but reality seeped in and once again I tensed before pushing back against his chest with my back until he allowed me space by stepping away. Then I slipped through the gap whilst saying,

"I can't...not here remember." But as I started to walk away he grabbed my hand and quickly pulled me back. Then, just as my mouth opened to tell him again, his leather hand framed my face as he pushed me back against my father's throne. Then once trapped there, he told me fiercely,

"No, but I can!" Then he kissed me. And when I say he kissed me, what I mean is...*he really kissed me.*

Meaning just like that all thoughts of my past seeped away, being set alight by the passion of his kiss and laid to rest as ash dusting the floor of fears my mind had forced my feet to walk upon. Because that was the power of Lucius' touch. It had the strength to ward away anything that had the potential to cling to my fragile heart. It brushed away the cobwebs from my sensitive soul and commanded all my thoughts be centred around him, the man who owned my heart. Which was why, instead of pushing him away like I should have been doing, I was clinging to him. Clinging to him with fists clutching the lapels of his suit jacket with a fear that if I let go, then I would simply float away.

That was of course, until I heard the clearing of someone's throat and I quickly tore myself from him in utter fear of who it was that could have caught us.

"I may be blind but even I know what you are doing, so unless you wish to get caught by someone else, say someone with a lot more roar to his bite, like the Vampire intends, then may I suggest you make your way to the drawing room before Pip eats all of the cake like your mother fears."

"Rue!" I shouted quickly and looked to where my father's witch stood looking about as witchy as a three year old on Halloween. Meaning she was about as far away from the stereotype as you could get and looked more like an eighteen-year-old skater chick/punk rocker, than who you would have ever believed enough to call sorceress.

She had black spiked hair that was shaved on one side, a white Tee with the black words 'Chicks dig my ride' over a skateboard (seeing as she was gay) which was worn with jeans that were cut off just below the knee and a plaid shirt tied around her waist. She also wore worn looking high-top converse shoes in a black and white checked design and had black bands up both wrists.

Oh, and like she said, she was also blind. Something that was easy to see with puckered burn scars down her cheeks and around her white eyes, a pair that only held a black dot at the centre. But even with the evidence on her pretty face, she still had some sense of sight with the help of the two tribal tattoos on the palms of her hands that were left over as part of her curse. A curse cast from the once Titan, Theia, Goddess of sight, which I thought was a cruel twist on irony.

I didn't exactly know much of the details surrounding why she was cursed, as it had been a conversation I had overheard once when she had been put under pressure to speak of it. Unbeknown to those included at the time that I had actually been there to overhear.

"Hey, Faery girl," Rue said, having called me this since I had been a child, one I was very much not now, especially since she had just found me kissing Lucius to the point I had been three seconds from climbing him like a stripper pole.

"Oh shit!" I said as the situation came crashing down on me like a wave of 'Oh Fucks!' as I had literally only been home for enough time to use the bathroom and I had already been caught tongue duelling with my boyfriend! Although, I had to say, it wasn't like we were making much effort to hide it, which was going to change right that moment…well, that was if there was still any point. Which was why I quickly said,

"Please Rue…please don't tell my dad, if he found out…" I stopped the second she held up her tattooed hand and said,

"I am not going to tell him, besides, it's not like I am shocked here, Faery, after all, I was the one who returned your lost diary that day…you know the one covered in hearts and…"

"Yes! Yes, yeah…well, okay then, thank you, Rue…I uh… appreciate it…now let's go should we." I said turning back to Lucius who was looking more and more intrigued by the minute and my blush wasn't helping much. That or my freaked reaction in getting her to stop talking and one look at her smirk told me she knew it. So, instead of giving her any longer to mention what would no doubt make me first place winner in the embarrassment of the year contest, I grabbed his hand and started to pull him towards the doors off the VIP. They were the ones that led into the main building of Afterlife, ones that only those who were welcome or lived there were permitted to enter through.

However, my hopes of getting there unscathed were dashed the second Rue commented as we passed,

"Welcome home, Faery. Oh, and I would definitely hide that one page I did catch, 'cause boy, it certainly looked like an interesting read, especially for a certain Vampire." Then she winked at him making Lucius grin down at her as I tugged him forward, commenting dryly,

"Helpful as always, Rue!" I could still hear her chuckling as the door swung closed.

"So, feature in this diary of yours, do I?" Lucius asked me when pulling back slightly so as I followed and stumbled back into him. We were currently standing in a large corridor and barely past the first door on the right that was where my father's office was situated. I glanced at it and then back at the door at the very end of the overly large, stately hallway where my parents' private chamber was.

"They are not in there…so have no fear, *the coast is clear,*" he told me making me snap back,

"Well, excuse me if I am not entirely willing to trust in that 'Vampy sense' of yours, as according to Rue, you want to get caught." Lucius just shrugged his shoulders, which was all the reply to this I got. So, I rolled my eyes and turned, only making it one step before his arm banded across my front from behind, now stopping me from going any further.

"Was that an eye roll I just witnessed?" he asked in a tone that told me this was all a game to him, making me snap back,

"It was and one you deserved…it was also one you can do

nothing about, as I am just guessing here, but I think even you would draw the line at one of my family members finding me bent over your knee being spanked in a hallway."

"Is that a challenge, Pet?" he whispered making me shudder against him hearing the amusement I could sense in his tone.

"No, it's a fact if you want to wake up tomorrow knowing you still have a secret girlfriend," I replied making him growl before playfully biting my earlobe.

"Yes, well may I remind you, my secret love…there are plenty of places this old castle holds where no-one would find you restrained in my arms…or hear you scream, *for you are not the only one who knows these walls well,*" he said in warning and this time I sucked in a knowing breath, unable to ignore the explicit images he invoked and feeling them down to my belly.

Then he snagged my hand with his leather clad one as he walked past and I soon became the one he was pulling down the hallway.

Only now doing so with one demand being voiced by his perfect, kissable, very forbidden lips…

"Now tell me more about this diary of yours."

CHAPTER SEVEN

IT'S ONLY CAKE

After this we reached the drawing room where Rue told us everyone was waiting and I couldn't help but pull him back, looking panicked. And Lucius knew this with one look back at me. So, without a word, he hooked the back of my neck with his palm and yanked me forward, tipping my face up and telling me,

"If you fear what they don't know, then they will discover it through guilt and nothing more." Then he quickly kissed me one last time before turning and walking through the double doors as if he owned the place. But that was Lucius all over. He didn't just enter a room by slipping inside unheard. Not unless that was his intention.

No, when Lucius walked into a room, you knew about it, sat up and took notice. Me, however, well I just thought on his words and knew he was right. If I followed him inside with the look of guilt already written upon my face, then my father would know something was going on between us in a heartbeat.

Which made me realise that, despite Lucius wanting nothing

more than to tell the world about us, he had taken one look at my worried expression and tried to ease it. Doing so by giving me the knowledge needed to keep it a secret, even though he himself didn't want to. And he did this for me...*because he loved me.*

So, I took his advice and followed him inside, doing the same as I would any other time at the sight of my mother's famous chocolate and strawberry cake sitting on the table facing me.

"Pip! You ate like half of it already!" I complained, which trust me, hadn't been the first time when my mum's cooking was involved!

"Huh?" Pip asked sat cross legged in an armchair with a mouthful and her head popping up over a huge slice overflowing the sides of a tiny china plate.

I just rolled my eyes and took a plate from my mum, getting ready to complain about the size when she grinned wide and said loud enough for the whole room to hear,

"Go take this to Luc for me and tell him not to be put off that the red bits aren't body parts." Then she winked at me after hearing Lucius sigh and roll his eyes at the comment. I couldn't help but chuckle and was secretly grateful for the excuse to go over to him as he stood next to one of the sideboards that held a tray of both tea and coffee. Of course, he was pouring himself a cup that I knew he would be taking black.

"I hope you aren't forgetting your husband whilst cutting up those slices, or I may have to take over that hand again as I did the night you first made me this cake," my dad said after wrapping an arm around my mum's waist from behind, making her look even smaller than she was.

"I didn't make the cake just for you!" she argued making him grin at her back before winking at me to tell me he was teasing her.

"That's not how I remember it."

"Oh, and just how do you remember it, old man with an aging ancient memory?" my mum replied sarcastically, making me laugh.

"I remember you trying to impress me with your skills in making it for me, that is what this *old man* remembers." This was the last of his reply I heard before walking away chuckling at the pair of them. Of course, the second I heard my mum slapping his hand and telling him things like, 'not here' then I was just glad I had turned my back on them both when I did.

Lucius, on the other hand, had turned with cup in hand so he could casually lean back against the sideboard and leisurely watch as I approached… and doing so with a very obvious smirk playing at the corner of his lips, I should say.

"Erm…my mum told me to give you this," I said trying to hand him the plate and fork that was stuck in the wedge of cake. He looked down at the plate in my hand and then back up at me, doing so slowly, which I knew was a tactic to keep me there longer. This was confirmed when he twisted at the hips so he could first place his cup down on the side before taking the plate from my hand, making sure our fingers touched when he did.

"Enjoy," I said, this time trying not to smirk myself before turning around, ready to walk back to where my parents still looked occupied. This was before Lucius' voice stopped me.

"Well, don't you want to wait and find out if I like it, after all, your mother most likely would like to know what I make of this famous cake of hers." I turned side on to him and my look asked silently if he really thought the conversation we were having was safe, as I most definitely considered it as flirting. Which was why he leant his head forward slightly and with a secret grin said,

"Relax Pet, after all…*it's just cake.*" This made me blush

before he cut a piece with the side of his fork before popping it into his mouth, winking at me as he chewed.

"Well?" I asked after he had swallowed.

"Mm, its good but…" he paused a second so he could once again shift forward a little and whisper,

"…it's not chilli fries and roast potatoes good." At this I blushed again and couldn't help it when a fingertip found its way to my mouth for me to bite. Lucius watched the action with great interest and a flash of crimson in their depths told me exactly where his mind had travelled back to, seeing as my lips were involved. But then his gaze snapped up and over my head, telling me without words that my dad was on his way over. So, I whispered,

"Bye, Lucius," and in return he almost purred,

"Until later, Pet." I turned and walked back to my mum for my own piece of cake, nodding to my dad as I passed. My mum too was blushing and I really didn't want to know why or what my dad had said to her before walking this way to have her now biting her lip, looking almost as giddy as a naughty schoolgirl. So, without commenting, I took a slice from my mum, who knew me well as she had cut me a similar size to Pip's and handed it to me with a kiss to my cheek.

"Welcome home, honey," she said making me squeeze her shoulders after first wrapping a free arm around them, telling her a little white lie,

"It's good to be home too, mum." And for some reason I couldn't help but sneak a glance at Lucius to see that he had heard and raised a brow at me as if silently calling me on my bullshit. But then I watched as my dad finally approached him and I quickly looked away before he looked to where Lucius' gaze was rooted. After that I tried not to look again, which was hard seeing as my dad and Lucius remained in what seemed like a deep conversation for the rest of our time in there.

"So where is everyone?" I asked the second we took our seats in what could have been a living room in some stately manor house set back in the seventeen hundreds. It also looked like some antique dealer's wet dream, minus the fact that none of us were naked and actually draped across the antiques, which I assumed would have played a part in it.

"Well, Sophia and Zagan should have been back from their business in New York, but knowing your aunt's love for shopping, then she probably got side-tracked," my mum said, curling her feet up in the large chair and tucking into cake like I was.

"Oooh, you know what that will mean, jellybean, more presents!" Pip said excitedly, jabbing a fork my way. But then Adam, as he walked past her, swiped a fresh strawberry from the cream filling on her plate and she was quickly trying to use that fork to stab his hand with.

"Oi! You thief! Don't make me tie you to the bed again whilst I eat this off your face…you do remember Mexican night don't you!" Pip shouted and Adam took off his glasses and cleaned them with the edge of his sweater before commenting dryly,

"How could I forget, my darling…*or the extra chillies.*" Pip giggled with a hand held straight over her mouth like a naughty child and said,

"Oh, these men we do love to tease…uh and by men I mean Adam and Big Dom man because you know, these two kids are still single…okay well, off to eat cake the way it should have been made to be eaten…Oh, Hubby Sugar soon to be cream in your face!" Pip said making me wish in that moment I was free to smack a palm to my forehead and let out an 'Oh Lordy' groan. But with my mum there now hiding half her own expression behind a steaming hot mug of tea, I was only left to laugh nervously and shrug my shoulders saying,

"Crazy that one."

"Huh uh," was my mum's agreeing cryptic reply.

A little time later and I could stand it no more, just being in the same room all together felt like one big lie screaming at me to do the right thing. Of course, it also didn't help that Lucius and my dad were still deep in conversation and from the looks of things, it was one that was growing more tense by the minute. So, with a yawn, I excused myself, first telling my mum that I was tired, something that wasn't a lie. So, I told her I was going to try and get some rest before the evening.

I was just about to slip out the door when my dad called me back asking me to join them for a moment. I froze with my hand on the door, wishing in that moment I had just slipped out sooner before he had noticed. But instead I was now faced with walking over there only to have to stand next to who I was pretending existed very little beyond friendship. When doing just that felt as if I was going against the grain of the Fates.

"Amelia, my beautiful girl, by the Gods I am so proud of you!" my father said curling me to his side the second I was within reach and giving me a squeeze. This naturally shocked me and one look at Lucius and those knowing eyes of his was taking in my reaction with a barely contained smirk playing at his lips and let's just say it made it ten times harder for me.

"Uh…okay…what did I do exactly?" I said not knowing what else to say…well, that was until my dad continued on,

"What did you do!? Amelia, Lucius told me what you did, on how you disarmed the hijackers and then you flew the plane all the way here and not only that but landing it also. Gods Amelia, but I would even go as far as saying you impressed this cold hearted bastard, as he certainly spoke highly enough of you," my father said laughing and I couldn't help it, but I blushed before finding my feet and only braving raising my gaze just enough to see his own staring openly back at me, with again that knowing smirk firmly in place.

But then, just knowing that Lucius had been telling my father of how I saved the day by flying the plane was enough to cause butterflies in my belly. The kind that were warm, fluttery and decided to stay a while. Because having Lucius in my life was powerful enough to make those butterflies thrive and multiply daily, instead of them just disappearing one day. For it was possible, as I still witnessed it between my parents. Especially with the way my dad, after all this time, still managed to make my mum practically swoon with only a few spoken words and that was after thirty years together.

"Well, you taught me well so I can't take all the credit," I said smiling up at him making him scoff before telling me,

"You are too modest, my girl… she always has been." This last part was said to Lucius who openly stared at me and replied,

"Yes, I discovered that during our time together, along with other personality traits I found most interesting." This last part made my jaw go slack as I couldn't believe he had said that, along with the wink he shot my way the second my father's attention was back on me and thankfully missed it.

"My daughter is full of surprises, this is true and holds a mind like no other, for her intelligence outshines us all." I blushed at this and leant into my father's side for the compliment and mumbled a chuckled,

"I think you're a bit biased, dad, but thanks."

"Nonsense, for I speak the truth despite my heart, but what of you Luc, you are not biased and what do you say, is my girl not too smart for her own good?" I laughed at this and rolled my eyes, but Lucius being Lucius still answered and did so with a certainty in his tone that couldn't be masked,

"Most definitely."

"There you see, and that is a true answer for he does not speak with his heart as I do," my dad added making me inwardly wince as Lucius' expression hardened. And my father thankfully also missed the way Lucius' hands curled into fists for a few seconds at his sides, telling me his famous cool façade was slipping. This especially showed when he spoke.

"And added to that intelligence is a willful nature and one that makes for a stubborn girl who thinks she knows what is best and rarely trusts in age and experience over her own intellect." I swallowed hard knowing why he had said it and tried not to let it hurt me the way it had already started doing.

But this, combined with his hard features when I was already used to seeing soft and tender when around me, well it was like a double blow. However, it was what my dad said next that really did it for me as he unknowingly cut the deepest injury,

"Yes well, I think we both know it is a case of like mother, like daughter there." I closed my eyes for a moment as those words carved deep and not in the way they were intended to do, as they had been said in a light-hearted way. But Lucius could see the truth. He even opened his mouth to say something more on the matter, but I beat him to it, knowing there wasn't much more I could cope with after that.

"Yes, well on that note I will leave you both to it," I said in a deflated tone that couldn't be helped. My dad looked down at me with concern in his eyes and hooked my chin to raise up my face,

"Are you well?" he asked making me grant him a little smile before raising on my tiptoes to kiss his cheek, telling him,

"I am just tired." Then I turned my attention back to the

other half of my soul and as way of goodbye snapped a short and curt,

"Lucius."

After this I turned my back on him without taking notice of the look of annoyance at being dismissed so easily and I walked out the door. And it was hard to miss the curious look my mum had on her face, as it was clear she had been monitoring the conversation closely. Once on the other side I couldn't help but find myself leaning against the wall next to the door and releasing a deep sigh. I even felt my hands shaking and I didn't know which emotion exactly was causing it. I was angry, upset, frustrated and confused. Half of which I knew Lucius was no doubt feeling as well, with frustration definitely being top of the list!

I just wanted to make my excuses and get back on that plane with no destination in mind just so long as it was far from here. Somewhere I had the freedom to do as I pleased and more importantly, free to do as I pleased with a certain someone.

But with this looming threat on all his people, then I knew I needed to focus not on our relationship, but more on the bigger problem we all had on our hands. For Lucius and I would just have to wait. Which, admittedly, was a lot easier said than done. Because all I could see was Lucius and the annoyed hard look in that steely blue gaze when he was being denied what he wanted.

This was the reason I closed my eyes and put my head back to the stone with only one thought on my mind…

Shit just got a lot harder.

CHAPTER EIGHT

HOTTER THAN HELL

"*Here we go again.*" I had just muttered after finding myself right back in the deep end stood opposite the doors into the VIP area. Because now it was night and I found myself out of any more excuses not to do this. After what happened in the drawing room, I had done as I said I was going to do and walked back to my old childhood bedroom and crash landed on the bed before passing out. During which time I swear I had heard someone entering my room. But as I hadn't stirred enough for them to stay, they obviously realised that I had needed the sleep and left.

However, it was shortly after this that my mind had continued to nag me to wake and once I lifted my head off the pillow, I tapped my Starship Enterprise alarm clock that projected the time onto my wall. A red glow of numbers appeared, telling me it was gone eight at night and therefore I was overdue for getting my ass into gear. So, I had dragged my tired butt from my kick ass Landspeeder queen sized bed. It was one my dad had surprised me with once my Star Wars' obsession had really hit, so he'd had it custom made for me for my birthday one year. It was made to look as if it was floating with a mirrored base unit, so it gave the illusion that it hovered as it reflected the floor. It was grey and orange, with a curved surrounding frame with 'engine' side tables holding round spaces for storage inside.

There was even a Tie fighter desk to match that had a glass top held suspended in between the wings and a Tie fighter desk lamp to match. I also had a huge mural hand painted on one wall, that made it look as if you were on the bridge in command of a spaceship and looking out into space, with an intergalactic war being fought beyond.

The rest of the walls were a muted shade of grey to continue the theme, with artwork, posters and other bits of my geek collection on display. There was even a light my mum had painted to look like the Deathstar that was actually a lamp bought at Ikea that opened up when you pulled on the hanging switch. Then, in one corner, I even had a giant floor pillow that was a Millennium Falcon and was basically the size of a bed. There was also another wall that held nothing but blueprints for Starfleet ships, all framed and arranged around the biggest one in the middle, that being the Enterprise.

But then, continuing the homage to my other geek loves in the world, there was a bookcase made to look like a Hobbit door, still containing my favourite collection of research books in my field. Not surprising really as I used to spend most of my time studying, with little else to do. There was also another shelving unit in a Harry Potter style with two shelves each in the colours of the different houses, Gryffindor obviously being my chosen house after taking an online test, because unfortunately the sorting hat wasn't real. This housed all my favourite movie memorabilia, which was more extensive than the ones now displayed in Lucius' private cave.

I even had a Doctor Who rug which was a giant Tardis, and surrounded the open doorway that led into my private bathroom and beyond that into my large walk in closet. One that was admittedly more than half the size of my flat back in Twickenham. Two places I had spent the next hour in getting ready and picking out one of the many dresses my Aunty Sophia had filled one whole wall of my closet with.

And it was one of those dresses that I also ran my hands down now as I took in a deep breath before entering the VIP. Of course, this time I had dressed with only one person in mind, and he was the first face I had seen sat at my father's table with features set in stone as if tense while waiting for me to arrive.

I took another look down at myself and couldn't help but question my choice of dress for what seemed like the millionth time. It was a pink blush coloured, knee length dress with a black sheer overlay. It had a pretty and delicate black lace top that was made up from two sections of material over lapping, creating a V neck. It was also what would have been classed as a 'booby top' if it hadn't been for the black overlay that continued up from the skirt and covered up a decent amount of my cleavage. It also meant that the top half of the dress created sheer three quarter length sleeves and cut across my collar bone with the edging being the same thick lace flowers on the top.

As for the skirt, the lace flowers continued down, trailing off to one side where the cross over top was ruched. It was also heavily layered, where the silk blush material underneath was cut inches above the knee and the overlay finished three inches past it. This continued around to the longer tear drop design at the back that brushed the backs of my legs.

I combined this with some simple black strappy heels, a sweep of curls twisted off to one side and what I hoped was elegant makeup to match. I had used dusky pinks over my lids, with a blend of darker shades in the creases and sides. A thin line of black liner, a swipe of mascara to darken my already long lashes and a dusky pink matt lipstick completed the look.

But no matter how much I liked the dress or how well I thought it fit me, I still felt self-conscious wearing it. Of course, walking in late and having the whole of the VIP turn all as one to watch as I entered wasn't exactly a confidence booster. But then again, hadn't it been a thousand times worst when finding myself walking into Lucius' ballroom with him stood at the centre of it all waiting for me.

So, I took from that experience a slice of the self-confidence I gained that night and called this a piece of cake. Then, by doing so, I straightened up before taking the steps needed to reach my father's table. Of course, I told myself not to look at Lucius, not to focus on him, not to even sneak a glance.

Then I failed.

As everyone on the table turned my way to watch me, they each took my dad's lead by standing up from their seats as I approached. Which was when I finally braved a glance at Lucius seeing as he too stood, doing so now in an almost a predatory way. This was with his eyes travelling the length of me as he rose, doing so in that knowing way. It was the look of a man who knew what lay beneath the material and was currently focusing more on the recollection of naked skin he looked to have memorised when last exploring it. His hooded gaze said nothing else but need, want and desire. Which was why I could feel myself blushing before I even reached the table.

Of course, my father was dressed for the occasion as he did most nights, along with everyone else. He wore a black, three-piece suit with a black shirt and purple tie, one I knew my mother had bought him years ago and was one of his favourites for that very reason. He had also allowed a few days growth to show peppering his jawline and around his lips, creating a shadow around the lower part of his face with dark hair. Done, no doubt, as I knew my mum liked it like this and no doubt teased him about it too.

As for my mum, she was sat next to him in her own throne style seat which was a mirror of my father's, only being white instead of black. She was wearing a stunning purple satin floor length evening gown that fell off the shoulders with over lapping material creating a plunging neckline. One that was tamed slightly by the over lapping black velvet that edged the top and bottom parts of the dress. Her golden locks were also tamed back into a high ponytail that had been twisted and knotted in a way so as a length of waves cascaded down her back. Her makeup as usual was light, with only a slight brush of colour over her lids and tint of red to her lips, colour that mostly looked to have been kissed away already.

Both of my parents' eyes lit up when they saw me approach and my father took a few steps away from his seat and held out his hand for me to take to lead me up the step to the raised dais. So, I curtsied with a cheeky wink telling him,

"Always the gentleman eh, old man?" To this he placed a large hand over his heart and feigned the hurt inflicted telling me,

"Ouch, you wound me, little one." I patted him on the chest as I stepped up and said,

"You have survived worst, Pops." My mum chuckled and my dad grumbled,

"I am beginning to think your mother is a bad influence on you."

"Or the right one." My mother replied before embracing me as I walked over to her, then telling me,

"You look stunning, Fae."

"Thanks, mum," I replied before looking around the table, to see Pip and Adam were already there and Adam was also wearing a suit. This time it was one of grey tweed with a dark red shirt beneath and grey bowtie. He straightened his glasses from where Pip had been purposely walking her fingertips along the top and tipping them crooked.

"Little Bean," Adam said nodding and Pip shot two imaginary guns at me and said,

"Looking bang, bangin' smoking hot there, PetalPants!" making me smirk before motioning to her own outfit and telling her,

"Back at you, aunty Pip." This was referring to her own dress that was in two parts, with the top half being a cropped halter neck top that showed off her belly. The bottom part was a full skirt that had a huge slit up one side to the waistline because obviously just showing off her belly wasn't enough skin exposed for one night.

The skirt part was also a navy blue and purple tartan, and the top was black leather with two rings of material roses in the same tartan as the skirt, all sewn on the top in circles around her breasts.

Her hair was in pigtail buns with longer pieces framing her face and leather flowers pinned there, each with barbie head centres that were made up to look like mini Pips. This was complete with green and pink hair, and matching makeup, that was thick black with neon eyeliner with large flicks at the sides. Her lips also matched the theme.

They were both sat on my mum's side of the table, which also just happened to be at the same side as Lucius, with a single seat in between them. On my dad's side were two empty spaces and then Takeshi, his seeker, who was also standing upon my arrival. He was a handsome Japanese man dressed as he usually was in a black and red robe style tunic top with long wide sleeves that covered his hands, combined with loose pants.

So naturally I took one step towards my dad's side ready to take a seat when my mum stopped me,

"Fae, you are better sitting on this side as Sophia and Zagan said they should be back shortly." She then nodded to the only seat free that just so happened to be next to Lucius. This then meant that I had no choice but to do two things, the first was finally look at him and the second was walk his way ready to spend the entire evening sat next to him.

And with that one look, it meant that the first, only ended up making the second so much harder. And why?

Because simply put, he gave new meaning to the saying…

One Handsome Devil and Hotter than all of Hell.

CHAPTER NINE

VERY IMPORTANT PET PEEVES

"*Gods,*" I couldn't help but mutter to myself as hot as Hell and dangerously sexy was the only way to describe how Lucius looked. He was wearing a navy-blue suit that fit him like a glove, being tight in all the right places on his large upper body. I could also see the waistcoat beneath the jacket knowing that it too would fit him perfectly, tapering in at the waist in that delicious way.

He wore a crisp white shirt beneath it, open at the neck, with no tie and he lowered his gaze enough to pull his shirt cuffs further down past the jacket sleeves as if using this as a reason to hide his knowing smirk. This gave me a glimpse of both the black skull cufflinks and black leather glove he was never seen without. Even his hair had been styled back and his face freshly shaven for the occasion. It was also a look that slammed me right back to the first night I had stepped foot inside Transfusion seven years ago. The intimidation level was most certainly that high.

He was utterly stunning and right there and then, it felt as though I had lost all claim to him. Because we were no longer in his domain, in his Kingdom under his rule. No, we were in my father's and here he was back to being the forbidden fruit I had only ever dreamed of possessing me. Which was why, looking at Lucius, I swear I didn't know whether to run or just keep standing there like a cartoon character with my mouth open, my tongue lolling out and my eyes bulging from my head.

But then he looked right back at me and his look said it all, he wanted to know what I was going to do next. But then something in my gaze must have indicated my hesitation. Maybe it was the fight or flight response he was seeing. The one that was currently swinging more to the flight side of the spectrum, because suddenly Lucius pulled out the chair next to him and said,

"What are you waiting for Fae, I think you know that I won't bite you by now?" There were some chuckles around the table and Adam purposely chose that moment to kiss Pip the second she opened her mouth to say something that most likely would have blown our cover. I laughed in a way that was total bullshit and mumbled a,

"Yeah, I know." Then I walked over towards where the seat was waiting for me and Lucius, acting now as gentlemanly as my father, held the back of the chair out for me. It took me back to what might have been classed as our first unofficial date when he had done the same for me in his favourite restaurant. I mumbled a thank you as I took my seat and the moment I was down, he pushed it in towards the table and whispered so only I would hear,

"Now, as for later..." This was said as an addition to his biting comment and I quickly looked up at him over my shoulder, watching as he re-took his seat along with everyone else now that I was settled in mine. I nearly choked when he

winked at me. Oh yeah, 'cause this night was going to be easy…NOT!

But then he also must have seen how tense I was, as he turned my way slightly and said under his breath,

"Relax, Pet." I gave him a strained look in return and then the second I felt my dad's eyes on us, I said quickly,

"Sorry, I was late, did I miss much?" Alright, maybe I should have taken Lucius' advice seeing as my voice came out a little higher pitched than normal. But hopefully my dad would simply put this down to the stress of the day, or more like the last few weeks. Which also made me wonder…exactly how much of what had been going on or had happened had Lucius told my dad?

"Only your mother trying to convince me it would not be healthy to have you sent straight to a Scottish tower and surround it by guards and have no one enter until the threat has passed," my father said making me sigh before telling him in a serious tone,

"Then I am inclined to agree with her."

"Um, funny, as Luc said the same thing," my father said in a way that seemed to be questioning why, before taking a sip of his drink, one that was smooth honey amber in colour, so was no doubt some expensive scotch. That was when my mum placed a hand on my dad's arm and said,

"That's because it's as barbaric now as it was when you used to threaten to do the same with me. Which does make me wonder when you will realise that us 'little women' do tend to have a problem with the idea of being locked up like the family crown jewels that need protecting." My dad simply put down his drink and told her,

"Fuck the family jewels woman, you are my Electus!" he snapped making my mum quickly remind him,

"Yes, and if you recall I am also an Electus that has proven time and time again that she can protect herself." My father growled at this, especially when she patted him on the cheek in a teasing way that most with their sanity intact wouldn't have dared to do, considering my dad's temper.

"Seriously, I used to think your father was one step away from becoming a caveman and just hitting me over the head with a big club before dragging my blonde ass back to some cave somewhere," my mum said laughing, making my dad grumble,

"Yes, and simpler times those were, I've no doubt."

"Oh, trust me, my broody King, I very much doubt women back then were much different, they just took their time and struck at the right opportunity, knowing when to bite back," my mum replied making everyone laugh, all except my dad and Luc. No, instead my dad simply caught my mum at the back of her neck and pulled her to him for a secret promise,

"I will be reminding you of these words later...*when I will make you pay for them with those witty lips of yours.*" Her reaction was to melt as was usual, at the same time biting her lip, whilst mine was to groan aloud, raise a hand and say,

"You do remember your daughter's home, right...and like, right here?" I then waved at them both, making my mum chuckle and my dad say,

"And?"

"And I do not need you two painting pictures in my head that no daughter should ever have, only to need therapy to try and remove them," I said making mum laugh before my dad argued,

"Is it not healthier for you to see your parents in love?"

"In love, most definitely...announcing what you are going to do to one another later in the bedroom whilst mum feels you up under the table in front of your daughter...as yes mum, I see you..." At this she blushed and coughed a little before shamefully bringing her hand back up from under the table like a child that had been caught stealing cookies from the cookie jar.

"...then that would be a no. But hey, mazel tov and all, on what is blindingly obvious a cracking sex life but as far as having your daughter trying to function in every day society, without my random answers to things being, 'Oh yes, I am ready to order dessert now, but first, did you know my parents still shag like bunnies, oh yeah, the death by chocolate cake sounds like a good choice right about now, thanks'...then I suggest that be the first thing you protect me against, Pops," I said making Pip burst out laughing, along with my mum who started snorting uncontrollably. Even my dad laughed, and I smirked because hey, making people laugh felt good. But then I felt Lucius' hand grasp my leg under the table and I swear I nearly shot out of my seat.

"Then I promise to pay for the best therapist money can buy for there is no will on Earth, Heaven or Hell that could prevent me from being as I am with your mother," was my dad's reply and Lucius muttered under his breath at me, before taking a swig of his beer,

"I know the feeling, only with your daughter." Then he squeezed my thigh tighter to emphasise his point and I sucked in a quick breath before putting my hand under the table to try and pry his fingers off me. An attempt that seemed pointless when trying to prevent Lucius getting what he wanted. So, naturally, this was to no avail, as he simply turned to me and mouthed the word,

'Sneaky,' then slapped my leg the same time he moved his chair back to hide the sound, before going right back to holding it again, and the warning was clear. Meaning, I had no choice but to go back to pretending it wasn't even there...something that was most definitely easier said than done! I also had to

wonder why my father hadn't heard what he had muttered under his breath, as for a supernatural, then they would easily have heard this with their heightened senses.

So, the question in my mind became...*was he controlling certain aspects of people in the room?* I had been told of his extraordinary powers of mind control before and even heard that it was once used on my dad. But seeing as this witch had the power to make those rogues immune, along with humans who stood with them, then I was yet to see it fully in action.

"Gee Pops, thanks for the offer and all, but I think I will just stick to closing my eyes, singing la, la, la and believing the stork delivered me to your door," I said and before thinking about it I grabbed Lucius' beer and tipped the bottleneck my dad's way before taking a long swig. Of course, my eyes widened as I was still mid swallow, thinking shit, shit, shit! However, it was Lucius who came to my rescue as he burst out laughing and swiped the bottle from me, telling me,

"Like I keep telling you, little Draven, that one is mine...By the Devil's hands, but I don't know what you have been teaching your daughter, Dom, but she keeps stealing my drinks," Lucius said, now giving reason to the action and making a joke of it. Which, thankfully, made my dad smile and lose the questioning look I saw starting to brew. My mum, however, strangely was smirking at the comment, like I often found her doing when watching us...*did she know something like Pip had suggested?*

"Get this girl a drink before I find myself dry!" Lucius shouted with a gesture of his hand in the air, gaining a waitress named Candra's attention. Of course, Candra was also a stunningly, beautiful brunette with blue streaks in her hair and someone I wanted to hate the second she winked at Lucius. But then I couldn't, because I had known her since being a child and she was actually a really nice Angel. Plus, she had no clue that we were together, so as far as she was concerned Lucius was just a single hot King who might be in need of some company to help warm his bed for the night. Meaning Lucius was right…

This was painful.

Which was why, by the time she came back with a beer for me, one Lucius had ordered, the second he thanked her and she flirted back, I grabbed his leg this time and squeezed as hard as I could. But then when he smirked and asked,

"Candra isn't it?" I used my nails and dug in to make my point, giving Candra a strained smile in return, before telling her,

"I think my mum could do with a top up." She bowed her head at me and said,

"Yes, Princess," thus making me wince at the title.

Lucius, obviously feeling smug, took another swig of his beer and at the same time his free hand left my leg to cover my own hand instead. I had expected to feel him trying to peal my fingers from him but instead he shifted my hand further up until I could feel for myself the obvious bulge behind his suit trousers. My hand tensed and I tried to pull back, but with his hand covering mine it wasn't easy without making shit look obvious. So, I looked desperately around the table and suddenly stood so I could bow to Takeshi and Lucius had no choice but to let me go.

"Mana no ketsujo o yurushite. Konbanwa, Ohayo gozaimasu," I said starting off with 'forgive my lack in manners' and finishing it with an evening greeting in Japanese. He bowed in return and granted me a soft smile before telling me I had caused no offence and then went on to ask me how I was in the same language.

"That's it, my next year's resolution is to learn more languages!" My mum declared making me laugh as it was the same complaint I had heard many times before. Along with my dad's reply, as he took my mum's hand from where she had banged it on the table at her declaration and started kissing it, after saying,

"I believe, wife of mine, that I have spent a good few years trying to teach you...*alas, to no avail"* At this she rolled her eyes and said,

"Yes, well, that is because you are too distracting."

"And what is it that distracts you, my love?" my dad asked in that tone, one I knew was flirtatious and only ever reserved for my mum. She snorted a scoff like she typically did and counteracted,

"Ha, yeah like you don't know!" His eyes flashed purple for a few seconds as they usually did when banter was on the cards between them and replied with feigned confusion,

"I am but at a loss, Sweetheart, so why not enlighten me."

"Oh yeah, that's all you need, your ego stroking," was her answer. To which my father replied not as quietly as I would have liked when cupping her cheek and pulling her closer,

"It's not my ego you can stroke, Vixen."

"By the Gods, I swear, it's like I am not even here?" I muttered as I took an even longer swig of my drink, wishing now it was something stronger that burned when it went down just to give my brain something else to concentrate on.

"I see you, Jelly Bean...Jelly Bean?" Pip said offering me a sweet from the packet she had in her hand and smiling, showing me that she now had a green one stuck in between her teeth where her gap was.

"You keep eating them by mistake, don't you?" I asked her before she sucked it back in her mouth creating the gap again, whilst answering,

"Yup, sure do!" Then she grabbed a red one and stuffed it in the gap again after chewing. Meanwhile, my mum was still complaining about languages.

"You know, I never had any problem learning Spanish, so what does that tell you?" she asked complaining and making me smile.

"That clearly you were more focused back then," was my dad's reply, making her snap back,

"Oh, I have focus, Draven, in fact I have it in spades and buckets and hidden vaults full, that is not the issue," she said making me chuckle and shake my head, before commenting,

"Then perhaps too much focus…*in the wrong places."* My dad chuckled and my mum faked a scowl at me before telling me,

"Hey, you're on my side, remember?"

"Am I?" I teased back,

"Yes, you're a girl, therefore we are on the same team…plus you're not too old for me to ground you," she teased back and with a smirk in place I replied,

"I'm pretty sure I am but…auch immer du sagst, Mutter." This of course made Lucius laugh as I had said, 'whatever you say, Mother' in German. My mum, in response, pretended I was in trouble by shaking the neck of her usual Corona at me tutting, and muttering before taking a swig,

"Bloody Draven smartass genes."

"I heard that, little one," my dad said on a playful growl taking her fingers in his hand and biting the tips. So, in return, she pulled his hand closer and bit the fist around her hand making him fake a silent *'Oww'* before she silently, mouthed back, *'Baby'*.

"Aww, aren't they just adorable?" Pip commented in a breathy dreamy way with her head now held in the frame of her hands and her elbows to the table.

"Oh, just darling," I commented drily making Lucius again chuckle next to me.

"And like I said, my focus isn't the issue," my mum went back to saying.

"Entonces que es, carino?" my dad asked in Spanish, meaning, 'Then what is, Sweetheart?', a language my mum actually knew, hence the reason he picked it.

"Well, for starters, my Spanish teacher was in his sixties and looked like one of the Twits." Everyone frowned in question except me, as Roald Dahl wasn't exactly in the Afterlife library. Of course, I knew the story from my mum who used to read it to me as a child, meaning I was the only one who burst out laughing.

"What's a Twit?" Pip asked making me tell her,

"A book about a crazy couple that are disgusting to look at and are horrible to each other...don't worry, you would love it." At this she nudged Adam and muttered only two words,

"Amazon prime." This made Adam roll his eyes before getting out his phone and muttering,

"Time to make the richest human, even richer." I chuckled at this, as technically my father was actually the richest man alive, it was just that no one knew it but his people. But then, being thousands of years old and for most of them being known as a King even in the human world, well then it was no wonder really as he had investments older than most the buildings in England.

"So, this Twit fella?" Pip asked my mum who replied,

"Basically, he had a beard so long he would sometimes come to class without realising he had cornflakes in it, he used to scratch his ass as if he wore a thong and smelled like mould, so I am pretty sure he lived in his attic...that, my dear, is why." She said this last part directed at my dad, making us all burst out laughing and Pip ask,

"Sounds like a fun guy to me, but why weren't you focused on that?!"

"Yes, well, he also had the personality of a hermit that would throw a travel book at you if you knocked on the door, hence why it was easy to focus on the actual learning part of the class," she told Pip.

"And why was that, Mum?" I asked.

"Well, nobody wanted him to come close to them because he smelled so bad, the only way that wouldn't happen was if people actually handed in their work and legged it out of class at the end," my mum replied making my dad laugh before pulling her in for a kiss, whispering over her lips,

"I can think of other ways to help you concentrate." She raised a brow at him in question, to which he whispered this time,

"Class Incentives." This made her bite her lip. So, once again I closed my eyes, placed my hands over my ears and repeated,

"La, la, la… the storks are real!" This made my mum stick her tongue out at me like a child and say,

"You will understand one day, Fae, when you find yourself a man." Then she winked at me, but I just rolled my eyes and said,

"Yes, and does that mean I could get my own back without Dad wanting to kill this mystery person when he is whispering sexual sweet nothings in my ear?"

"Yes," was my mum's reply.

"No," was my dad's firmer reply and I had to say, it was one way to drive my point home to Lucius. But of course, everyone laughed except him, who instead downed half his bottle, looking thoughtful whilst doing it.

"That's what I thought and precisely why I am in no rush to bring a guy home for dinner, especially one where the tour of the house would include comments like, 'let me show you my dungeon' or better yet, 'and now for my weapon collection'," I said making my dad laugh before shrugging his shoulders and telling me,

"Fathers protect their daughters, Amelia, it's what we do." I opened my mouth to argue that point, when suddenly Lucius did it for me.

"Or they teach them to protect themselves and trust in their capability to do just that," he said whilst putting down his bottle and looking straight at my father with nothing short of a challenge. Pip even whistled as you would when a fight was about to break out on the school yard. Adam wisely clamped a hand over her mouth and when she looked back over her shoulder at him, he just shook his head telling her no.

My father took a deep breath and calmly placed down his drink before addressing Lucius on his comment.

"You seem to take a great deal of interest in my daughter and her capabilities, for since you arrived here you have had a lot to say about them," my dad said making me shoot a look at Lucius and before I could stop myself, I asked,

"You have?" However, he ignored my question, or the way he could no doubt hear the pounding of my heart in my chest.

"As would you, had you seen for yourself first-hand exactly what she is capable of," was his reply, making my mum secretly smile, even though my dad was doing anything but.

"I know what my daughter is capable of!" he snapped losing his cool. Now Lucius, on the other hand, was keeping his firmly in check like he usually did. Even when he said,

"Bullshit."

"Lucius, stop it," I hissed, which was something he ignored again and his fist clenched around his beer bottle.

"Excuse me?" my father said dangerously, leaning forward and my mum's hand moved to rest on his forearm before squeezing it as way of containing his rage.

"You heard me, Dom."

"You don't think I know my own daughter?!" he snapped, and I muttered,

"Oh, here we go."

"No, in fact, I don't think you do, for if you did, then you would most likely let her lead your armies!" Lucius snapped back making me suck in a shocked breath, because in this house, then it was one of the nicest things anyone had ever said about me. Because no matter how much I knew my parents loved me, all I had wanted was enough respect to feel a part of their world. Which was the biggest battle of all and one that continued when my father snapped cruelly,

"Is that a fucking joke!?" I hissed air between my teeth at the blow and my mum snapped,

"Dom!" But my father was too far gone to realise how far he was taking this, so the argument continued,

"The only joke is how blind you have become to the fact, Dom," Lucius replied but it didn't matter because my dad had the last blow before I exploded and it happened the second he threw back at him,

"She's a fucking human, that is fact enough for me!" My mum even sucked in a startled breath and snarled,

"Dominic!" But it was me that put a stop to it after officially losing my shit.

"ENOUGH!" I shouted erupting out of my chair and slamming my hands down on the table, causing everyone in the room to shut up and take notice.

"Amelia, what is…?"

"NO! I said enough and that is what I fucking meant!" I snapped cutting my dad off quickly and continuing even after he said,

"Now listen to me, my girl, you do not get to speak to me…"

"Well, that's where you're wrong, dad, as I am not a child

and therefore you don't get to treat me like one! You want my respect, then try earning it, because Lucius is right, you have no idea what I am capable of! But then again, you never will know because all you see me as is some weak little human you had by mistake, instead of my golden balls brother!" I said panting and my mother covered her mouth with her hands in shock and my father actually looked as if I had slapped him! So, I calmly kicked my chair back and snapped,

"Now, if you will excuse me, I think I will go and join my own kind, after all, it's where I feel more welcome!" Then I walked over to my mum, kissed her cheek and said,

"Sorry, mum." Then I continued on despite my father growling my name in warning and walked down the steps of Afterlife without looking back. And by the time I got to the bottom of them I was shaking I was so angry.

Meaning that I ignored all the startled and gossiping looks from a club full of people and walked straight to the bar to order myself a drink, one much stronger than beer this time.

So, when a barman came and took my order, there was only one thing on the menu...

"Tequila."

CHAPTER TEN

LUCIUS

BREAKING CHAINS AND MAKING CLAIMS

The second Amelia was up out of her seat so was I, with the full intent of going after her, damning all the consequences of doing so! But then I wasn't the only one as Dom was also out of his seat and now looking at me in both a challenging and questioning way. However, it was when Keira slammed her bottle down, rose out of her chair and snapped,

"You two sit your asses down whilst I go and deal with this!" But when neither of us did, she then allowed that slice of power to slither from beneath her fingertips, making all glassware on the table start to shake, rattling along the onyx top. Then she hissed one word with her eyes turning black and dangerous,

"Now!"

Wisely her husband decided it was perhaps best to listen to

her and even though I could have controlled this demonic side of her, being the one who sired her, I too decided against it. This was only out of respect I had for the girl and also the fact that she was mostly likely the best person in this situation to comfort her daughter's outburst. An outburst that had been more than warranted. Something Keira also knew if the way she turned those deadly eyes to Dom and said in a dark tone,

"And you had better have your apology at the ready…"

"I will not, for I have done nothing…" Dom started to say, but Keira cut him off and when doing so, the sound of everyone's glasses cracking drove her point home.

"You were in the wrong and *you* will apologise, Dominic, so help me God or tonight you will find yourself sleeping on the damn couch!" Then with that, she stormed off angrily, ignoring the way he said her name in hopes of containing her fury. However, she ignored him and instead continued on towards the staircase, slightly skidding on a heel. Because not even her clumsiness would cease its antics in the face of her anger and any other time the sight would have made me smirk.

Dom then held the bridge of his nose in frustration before his gaze snapped to mine and he demanded in a demonic growl,

"You and me…office, now!"

"With fucking pleasure!" I snapped back slapping my hands down on the table and pushing back my chair before I simply exploded out of it and destroyed the fucker! Then I walked away from the table with Dom mirroring my actions, doing so now to the sound of Pip asking,

"What just happened?"

Then, as we both very near cracked the floor with our determined steps from the VIP, this was the moment Sophia and her husband Zagan appeared.

"Now where is that gorgeous niece of mine?" she asked as

Dom's only answer was a growl down at her and my own was a snarled,

"Ask your hothead brother!" She looked confusingly between the both of us for a moment and then turned to Zagan,

"Seriously, we have been gone for what…two days?" We both ignored her comment and continued on back through the double doors, entering his home. Then we stopped at the first door on the right that led straight into his office. Once inside he took his angry ass over to his desk and slammed the door with his mind, making it rattle on its hinges. Something that I knew with his temper, had he touched it, then it would have been in pieces. Although, I had to say, he wasn't the only one close to losing his shit, as my usual calm facade was slipping and fucking fast at that!

But then again, it usually was where Amelia was concerned, as it seemed losing your head was an occupational hazard when finding your Chosen One…something right now I had to try not to do.

"Now, would you like to explain to me what the fuck that was?!" Dom snapped, getting right to it and in that moment, I wanted nothing more than to tell him to go fuck himself, as I explained myself to no-one! But then Amelia's heartbroken face came to mind and the second my memory reminded me of the sight, I knew I couldn't burn her bridges just yet. So, I took a deep breath and told him,

"It was exactly what it fucking looked like."

"Yeah, well what it looked like was you interfering in my private family life when you have no fucking right or say, to do so!" I curled my lip at that, once I wisely turned my back on him after first raking a hand through my hair before facing him again. Because I was furious and quickly finding it was getting harder to keep a lid on it. So, for those short quick seconds I focused on anything in the room but the man I had to face, once my king and now father to the girl I was in love with.

The room was as I remembered it, a long open room with the same bare pale stone walls that ran throughout his home. A huge carved desk was situated off to one side with a heavy seat behind it ready for his ass to calm down and sit in it! A small seating area was on the other side with a fucking Gods awful teal velvet sofa that screamed the likes of his sister. Stone pillars connected to the arched ceiling above and stood like sentinels throughout the space. Then, at the far side opposite the door, was a wall of glass. It was one that folded back and led onto an open, arched balcony that at the moment showed black skies and stormy weather. A sight that mirrored both of our moods which was why I reminded him,

"You brought her reaction on yourself! I was merely making a point." I told him wanting to say oh so much fucking more!

"Yeah, and a fucking big one it was, Luc! Which begs the most important question as to why?"

"Why?" I repeated the question knowing that I was stalling for time and I hated the fact that I even needed to.

"Yes, why, or is being questioned now so much of a foreign concept for you these days, for I am owed the fucking answer!?" Dom snapped and in turn so did I.

"I don't owe you shit!" I snarled at him, making his demon growl back in return.

"What the fuck do you want from me anyway, I kept the girl safe and just because I made a point to speak on her behalf, you think you have the right to make fucking demands of me!"

"She is my daughter," was his answer, whereas mine should have been, 'and she is my Chosen One!' Something that felt like swallowing a bag of nails and demon teeth when not being able to say it.

"That maybe so, but you do not get to throw allegations my

way and to what exactly…what the fuck are you implying, because if you are, then just come out and fucking say it already?!" I snapped.

"Who is it that is dating my daughter!?" I frowned at this and couldn't help but jerk back a little.

"Excuse me?!" Was he fucking joking?!

"You heard me," he snapped telling me that he wasn't.

"Yes, I did but that doesn't mean I fucking understand you!" I told him thinking that this was the Gods' version of taking the piss and amusing themselves.

"I know you know who it is and I swear if it is one of your own and you are protecting them, then I will find out and guess who I will hold accountable when I do!" he said and I swear I couldn't help myself but I actually laughed! Because the irony of it all was most definitely worth the reaction.

"You think this is fucking funny?!" he snapped, and I dragged a hand at the back of my neck and released another disbelieving laugh before telling him,

"By you asking me who is dating your daughter, then yeah, I think it's fucking hilarious!" I told him boldly, making him slam a fist down on his desk and roar,

"I will kill him!"

"Oh, relax Dom, you will do no such thing, even if he existed," I told him having no reaction at all to his outburst, coming to expect it by now.

"No, you think I wouldn't?" he challenged.

"No, I don't." I told him boldly and before he could say anything more on the matter, I reminded him of exactly what would happen if he did…*or try, seeing as that fucker was me.*

"Not unless you want to lose Amelia and never see your daughter again," I reminded him and his outburst, making him finally get a hold on his rational thoughts and start using them.

"Besides, what is the harm if she is?" I asked knowing that I was walking a fine line here with this question, but I had a point of my own to make.

"Are you fucking serious?" he barked, making me roll my eyes before trying for reason.

"You're the one who fucking threw the fact that she is human in her face like a fucking insult." He growled low before raking a hand through his hair hard enough I was surprised he didn't rip the fuckers out.

"I didn't mean it like that!" he argued and unbelievably, I knew it as well, despite how it sounded to Amelia.

"No, you didn't but nevertheless, that is how she took it and that was exactly how it sounded," I reminded him leaning back on one of the pillars in the room, now taking in a man who looked guilty and was frustrated by the fact, which was why he hissed,

"Fuck." Then dragged a hand down his face.

"Look, I am not telling you how to be a father, Dom, I am simply pointing out that by her dating one of our own would in fact mean prolonging her life in the very same way you originally planned with Keira…after all, she is destined for someone and I very much fucking doubt he is human." At this he finally started to think on my words, and I had to say he looked torn between hating the idea and focusing on the benefits it would bring.

"I am not ready for that," he admitted making me unable to help scoff a laugh before telling him,

"Perhaps she is."

"So, there is someone!" he snapped making me decide it was time to back track.

"That is not what I am saying." At this he seemed to relax a little but not enough that he didn't see past my obvious interference.

"You seem to take a great deal of interest in this?!" he asked suspiciously and this was when I knew I had to give way to caution. So, I shrugged my shoulders casually and told him,

"During our time together then I will confess I felt somewhat responsible for her," I confessed and continued quickly knowing what I said next would make him think twice about questioning me again.

"Something which I will assume is acceptable to you, seeing as it is undeniably better for your sake when making choices that benefit her safety, than doing so based on thoughts of indifference for the life I am charged with protecting whilst in my kingdom." At this he scoffed once but the lack of response told me I had hit a nerve for he knew my words to be true.

But then I also found myself adding more for I couldn't let it go unsaid, hinting at my feelings for her and testing the waters so to speak.

"Besides, she has an infectious nature and I enjoy her company, for I feel as though during this time we have developed a friendship. One she seems reluctant to show in fear that you would…well, behave as you are now." I told him hoping this would account for any further contact or conversation together and not fuel his suspicion.

"What else do you expect? She is my only daughter," he said as he deflated into his office chair like a father who had no clue what the fuck he was doing.

"I expect nothing…but Amelia on the other hand, well my best guess is that she expects the respect she believes she deserves through her past actions and proving herself more than capable to be a part of our world," I told him in a calm tone now that his own rage had simmered somewhat.

"She is my world! She should know that!" was his reply and as sentimental as it was, the proof of his words had yet to be shown.

"I am not speaking of the love of a father, Dom."

"Then what?! I give that girl everything she needs!" was his argument and in that moment, I wanted to ask if he really was that clueless. He was speaking merely of material possessions, when all she needed from him cost nothing but trust given. Which was why I challenged,

"Everything?"

"She is human, Luc, what the fuck would you do?" Oh yeah, he understood me now.

"Fuck, Dom, have you actually seen this girl fight!?" I told him making him sigh and shake his head as if it wasn't enough, so I told him,

"Look, a few weeks ago I would have been with you on locking her in some fucking tower somewhere and throwing away the key. But since then the things I have seen her do, well fuck me, I am over two thousand years old but even I am fucking astounded!" I told him and he raised his eyes to mine now looking hopeful.

"You don't exaggerate?"

"When have you ever known me to?" I answered his question with one of my own and again he started to look thoughtful.

"She's that good?" he asked and I laughed without humour and told him,

"In all your years, Dom, *all your fucking years*, have you ever witnessed a human girl bring down a trained killer with nothing but a piano stool and a fucking pencil?!" I asked him, making his eyes widen before asking in return,

"She really did that?"

"Fuck yeah, she did and that was after dispatching the threat of another with shaving foam and then killing another with a lamp cord that nearly severed his head! Now, if that isn't skill, then I don't know what is, because it's that or your daughter has more lives than a fucking cat in Hell!"

"I know my daughter has skills, Luc, that is not an issue here."

"Then what the fuck is?" I questioned in a dumbfounded tone.

"They were all human, and as you know in our world then being a good fighter is not enough." Okay, so he had a point, but there was more he didn't yet know.

"I would have agreed with you, had I not only days ago witnessed her being surrounded by rogues and killing them without gaining a fucking scratch, two of which Liessa told me she did with a fucking shoe and a sink!"

"Fuck!" he hissed as if he could barely get his head around the idea.

"So, you tell me, Dom, don't you think she deserves a little more credit and belief in the ability to take care of herself?" I asked, knowing that I had driven my point home, especially when his head fell to his hands and he muttered,

"Fuck me…she did all that?"

"Saw it in the flesh, Dom, along with the one she used my own sword to impale before I freed him of his head," I replied making him shake his own as if he was trying to picture it all. I knew this when he said,

"I knew she had skills, but Gods, I had no idea it was to that level."

"Yeah, well, don't even get me started on how many bones she has broken in between those mentioned and more," I commented thinking back to it myself and now shaking my own head.

"She certainly sounds resourceful."

"Oh yeah, she's resourceful alright, for there should be a whole new word invented for what that little girl of yours is!" I replied scoffing a laugh once more and thinking about Pip's bloody keepsake from the plane ride here.

"You respect her?" he surmised and I didn't bat an eye or let it go more than a heartbeat before I told him,

"Fuck yeah, I do, as do the rest of my council, for there is more."

"Gods, but what else could there be!?" he asked in a tone that was pure disbelief.

"She saved Liessa from the Mercs and for my Enforcer, I think you know what that means." Dom hissed and said,

"Caspian vowed a soul of life to my daughter?"

"He did, and one she tried to give back telling him that the next time he wanted to say thanks, for him to trying doing so with flowers or chocolates." Dom laughed at this and said,

"She certainly has her mother's humour all right."

"And her strength of will and courage," I added because it was true…in fact, I was in mind to believe she even surpassed it at times.

"You really do admire her, don't you?" I shrugged my shoulders and played it as cool as I was capable of doing in that moment,

"She reminds me of a stubborn King I used to work for once." And I wasn't lying, for as much as Dom and I had been faced with our issues, those grown from the seeds of his betrayal, our battle was long over. And as for now, well then, I couldn't help but remember our time spent as brothers at arms, rather than those spent as enemies at war. But he also had to understand that now we were stood on equal ground and he wasn't the only one with a Kingdom to rule. And seeing as now those Kingdoms were about to cross, and in a big way, then it would seem that we were all in this shit together whether we liked it or not.

But getting back to daughters like their mothers, I told him,

"And speaking of stubborn…I suggest bracing yourself, Dom, for your wife is on her way up here and is on the warpath," I told him as he had obviously been too deep in thoughts to sense her coming like I had. But then, as her Sire, perhaps it meant my senses to such were slightly quicker than his own.

Dom's head snapped up and he took a deep breath, as if doing as I suggested by bracing himself. Because seconds later the door was being opened by a blonde fury who looked similar to the day she squared off to a God and won.

"Just what the Hell do you think you two jackasses were playing at in there!?" she roared slamming the door and this time the wood cracked. Not that she noticed the lightning bolt splitting the length, being too far gone in her rage to do so.

"Keira!" Dom said in warning and I swear I almost laughed for the good it did him.

"Don't you Keira me in that tone! Do you know how much you just upset our daughter, and one, may I remind you, that is barely fucking here to begin with?!" she snapped back, now holding her arms rigid and hands balled into small fists.

"She took my words…"

"As the insult it sounded, Draven!" she said cutting him off and I always questioned why she chose to call him mainly by his last name. I had done so myself after the discovery, but that was done so in mocking when…well, admittedly I wanted to piss the bastard off.

Dom sighed before getting to his feet and no doubt spending the time trying to ask the Gods to grant him the patience in dealing with his angry wife.

"I did not mean it as an insult, and she should not think of it that way," he said and after speaking with him of his fears then I had to say, I was starting to feel sorry for the man.

"Then go bloody tell her that, because tonight you just broke your daughter's heart and in all honestly, I am not sure that my own survived the experience unscathed." Dom's entire body jerked as if he had just been struck and now that father's worry turned into something much more profound. Which was why, before she even had chance to physically react, he was around his desk and in front of her in a heartbeat, taking hold of her face by cupping her cheek to then utter a whispered term of endearment,

"My heart." Keira closed her eyes and held herself rigid, unable to yield just quite yet.

"I will fix this," he said and I hid my knowing grin. Because if there was a single person in this world who had the power to bring Dom to his knees then it was his wife...and in all honesty,

I, unashamedly, knew the feeling.

"You'd better, Draven, or I swear…"

"I will fix it, I swear it, my love," Dom said not letting her finish, and no doubt too afraid that she would.

"You get that you were in the wrong here…right?" she asked raising a brow as if surprised that she didn't have more of a fight on her hands at convincing him of that fact.

"I was, as I spoke too harshly and should have handled the situation…"

"Like a father, not a king," Keira finished off for him and this time he was the one closing his eyes before he nodded. Especially when with tears in her eyes she said in a quiet tone,

"It feels as if I have already lost one child, and I refuse to lose another…do you understand what I am saying?" Dom took a deep painful breath and told her whilst placing his forehead to hers,

"I do…*I do, my wife."*

After this moment between them, Dom looked back at me and told me,

"I thank you for your council once again, my old friend, for it seemed to be what I was in need of, and our daughter is in your debt also for speaking up on her behalf when she could not." And with his words being said, then I had to confess that throughout it all was when I found it the hardest not to speak the truth.

To not be granted the freedom to tell him that Amelia would never be in debt to me, for she was the other half of my soul and for that, I would have done anything for her. I wanted to tell him it was my right to speak up for her and it was not done solely to be the voice of reason like he foolishly believed.

But then there was also the other part of me that now felt as it had that fateful day Dom had betrayed me, only now, the roles had reversed, for *I was the one to betray him.* And one look at his wife who also knew the truth, showed the guilt my conscious felt but didn't show. A foreign feeling that was starting to seep into my once cold heart and one only recently thawed by my Amelia.

Because Keira too had betrayed him, doing so with the knowledge she held and yet still hadn't spoken of once. And why, because I had asked her not to and because she owed me that loyalty. But it was also because she wanted her daughter's happiness above all else and she knew it was one day fated that I would be the one to give it to her. A happiness that was threatened if Dom knew the truth and acted the way we both knew he would.

Which was why, in that moment, it affected me in a way that I couldn't stand and therefore needed to get out of this fucking office before I suddenly crossed the point of no return and told him.

"There is no debt…now if you will excuse me," I said in

reply to his thanks, leaving then without another word and ignoring either reaction from them. After which I quickly stepped into the hallway near desperate for fucking breath! I looked both ways for the indecision of which way to go felt far too fucking profound than I would have liked.

Because he had been free to claim his wife, yet I felt as if my queen was shackled to this place and in order to finally make her mine, I had first to figure out how to break those chains.

Break chains and not…

Her heart.

CHAPTER ELEVEN

AMELIA

TEQUILA, CHAMPAGNE AND COCKTAILS

"I'll have the same again," I said to the new employee that I didn't yet know, and had I been in a better mood, then I would have most likely introduced myself and asked his name.

But not tonight.

"Fucking mistake," I muttered to myself and the second the bar stool moved next to me I didn't even glance at it, as I knew who it would be.

"I see Lucius is rubbing off on you," my mother commented before nodding to the barman and saying,

"I'll have what she's having please, Martin." Ah, so that was what his name was, good to know I guess. Then, before I could stop myself or the three shots before it, I said,

"Oh, you have no idea." Then I downed the fourth that had

been put down before me, ignoring the salt and lemon like all the others and sucked in the air through my teeth at the burn.

"You waiting until you have a whole one?" my mum asked, making me finally look at her to see her nod at all the wedges lined up on one of the fancy Afterlife branded napkins.

"Well, you know what they say when all you have is lemons," I commented dryly before going back to looking head on at nothing in particular and taking a swig of my beer.

"Throw one at your father and hope one gets in his eye?" was my mother's witty reply finally making me laugh, despite it being one that was short lived.

"Yeah, well, you can be the one to throw it for me as I would probably just end up missing…you know, on account of being human and all," I replied in a cutting tone that made her release a deep sigh.

"I know this might not be much consolation here, but will it help to say that I understand what you're going through?" This time it was my turn to release a sigh before rubbing a hand over one eye in frustration and turning my head to her, saying,

"Why, did gramps want to throw your ass in a tower and let you die a virgin?" I asked making her scoff and obviously hiding the fact that I wasn't one anymore.

"Hardly, in fact I think he couldn't wait for someone to come along and take me and your Aunty Libby off his hands," she replied making me mutter,

"Lucky you."

"Look, I get it okay, your dad takes possessive to a level even Lucifer would cringe at, but I know for a fact that he doesn't think any less of you for being who you are, Fae," mum said and as comforting as her words were, it also was coming from the wrong person.

"Oh, you mean human?" I snapped making her look around at who was close by and shake her head as if trying to get through to me wasn't going as easily as she hoped it would. So, quickly feeling guilty, I sighed and said,

"Look mum, I know you are only trying to help, but nothing you say right now is going to make what he said okay…it didn't back then, and it especially isn't right now."

"But that's where you're wrong, I am not here to make excuses for him as what he said wasn't right," she told me putting her hand over my arm and squeezing it.

"Then why are you here?" I asked turning to face her once more.

"To see if my daughter is okay, because I miss her, and I love her, and I hate that you have been home for not even a day and you were made to feel like that." She paused and shook her head as if she still couldn't believe this had been my homecoming.

"Mum, it's not…" I was about to tell her that it wasn't her fault, but she continued on,

"…To be made to feel as if you're not welcome here, made to feel as if there is a line between us and that Theo is somehow more important to us because he is like your father," she said making me tear my gaze from her at the mention of my brother's name. As let's just say that we weren't exactly on what you would call speaking terms and felt more like two people that just so happened to have the same parents, rather than being siblings.

Because, once he came on the scene, that was when things got complicated and things for me changed more rapidly. And no matter how much I knew at heart it wasn't directly his fault, my mind still blamed him. It was when I started to feel more and more like the outsider as he seemed to just step into my place and embrace the life I craved. That was why I never spoke about my brother…

Because it was too painful.

Now, as for my other brother, well that was where shit got even more complicated, for he just blamed everyone for what he believed was his curse. Because, whereas I craved to be one of them, he craved the opposite…

He wanted his human life back.

He hated and utterly loathed who he had become and the demon inside of him that was said to battle him daily for control. The demon he despised that was simply waiting to consume himed, feeding from his own hatred of what hand the Fates had dealt him.

Thane, my brother, was complicated and broken.

That was what they said and to be honest, I had no clue seeing as it wasn't as though I had ever spent much time to get to know the man I called brother. However, Theo I knew. And he wasn't complicated, and he certainly wasn't broken.

No, Theo was a hero.

Thane was the runaway.

And I…

I was the human disappointment.

Not that my parents would ever say as much, but really, with my father's words spoken only four shots ago, then what else was I supposed to think? Sure, it was only earlier he had been saying how proud of me he was for flying that plane. But how long had that lasted before I was back to having being human thrown at me like an insult?

"I'm fine, mum," I said before lifting my empty shot glass, one etched with the club logo and shook it at Martin stood at the end of the bar, who got the hint pretty quickly.

"Really, 'cause you could have fooled me," my mum commented before telling him to just leave the bottle and hold the lemon.

"Answer me something, mum, did you ever feel torn between the two?"

"Of course I did. I wasn't exactly born into his world you know."

"Yeah, I know," I replied but she wasn't finished.

"And I most certainly didn't feel a part of it, not for a long while anyway," she told me pouring us both another shot and showing me her leftover skills from when she worked behind the bar all those years ago. Doing so now with a little trick that looked like she made the glass disappear from her hand and ending up in the other, after drinking from the shot glass.

"So, what changed?" I asked being curious.

"Mainly...*your father did.*" I frowned at her answer and therefore asked,

"How so?" Then she smirked at me, grabbed a piece of lemon and sucked on it before dropping it in the empty glass and telling me by getting close to my ear,

"He found his humanity." I gasped a little at hearing this, as what she just said felt far too profound to ever leave me. Then she gave me a kiss on the cheek and left me to continue drinking and it wasn't alone as I would have liked. Not when I heard her talking to her posse behind me.

"Don't let her puke on her hair." I rolled my eyes at this, as I heard the stools either side of me sliding back this time, before both spaces were taken up by my aunties. Both of them I adored but with that being said, then I knew this meant that my chances of drinking alone, getting shitfaced drunk and wallowing in my own self-pity, was now off the cards.

"So come on, what did my dumb brother do this time?" My aunty Sophia said, leaning in and kissing me on my cheek as a way of welcoming me home. As usual, she looked utterly stunning and reminded me of a porcelain doll, with her utterly flawless skin and black glossy curls. Curls that at the moment were tamed and all swept off to one side. They were held there with a row of deep blue diamonds secured and clustered on a hair clip, with a few curls purposely escaping and hanging loose around her face. She also had eyes like my father, that were dark and framed with thick black lashes, with lips that always looked naturally tinted red. And like always, she was looking as though she had just stepped off some fashion runway in Paris or should I say this time, more like New York.

Her dress was a navy-blue halter neck with a silk handkerchief style skirt that hung in pointed waves around her slim legs and was a pattern of thick and thin lines in different shades of blue. She also looked like an Angel but was, in fact, a very powerful Demon. And if the barman who came over to her had known this, then I think his reaction of awe in sight of her beauty would have been quite different.

Of course, he then asked if she wanted a shot glass before nodding down to the bottle of Tequila. She frowned, looking slightly disgusted and said,

"Do I look like I would drink this shit? No, get me a bottle of champagne from the reserve, please." Martin then nodded, obviously being too tongue tied to do much else and instead turned to Pip and asked her what she would like. Pip grinned big and as if she was on autopilot said,

"I'll have sex on my face, please." To which I groaned the second the poor barman looked like he was choking on his own spit,

"Oh, Lord."

"Gods almighty," Sophia said and Pip shrugged her bare shoulders and asked,

"What...what I say?"

"She will have any colourful fruity cocktail you have that doesn't have the word sex in it," Sophia asked for her, making me chuckle.

"Gottcha," the barman said looking thankful that she had intervened.

"So come on, what did he do?" Sophia asked and I released a deep sigh, my millionth of the night and said,

"How long have you got?"

"For you, gorgeous...*I've got an eternity,*" was her awesome reply.

"Oh dear, do you think we will get into trouble, because do you remember that time we got Keira shitfaced just before her first wedding?" I heard Pip ask somewhere next to me, but seeing as I was now the shitfaced, drunken one, then it was kind of hazy.

"You mean *you* got her shit faced, as you're the one who gave her too much!" Sophia replied to Pip over my head, one that was currently resting against a hard surface that could have been the bar...although I wasn't sure as things got blurry pretty quickly after my...erm, I don't know how many shots of tequila and bottles of beer.

"Yeah, but look at this way, at least she isn't randy like her mother was and close to humping our legs...so win, without the second win as she is just drunk not drugged," Pip replied making me wonder what the hell they were taking about.

"Oh great, just great, I will remind Keira of that when she asks us why we let our niece get wasted and passed out in vomit," Sophia commented drily making me quickly lift my head up slightly and groan,

"Eeew."

"Oh, don't worry tipsy lipsy, that's just lemon juice off the napkin, you didn't puke...not yet anyhayway," Pip said making me sigh in relief before she turned her attention back to Sophia and said,

"Yeah, but she just said not to let her puke in her hair and look...still pretty." At the same time I felt my hair being lifted up making me giggle 'cause it kind of tickled.

"And plus, she's happy, so another win to add…no?" Pip asked at what must have been Sophia shaking her head.

"Hey, I flew a plane today, so that's a win for me too," I said lifting my head up and getting in on the conversation.

"She did?" Sophia asked making Pip tell her,

"Hell, yeah, she did, but that was after she stopped the plane getting hijacked and killed the pilot with an ice bucket…but don't worry, he totally had it coming."

"Holy shit? How did I not know any of this and how the Hell's blazing rivers do you kill a pilot with an ice bucket?!" Sophia asked, getting high pitched.

"Firstly, you were shopping and secondly by putting it over his head and shooting him under it, of course…and trust me, *it seemed very effective at 30,000 feet.*" I heard Pip add this last part in a whisper and think she did so behind her hand but couldn't really tell as she looked too blurry. Thankfully, whilst this conversation was happening, the bar had already closed and we had been helping ourselves to drinks ever since. Meaning I had no idea how many I'd had or what time it was, but I knew I was one drink away from passing out and needed my bed regardless. Oh, and preferably before I did vomit, as I had a feeling that was still on the cards. But then, that would have been my own fault seeing as I'd only had cake and a few sandwiches before deciding to skip dinner and sleep instead.

"Seriously sounds as if I have been missing all the fun," Sophia complained.

"Yup, it was Upic…get it, cause we were Up in the sky and…"

"Yeah, I got it Pip. So, what do you wanna do, grab an arm each or call ourselves a Ragnar?" I giggled at this which ended on a hiccup and made me bump my head into the top of the bar I was still face planted against.

"Oww," I complained making Pip rub the spot on my forehead I had hit as she continued on with their conversation,

"Only if we can call him a Ragnar Car…you know instead of calling a cab or…"

"Yeah, Pip, I got it…jeez I do live with you, woman," Sophia commented with a sigh.

"And?"

"And after thirty years, let's just say that I speak Pip," she replied, this time making me giggle.

"You two are funny," I said laughing again which was interrupted by another hiccup and then a burp and then finally finishing as the laugh it started off as.

"Nice… phew this chick could burn down bridges if I'd brought a match to that party stinkfest."

"Oi! Who you talking about, miss? I can spell sex burping," I complained in reply to Pip's comment, as yes, she had already done that once and unfortunately it had been before the club had closed.

"Yeah, I spelled it, I didn't set it on fire…*like the rain.*" Pip said singing this last part.

"Hey Adele, focus here, yeah?" Sophia snapped clicking her manicured fingers in front of Pip's face and again, I giggled.

"Just like when me and Lucius argued in the car, Gods, he is so hot!" I said making Pip laugh hysterically in a fake way that would have been obvious coming from anyone else that she was hiding something. But then this was Pip and she could get away with all sorts of behaviour without it being questioned. But just for good measure she also said,

"Wow, check out this one, eh, talking that crazy talk." I ignored Pip's comment, one that was probably trying to get me out of giving anything away and looked at Sophia with a big daft grin and asked,

"Do you think he knows how hot he is?" After this I heard

footsteps approaching and before I could look I took Pip's giggle as a bad sign. But then what I took as even more of a bad sign was when Sophia replied to my question,

"Uh…I don't know, maybe you should ask him."

After this came the worst and final sign and that was when the man himself spoke, now making me want to crawl behind the bar just to hide my shame.

Especially when I heard Lucius question in that sexy voice of his…

"Hot, am I?"

CHAPTER TWELVE

HOT, DRUNK AND TIME

"So hot, huh?" Lucius said and now instead of wanting to hide I threw caution to the tides of tequila and decided to embrace my drunken state. For I quickly melted at the sight of him…because even blurry he was hot.

"And handsome," I said hiccupping again after it. Sophia raised a brow in question and Pip said,

"As you can see, she's a little three sheets to the wind… although, I have not the foggiest idea where that saying came from or what it really means…let's ponder that a moment, don't you think?"

"Just in time as we were in need of some assistance," Sophia said making him reply,

"Yes, so I can see." Then he picked up one of the nearly empty bottles on the bar and shook it, making the small amount at the bottom swish. I giggled, raised a hand and said,

"Ooops, I did that." I then gazed up at him and noticed the telling smirk on his lips as he looked back down at me, telling me he was amused.

"So, that assistance, what we really mean is sneaking her back in her room without mummy Queenie and daddy Kingy seeing her and also making sure that she doesn't puke on her own hair, 'cause that part was specific," Pip said making Lucius look even sexier when he raised a brow in question. It was just a shame she let slip about the puke bit, as that kind of ruined the cute drunk thing I had been hoping to achieve.

So, I decided to try and prove that I was alright so he wouldn't have to deal with 'Elpukeo, Mistress of Tequila' should she threaten to make an appearance, because let's face it, no one wanted their hot boyfriend seeing that.

"It's fine, I am sure I can manage…right girls…whoa, why is the floor moving?" I asked the second I got down from the stool and started to sway.

"As fun as that would be, I'm not sure it is though," Pip said but the second I took another step I was falling as Lucius caught me and soon that floor wasn't just moving, it was disappearing.

"Easy now, I've got you," he told me softly, meaning I was now in his arms being lifted up so he could hold me closer to his chest. Which automatically made me snuggle my head into his neck and breathe deep,

"Mmm, you smell so good," I hummed making him chuckle before telling me,

"Also, good to know."

"Uh…I think we should come with you," Sophia said in a tone that told us all she didn't quite trust Lucius with her niece in his arms, especially seeing as I wasn't exactly acting as restrained as I should appear to be. Which was why I pulled back, tried to shake my drunkenness from my mind and said,

"Ooops, sorry Vampy." Pip laughed at this and finally so did Sophia. Lucius also looked as though he was about to reply with something I knew he shouldn't, but it was Pip who spoke up first, unknowingly saving us from discovery.

"Oh, I am sure Luc can get her back. Besides, Adam and Mr Paley will be waiting for us in your playroom." Sophia groaned at Pip's comment and said,

"Please stop calling him that."

"What, he's Albino, and a sexy one at that…I mean, what should I call him, Mr Needs a Tan…'cause that's a bit long?" Pip replied making me chuckle.

"How about Zagan like everyone else does?" she recommended.

"Well, that's not very personal is it…hey, what do you call him, Ziggyzigan, the wannabe Spice girl…see what I did there?" Pip asked making Sophia sigh before asking,

"Why does everyone need a nickname with you?"

"Because it elevates people to awesome status…duh," she said looking at me and Lucius and spinning a finger at the side of her head and mouthing,

'Crazy' in reference to Sophia's question.

"Alright, so what do you call Luc then?" she challenged with hands on her hips. Pip then looked us both up and down, (because I was in his arms and currently was part of that package) then she said,

"After tonight…His Royal Hotness." This made Lucius chuckle the second I slapped a hand to my forehead and mumbled,

"I am never gonna live this down, am I?"

"Oh yeah, 'cause that's not too long at all," Sophia grumbled and honestly, I could feel myself sobering up by the second.

"You know I hate to point out the obvious here, but I am pretty sure Lucius has better things to do other than holding me all night whilst you two bicker," I reminded them making Lucius hold me a little tighter and Pip burst out laughing muttering,

"Oh yeah, I am sure he does." So, I shot her a look that as soon as Sophia's back was turned, she made a 'zip her lips' gesture at the same time I was rolling my eyes...although admittedly, doing so made me dizzy. But, thankfully, after that we all made our way back up the staircase to the VIP and through the double doors.

"You know I am sure I would be okay to walk," I said ending it in a hiccup and making Lucius look down at me in a tender amused way. Then, with that trademark smirk firmly in place, he whispered down to me,

"Quiet, my little drunkard." This made me blush and shyly tuck my now loose hair behind my ear, the style long gone and escaped. This was due to some questionable head banging to one particular song from me and Pip...naturally, Sophia didn't head bang, but she had swayed her hips a little.

But then something that Pip said finally made it to the sense making part of my brain and I suddenly burst out laughing, telling everyone,

"I finally get it... Ziggyzigan, the wannabe Spice girl... genius!" Lucius looked like he was trying to keep in a grin and Pip threw up her hands and said,

"Finally, someone who appreciates my comedy genius!"

"She's drunk off her ass, Pip, don't get too excited," Sophia commented dryly making me scoff,

"Hey, I am not drunk off my ass!"

"Oh no, I am sorry, are those your legs you're using to carry your drunk ass back to bed?" she questioned, making me actually take the time to look down at Lucius carrying me and say,

"Okay, good point... don't get too excited, Pip, I'm wasted." At this last part I looked to Pip who patted my hand and said,

"That's okay, honey, drunken people still need comedy

genius in their lives, so I am still classing this one as a win." I then winked at her, clicked my tongue to the roof of my mouth and shot an imaginary gun at her saying,

"Gottcha."

We continued down the many hallways of Afterlife and soon came to the point that one way took me to my room and the other to Sophia and her husband Zagan's private wing. One that contained another club at its centre and what was known as Sophia's playroom. A room which naturally was a no go zone for me, back then, now and forever.

"I wonder if my Adam Picklebear picked up that bag of Jelly Babies I wanted, 'cause one of those squishy suckers is gonna be my new tooth!" Sophia rolled her eyes before ignoring her question, coming over to see me, pushing my hair back from my forehead and asking,

"Are you okay if Luc takes you to your room and puts you to bed?" At this Pip burst out laughing and muttered,

"Oh, I just bet she will be," and then tried to stop it quickly when all three of us shot her a look, making her nearly choke when she did and say

"What? I think we already established that he's hot and who wouldn't want a hot guy to take them to bed...right?" Well, as far as arguments went, then Pip was right but unfortunately for me it hit a little too close to the mark seeing as we were secretly sleeping together.

"I will be fine," I muttered quietly, turning what I knew would have been a beet shade of red. Sophia gave me a warm smile before then turning her serious eyes on Lucius.

"In, down and out, Vampire...you got me?" Sophia ordered in a stern voice at Lucius whose lips twitched slightly before telling her,

"In, down and out, Demon...I got you." His reply made her fight her own grin before she grumbled,

"You are lucky that you're hot, Vampire...I'll give you that." This made him grin before nodding and telling her,

"A title I will take over cold hearted bastard any day when faced with three beautiful women." At this Sophia smirked in a knowing way and Pip pretended to swoon into the side of his arm, making me giggle when she threw a hand to her forehead and sighed,

"Oh Lordy, take me to the cleaners for I feel oh so dirty!" Lucius, obviously being used to her antics, grinned down at her and told her,

"Then off you go to get even dirtier, little imp, for your husband grows impatient and will no doubt punish you for being late." At this she beamed back up at him and said,

"Oh, you do say all the right things, Vampy! Well, if you insist my Lordy bee!" Then she gave him a salute and left her swooning for the man whose name she had tattooed across her knuckles surrounded with hearts, flowers and kisses. Then I watched as she left together with Sophia, who looked over her shoulder at us before turning her head back to her friend and asking Pip,

"Did this happen often at Blutfelsen, only he looks very comfortable with the task?" I tensed in Lucius' hold thinking this was it, we had blown our cover.

"You mean Amelia passing out and Luc carrying her to bed...yeah, happened all the time," Pip answered with a bat of her hand, before granting us a cheeky look over her shoulder and winking at us, which was the last sight I saw before they disappeared around the corner. A reply that made me bury my head in his neck and mutter,

"I'm so screwed." He chuckled before kicking open the door to my bedroom and told me with certainty...

"Not yet, but there is still time."

CHAPTER THIRTEEN

LUCIUS

THE DEVIL'S BLOOD AND HIS BEASTS

I had to say carrying Amelia back to her room whilst drunk enough to feel free to act how she wanted around me, was an experience that I enjoyed immensely. Despite my amusement at her comments, it was the way she unknowingly held onto me, gripping my shirt in her fist as if she never wanted to let go. And I had to say, that choosing that moment to walk in on their conversation to hear her commenting on my physique didn't hurt either.

But, like I said, it was that freedom for her to do so that really stuck with me and at the time, unbeknown to her, it was like a soothing balm to my wounded soul. Because once I had left Dom's office, I had found myself storming through the halls of Afterlife until I reached the room I had been given. Doing so with purpose just so I could ignore all aspects of the room other than the balcony that beckoned me to step onto it.

I then released my wings, a pair that looked as though my feathers were blazing like Icarus who flew too close to the sun. After which I took to the stormy sky and soon found myself taking a seat under some covered pagoda in someone's private rooftop garden…most likely Sophia's as, if memory served me right, that was usually what she did when bored. Something that throughout the years happened often and much to her brother's dismay.

But I was thankful for being there for this was when I was finally able to take breath. Because being back at Afterlife, and once again I was fighting my own restraints. Only this time I knew the taste of her skin and the touch of her lips. I knew the true beauty that lay hidden beneath each layer of material she concealed herself with. And quite honestly, it made me fucking itch to rip it all off and touch her bare skin as it was made to be touched by my hands alone.

It was like being back to those torturous days where once again she was the forbidden fruit, only one I had now sampled and by the fucking Gods, I wanted more!

I was fucking addicted.

An addict that was sat trying to contain myself enough to get a handle on that addiction. To simmer the intense need I had for her to a level I could, at the very least, fucking breathe through!

I, King of all Vampire life…*fucking addicted to a mortal.*

But of course, I fucking was! Because Amelia wasn't just anyone, she was a fucking Goddess in geek clothing that hid the body of a woman who had the power to turn Saint to Sinner in a heartbeat. But her beauty wasn't the only aspect about her, for there were layers to the girl I was still peeling back and discovering. I hadn't exaggerated when trying to convince Dom of how incredible his daughter was and had he been right of mind in that moment, then he would have used that mind better in being able to detect so much more in my words.

She was constantly a fucking marvel to me, astonishing me at every turn. If I lived for another thousand years, I don't think I would ever forget the moment I walked into that fucking cockpit and found the sight that welcomed me. To see her with a gun in hand and a bloody ice bucket over the pilot's head to prevent the bullet from hitting a window. Her cunning nature was as deadly as the Devil himself!

But then it had continued as she had barked out her orders to me to get rid of the body before she seated herself in that blood splattered seat. One that, from her reaction to it, could have been covered in fucking glitter for all she cared, as she simply took hold of the controls, turned to me and said words I would never forget,

'Oh, don't worry, this one I know how to fly.'

"Gods alive," I hissed before pushing all my damp hair back against my skull, as it was wet from the short flight up here. I was angry with my thoughts, especially when it took me back to all that happened once we had landed. For that was when all her walls started to erect. I knew it the moment she had looked towards that convoy of SUVs that she would rather we sit back down, buckle up and take off once more. And I hated the fact that in that moment I couldn't give it to her. Because despite how much it pained me, Adam had been right. There was only one place safe for her and that was as far from my own kingdom as I could get her, which unfortunately, took me to her father's.

But what was worse, was that she still didn't yet know about my intentions to leave, something I knew I needed to do soon, because the longer I stayed, then more of my people would die. I already knew from my council, who were doing what they could by monitoring the situation, that the number of deaths were coming in hourly. It seemed that the first wave of my sired Vampires to turn rogue were the masses I had turned upon the cleansing. The first day I stepped foot back into this world not as a human man, not as one of Christ's disciples, but as a King.

I had been put here with a job to do and all that refused to kneel under my rule lost their heads and with them, their vessels. It was a bloody rising and at the time one done with far too much ease than my conscience liked to admit thousands of years later. But I had been a different being then, full of rage and twisted bitterness, with a clear disdain for not only human life but the mindless beings I had been charged with controlling.

However, all who did kneel then spent the coming weeks feeding from the Devil's nectar. One consumed from the Devil's veins inside me that he had pulled like strings on a new puppet. Filling them straight from the heart he had touched when punching a fist through my chest and flooding my new vessel with the life blood of the damned.

Bitterness indeed.

But I had quickly done the fucking job I had been given a second life for and once it was complete, I had walked away from the throne I didn't want. Instead, I had sought out one that did rule, for I wanted no part of ruling. So, I had become Dom's second in command and his right-hand man for the best part of two thousand years.

Until the day he betrayed me.

Of course, knowing now the reasons behind that betrayal had been beyond his control made that bitter pill towards him easier to swallow. For it was a betrayal that had been fated and done so that one day it would save who was to be his Chosen One, even if at the time she hadn't yet been born. Something that wouldn't have happened had I not stopped the second world war when I did and let her family line be deployed to the front line as he had been assigned to do.

But it was because of Keira that our personal war had ended, and another quickly took its place, now one in her name. For I foolishly believed the girl was meant to be mine. But it had all been a cruel trick of the Fates to get me to feel enough about her so I would protect her and continue to save her life. An act that unknowingly doing so also meant becoming the Fates' fucking errand boy in saving the fucking world instead. And my gift for that had been the loss of a hand and having to wait nearly thirty years to finally claim my true Electus.

And now that I had her, I knew the true power it held and as much as I respected Keira, she was never meant to be the girl for me. She was only ever supposed to be the one to gift me my Chosen One, and she knew that the same as I did, soon after Amelia was born. A fact I had fought against for a very good reason, and that reason was one I looked down at now and fisted beneath the leather.

My Venom of God.

I snarled down at myself before gaining my feet and punching it through one of the angelic statues situated next to one of the wooden posts that held up the structure. The pale face crumbled around my hand, one that had already taken far too much, that it actually brought me physical pain to think about its consequences. Other than the threat of taking Amelia's life, then her finding out the truth was the only other thing I was fucking terrified of happening and being here only drove that point home even more.

It drove it home the second she ran from my grasp and into the arms of her once personal guard, the former Viking King, Ragnar. He was a big bastard to be sure and had he not meant something to Amelia, then I would have put him on his ass for the disrespect he had shown me.

The difficulty of seeing her in the arms of another without first being able to prove my claim, was something Amelia wouldn't have been able to understand. Hence our argument in the car and why I had been left to watch her as she stared out of the window with the look of dread on her face the closer to Afterlife we travelled. It was the reason the gust of frustration left my sails and a calmer journey took its place. Of course, it helped immensely when she crawled into my lap and was soon kissing me. Despite it being done to aid her in achieving her goals in getting me to agree with her wishes...something I wanted to do about as much as I needed a hole in the head.

But I had not been able to say no to her. Hence my foul fucking mood and the reason I was removing my hand from crumbling stone. For the struggles of that agreement started the second we arrived and hadn't stopped since. Although, I had to confess, the bittersweet ache in my chest at seeing her embracing her mother outside the doors to Afterlife was a touching one. It was a sincere one, even for this once cold-hearted bastard. For it was obvious the love she had for her parents. Even despite her strained relationship with her father, her embrace had been one of the heart, not one of duty.

Of course, my situation had improved slightly when it became obvious Keira's interference in playing matchmaker, unbeknown to her husband, for it was subtly done. Hell, even Amelia seemed oblivious to it and trust me, Keira's acting wasn't that good! For one she had always been a shit liar but then again, she had once pulled off the biggest lie in history and on her own wedding day no less...so maybe she deserved more credit than I was giving her. Of course, coming back from the past and discovering I had sired her without even knowing it had been one hell of a surprise that day!

It even made me wince thinking about the circumstances that could have led to such a feat, as there was only one way to turn a human and it wasn't as simple as feeding from a slit in my wrist. No, it was one only accomplished through a fuck load of pain and near death on my part. Because that Devil's fist in my chest had been done for a reason and one drop straight from the source was all it took to turn human life...well, that and their death. It was why turning Adam had been an exception, first finding death at the hands of the woman he loved. Then once being accepted into Hell by the Devil himself it became a quick turnaround as moments later he found himself right back in his vessel as something new. A demon granted enough strength in the hopes of accepting the Devil's beast without first being ripped apart.

To be honest, I had little doubt at the time that it would have worked. But then again, the Devil had been determined to get Abaddon out of his Kingdom and let Earth's realm deal with the fallout...or should I say, to let me deal with it. Because as his Sire he was my responsibility and had in the past destroyed a whole island. This was because some idiot decided to try and use him by kidnapping Pip, thinking that he could hold her to ransom. That ransom being by forcing Abaddon to do as he wanted. But what many failed to realise was that Abaddon couldn't be reasoned with or controlled. He was the very meaning of fury and wrath. He had been forged in Hell by the souls of thousands in constant rage and the only thing that managed to calm him down was a shadow Imp named Pip who had been given to him as a plaything to snack on.

She didn't control him or even try, for she simply amused him. She took that rage and shadowed it by offering him so much more in the way of love and affection. Something that over time the beast had come to crave and should that craving, that addiction, ever be taken from him, then the shadows clouding that rage would lift. They would evaporate and leave nothing but destruction in its path to finding that cloud once more.

It was an addiction I and my Demon could understand.

It was also why, over these last fifteen years or so, I had come to understand Adam in a way like no other. Well, besides the other Kings perhaps. Or maybe it was why Adam understood me like no other.

Either way, here I was again, having stepped past the threshold of Afterlife and finding myself watching Amelia from afar only minutes after doing so. It had been like stepping back in time.

She had excused herself and gone to the toilet as if needing the time to compose her emotions at finally being home. So, I had watched as she had emerged and walked across the club in a way as if she had another's memories playing out in her mind. Perhaps it had been her mother's, for it seemed as if history was repeating itself for two Kings thirty years apart. For it was said that during that time he wasn't as free to claim Keira when she first set foot inside the club, as he would have liked.

A thought I had decided to crush the second I saw her taking a moment to herself by her father's throne, for I could watch her struggling with her own thoughts no more. And the witch had been right, I had wanted to get caught. I had wanted in that moment for her father to walk back inside the walls of his club and find out who had claimed his precious daughter.

A thought I now struggled with after speaking with him in his office, for he was right, it was like stepping back into the past and offering him council once more. I even remembered the days where I had spent time drinking with the man as he contemplated aloud when his Chosen One would finally walk into his world, struggling with the years as they went by. And still, I had offered him the council of my thoughts in a genuine desire to ease his suffering soul.

He had been a friend.

And now, he was the last obstacle to completely claiming my own Chosen One, just as I had once been his. Mirrored lives of two kings indeed. But the only question that mattered in regard to Amelia wasn't what type of King I wanted to be,

It was what kind of man she made me want to be.

Which was why I couldn't help the things I had said at that council table, unable to hold back on her behaviour. Just as I had done in his office and just as I knew I would do time and time again. Because no one took away what Amelia was rightly due in respect of her strength, her courage and will, as that was what I would fight for… that along with the ownership over her heart.

Which was also why my thoughts had finally led to the decision to leave the rooftop, having decided quickly that I needed to see her and what I had found stopped me in my tracks. Gods, but I swear she had the power to make my heart take pause and cease its beating. She was magnificent and so full of life it made my chest ache just to look at her.

Of course, she had no idea that I had then spent the rest of the evening sat in the shadows, watching her drinking herself silly. But even though I knew that she was in danger of making herself sick, I found myself far too mesmerised at the sight to stop it. So, I sat there, enjoying the show she unknowingly gave me and watched as she drank her sadness and anger away and had fun in between Dom's sister and the naughtiest Imp alive, and it was easy to see she adored them both.

And time seemed to seep into oblivion for life continued on all around me, buzzing like flies as humanity moved at a different speed. And all the while as only one beating heart held my interest. Lights changed colour, songs merged from one to the next and life came and went but my eyes never strayed…for there was only her.

I felt like I was a fucking stalker, memorising my prey and waiting to make my move. A move I made when I heard her comment. Because the second I heard her mention my name then that was when my limit reached its peak and it was time to put my little sun to bed.

And speaking of bed...

CHAPTER FOURTEEN

WHAT ABOUT BOB?

"Erm…okay, well this is my room," she said once I had placed her back on her feet, making sure she was steady. I looked down at her with my hand still holding her forearm taking care as she swayed without her own knowledge. She looked so shy with the way she nervously tucked her hair behind her ear as she had done when in my arms and I had to say, it was fucking adorable. But there was more in her gaze and it was then that I realised that she was shy because I was now in her room. Because this wasn't just her world, it was her *private world.*

She was nervous because being in this room now meant something to her... *my reaction meant something to her.* Of course, she didn't know that I had already been in here and seen a slice of her geeky world. Or should I call it more of a shrine to sci fi?

It had been when she hadn't joined her family for their evening meal, one I had only shown up for in hopes of speaking with her. This was after she had left abruptly because of what was said in the drawing room when I had let my frustrations get the better of me. It had been after Dom's comment about me not being biased that had struck the wrong nerve within me. And subsequently taking it out on her seeing as she was the reason he was still allowed to believe his words to be true, when they couldn't have been further from the truth.

But when I had walked inside her room the first thing that my eyes had settled on was her peacefully sleeping form very near passed out from exhaustion. For despite her denial, I knew that flying my plane all the way here had taken its toll on her nerves. She had done amazingly well, and I had spent half the fucking flight utterly astounded and the other half as hard as fucking rock! A particular aspect I had naturally held back when explaining things to Dom, for obvious bloody reasons.

So, I had let her sleep, for I knew she had needed it. Which had meant a restless wait once seated at Dom's council table for her to arrive, questioning every five fucking minutes in my mind if she even would. And then the moment she had walked through those doors, she had struck me once more with her breath-taking beauty. One that wasn't in any way less so now, despite her drunken state. No, now she was simply without the artificial colour upon her lips she didn't need, and her hair was cascading down around her shoulders and back in a carefree way.

But when she had first walked into the VIP, she had done so the vision of a princess, all poised and dignified. All the things that were expected of her when sat at her father's table. And now, well this was my Amelia and she was fucking perfect as she was, for no other version of her was needed when sat at my own table.

The girl who now looked at me nibbling on her fingertips looking unsure as she awaited my response to a room I had already studied. So, I couldn't help but be her cruel, playful bastard and tease her,

"Are you sure, only it looks like a spaceship to me." To which her fingertips fell from her mouth and she smacked my arm, putting more strength than usual into the move and whilst still holding back a grin she said in feigned outrage,

"Oi! It's not that bad."

"Bad? Who said anything about bad…No, I am simply hoping that when I walk into your closet I find a range of sexy silver spacesuits so we can indulge in a bit of role play," I said walking further into the centre and running a finger along the top of what I assumed was a Captain's chair. I then looked up to see that it was as I thought, a screen came down so this was where she could sit whilst watching her beloved sci fi.

Cute.

But my comment made her burst out laughing and I relished both the sound and the fact that I was the one with the ability to entice it from her.

"Why, are you going to be the Alien come to conquer my ship?" I laughed at her bold question and raised a brow at her, looking back and commenting,

"I see you have thought about this before…tell me, Pet, if I was to look through these drawers of yours, would I find a stash of sci fi porn?" I asked and her reaction didn't disappoint…*not that it ever did.* Her eyes got wide and her mouth dropped before she half whispered and shrieked at the same time,

"I don't have any of that!" I fought my grin as I usually did around her and said,

"No? I am surprised, for you seem to have the perfect setting for such a fantasy," I said making a show of looking around the room and wanting to shake my head at it, just as I had done the first time I had taken in the full extent of my girl's geeky obsession. Fuck knows what our shared home would eventually look like, but I had a feeling I was looking at a glimpse of what my future held. Not that I cared, however the bed might end up being a hard limit for me, as I was partial to a more…should I say, *dominant place to fuck*.

"Nope, in fact the only naughty thing in my drawers is underwear that's not white and BOB...*oh shit,*" she muttered quickly as she let something slip and I smirked, knowing that now I was getting somewhere.

"And who may I inquire is *Bob?*" I asked in what I knew she found a seductive tone, combining this with walking back over to her and taking claim of her chin so I could raise her face up. This way she could no longer escape my eyes, eyes that I felt seeping into the blazing sun at just the vulnerable sight of her and one that made my fucking mouth water. Gods, but the brutally beautiful things I wanted to do to this woman!

I wanted her tears on my tongue as she came screaming my name.

"It's nothing…I mean no-one…just what I erm…call my socks," she said struggling for the lie and making me restrain myself from the laughter that wanted to burst free and ruin what I knew was intimidating her. A weapon that worked well against her in getting what I wanted. A weapon that worked nearly as well as her own, when using her sweetness to get me into doing anything she asked.

"Your socks…um, I see," I said making her instantly wary. Then I gave her the only warning she would get, when I muttered,

"Well, in that case…" then I suddenly grabbed her and picked her up over my shoulder before throwing her down on the bed, being careful not to hurt her in doing so, with my quick and rough treatment. She screamed in an excited way and I continued to make my point when I pinned half her body back against the bed. As now I was facing her feet and had her legs trapped and locked tight under my armpit.

"I want to see what Bob is hiding, oh wait, no Bob…*lucky me,*" I said looking back at her over my shoulder, grinning as I knew her torment would be tickling her feet. Something she enjoyed as much as she hated, which for me was the perfect combination for inflicting torture.

"Don't you dare!" she said trying to be serious but with the impending doom my fingers could inflict, then she was already near to laughing hysterically. But then I thought back to my own reaction to when she had done the same to me and well, that was why I reminded her,

"Time for some payback, Sweetheart." Then I slipped off her shoes and attacked. Meaning soon my gentle and dancing fingers had her near crying in laughter. To the point that she needed great gulps of air in order to breathe and laugh at the same time. Something that was creating a cute and delightful noise I quickly became fascinated with. Of course, she was also struggling to free herself as I continued to keep her pinned where I wanted her, with my free arm held across her knees.

"Oh, Gods please! Please okay, okay please just…oh no! Stop have mercy, mercy, mercy… you shit!" she said making me laugh and I paused my fingers and she her pointless struggles.

"Do you yield?" I asked making her push all her hair back from her flushed face and say,

"Yes, I yield, you bugger!" I chuckled at this and asked,

"Now back to this Bob of yours." To which she tensed and tested,

"Okay, so it's not my socks."

"Yes, I gathered as much, Sweetheart…this is the time when you tell me what it is."

"Erm, would you believe it's my bras?" she tried making me roll my lips into my mouth as I shook my head telling her no.

"Knickers?" she tried again and I had to say, I was enjoying this game but once again I granted her a look and said,

"Try again."

"Pantyhose?" she said in a hopeful tone that nearly made me laugh and break the act. So, instead, I trailed my fingers down her soft bare legs, ones that were without the item she just mentioned, and said,

"Last chance, for I am getting very close to my target." I grinned in a knowing way when she started to squirm beneath my hold. But it was only when I reached her ankles that she finally caved and gave me what I wanted, shocking me when she shouted,

"Alright! He's my vibrator!" My grin got bigger the second I heard this sweet, dirty little confession of hers and instead of releasing her fully, I shifted my body. Now crawling up hers so I could pin her fully beneath me, facing her once again. So, with only inches between us, I ran a fingertip along her jawline before tapping her chin and telling her,

"See, that wasn't so hard now was it?" to which she huffed,

"Not for you it wasn't." Naturally I smirked at this response.

"Now for my next question."

"Oh no, please don't ask that," she moaned, obviously knowing what I was going to demand of her next. But of course, I asked it anyway,

"Why is your vibrator called Bob?"

"Does it matter, he's retired anyway," was her witty response and one I couldn't help but laugh at this time. Gods, but she was funny.

"Then if that is the case, surely he deserves the recognition for years of good service," I retorted, making her laugh this time.

"And he will get that, will he by me telling you what Bob means?" she challenged and I found myself only able to nod, because fuck me I was having too much fun playing this cat and mouse game with her.

"And what do I get in return if I do?" she asked in that cheeky tone of hers.

"Besides not torturing you further?"

"Yes, besides that," she said rolling her eyes at me and it was one I would have punished with my palm on her fuckable ass had she not been drunk. So, instead, I gave her what she wanted,

"A promise that it will be worth your while."

"Is that so?" she asked now waggling her eyebrows and making me grin as I whispered closer to her lips,

"It is a vow." And this did it.

"Fine…but you can't laugh."

"Now that I can't vow," I admitted making her roll her eyes yet again and say,

"Fine, I will just pretend you did."

"But I didn't," I reminded her.

"Not helping with the pretending bit here, Handsome," she said and I had to say, I fucking loved it when she called me that and it had fuck all to do with stroking my ego.

"My apologies, princess," I said teasing her and making her growl, so I dipped my head to her sweet spot and started kissing up to her ear before whispering,

"Tell me."

"Alright, fine! Bob means, battery operated boyfriend… B.O.B," she said and the second she did, I couldn't help myself for I threw my head back and burst into laughter, one that ended up against her skin as I buried my head in her neck.

"You promised!" she screeched and during my laughter I reminded her,

"No, I didn't." A fact I mumbled against her jaw after kissing her there.

"Alright, but at least you promised me it would be worth my while!" she argued and now this really made me grin, one that still remained when I lifted my face up and told her with the sexual intent burning in my gaze,

"Now that, Sweetheart, I did promise." Her reaction to this was to grin back at me, before brazenly putting her hands behind her head and making a show of it. Then, after looking down at herself still in her pretty dress, one I wasn't sure would survive the night, she said,

"Alright, cowboy…have at it." I chuckled once before taking the time to do as she had done. Only I guarantee that I enjoyed the sight more than she had when looking down the length of her. For when I did it, I did so looking like the hungry wolf I felt myself turning into.

"Oh, don't worry, Pet, I will but first…" I paused as I brought my predatory gaze back up the length of her and then I lowered my lips to her ear and told her on a sexual purr…

"It's time to bring Bob out of retirement."

CHAPTER FIFTEEN

AMELIA

BLISSFUL MOMENT INTERUPTED

Waking up the next day and the first emotion to hit me was shame. After that came the foggy sensation pounding at my temple, along with the taste of what felt like was a mouth full of bile-soaked cotton wool.

Needless to say, that due to a combination of these things, Bob had come out of retirement for all of about two minutes before he was once again cast aside and left without thought.

Because Lucius may have been turned on and I may have been horny with the promise of sex...but the overruling factor in all immediate future X rated escapades was...

I was still shitfaced drunk!

Which, therefore, meant that the moment I bent over to get poor once abused Bob, it was only to then throw him back to the bed as I made a mad dash for the bathroom with my hand covering my mouth. Once there I threw up a large amount of the alcohol I had consumed, telling Lucius to stay out and that I would just be a minute, in between hurling the burning vomit.

I didn't know who I thought I was fooling in doing this as it certainly wasn't Lucius. Because, despite my idiotic attempt at trying to make out that I was just innocently using the bathroom, he decided I wasn't doing so alone. I knew this when I felt him gathering back my hair in one hand and rubbing my back with the other, as I continued to get up most of the night's tequila.

"Please go, I..." I never finished as the next wave hit and Lucius told me in a stern tone,

"I am not going anywhere." I heaved and heaved again only able to stop long enough to try again,

"But I don't want you seeing me like this." This was said in a small voice that spoke only of my vulnerability and shame.

"I have seen far worse than vomit, Sweetheart," he told me, this time in a softer tone as he smoothed back the hair from my forehead.

"But it's *my vomit,*" I said pleading my case and making him lean closer and whisper,

"Ssshh, Pet, don't focus on me, just focus on getting it all up." So, deciding that he would do what he wanted despite my pleas, I did as he suggested. And it was only when I knew I was all done and 'Elpukeo, Mistress of Tequila' had pissed off for good, did he then take it upon himself to care for me. He started this by filling a cup near my sink with cold water and bringing it to me, telling me to swill my mouth and spit. I felt disgusted with myself but did as I was told regardless. Then, once he was satisfied, he picked me up and carried me to the bed, this time knowing that nothing fun was going to happen in it. Hell, it's not like it had been waiting long enough, I thought with sarcasm. But hey, I guess it was going to continue being a virgin

for a while longer yet and I should just be happy that its owner wasn't anymore.

But then he picked up Bob and with a wink, put him back in my drawer and said,

"Let's put Bob on a sabbatical this time." I smiled, appreciating the effort in trying to make me laugh and feel better.

"Bye, Bob," I said giving it a little wave and making Lucius grin at me before coming back to the edge of the bed and telling me to roll over.

"Why?" I asked confused.

"It's lovely on you, Pet, but do you usually sleep in a dress?" he asked and for some reason this made me look down at myself and was surprised to see that yes, I was still in my dress. He chuckled once and said,

"Turn around, Sweetheart." So, I did as he asked but instead of doing so lying down, I sat up in the bed and walked towards him on my knees to where he was still standing at the edge of the bed. Then I turned my back to him and couldn't help but shiver the moment I felt his gloved hand along my skin as he gently shifted my hair off to one side. I felt him pull the zipper down, doing so all the way to the base of my spine. I then felt his fingers trail the journey the zip made making me shudder.

"You looked so beautiful tonight...*I am a lucky man, indeed,*" he told me, whispering this last part by my ear from behind me.

"Thank you," I whispered, feeling shy.

"Ah, so that is the key," he commented to himself.

"Key to what?"

"In gaining your thanks, I must first give you half a bottle of Tequila and four bottles of beer," he said making me twist suddenly to look at him, despite my dress now slipping off my shoulders slightly.

"I say thank you all the time…at least I think I do…well, I am thankful," I told him pausing halfway through my argument to question myself. He smirked down at me before leaning into my face and informing me,

"I am teasing you, Amelia." Then he tapped my nose before standing straight once more.

"Now lie down before you fall down," he ordered and that was when I realised that I was swaying. Which was why I did as I was told and watched as he moved to the end of the bed before kneeling so he could get closer. Gods, but he looked so sexy, still wearing his suit but now minus the jacket. And like I knew it would it when first seeing him in the VIP, his waistcoat hugged his sculptured frame like a glove. His sleeves were also rolled up his forearms and I swear the sight made my mouth go dry and it was nothing to do with what just happened in the bathroom.

But then I felt my dress slipping down my body and instead of it being sexual, it felt more like he was simply taking care of me. Well, trying to, as I wasn't exactly making it easy on him. Especially when I bolted upright to sitting and asked,

"Hey, how did you know how much I had to drink?"

"Lift your ass," he ordered instead of answering me.

"Lucius?"

"I guessed, now lift," he told me and I narrowed my eyes at him before saying,

"Were you watching me tonight?" This was when he looked straight at me and said,

"I am always watching you, as is my right…now ass!"

"But you can't…" I never got chance to finish as after this I yelped when he swiped my dress out from under me so quickly that I fell back on the bed with the force.

"I didn't see you," I said as he now dropped my dress to the floor and sat himself next to me, running a fingertip around the top of my strapless bra and outlining the black lace cups.

"Well, that would defeat the object of stalking you," he told me boldly.

"Oh."

"Oh," he mocked back in return and suddenly I realised I was only wearing my underwear, so I looked down at myself and told him as much,

"I'm nearly naked here." His lips lifted on one side in a bad boy grin and he told me with a wink,

"Oh, I know."

"I need to brush my teeth, take my contacts out and put up my hair so I don't accidentally choke on it in the night. Plus, I could do with pyjamas and bed socks so my feet don't get cold as it can get a bit…" I stopped when he started chuckling and told me,

"I think a, 'Lucius, I need to get ready for bed' would have sufficed, Sweetness."

"Oh."

"Oh," he mocked again making me first hold down the urge to grin so I could narrow my eyes at him playfully and tell him,

"You know that's annoying right?"

"Then why does it make you smile every time I do it?" he asked and damn him, he was right!

"Cause I am a nice person." At this he laughed and said,

"That you are, Pet, now go get your ass ready for bed." I covered my mouth on account of the breath that could probably knock out a cow and pretended to kiss him by having my hand in between our lips. This made him shake his head at me in one of those amused, 'what am I to do about my drunken girlfriend' kind of ways as I scooted off the bed in my undies.

Then I went about getting ready for bed like I said I would, chuckling when I heard him calling,

"Don't forget to hydrate!" when he heard me brushing my teeth, making me stick my head around the door frame with the brush sticking out of my mouth to give him the thumbs up. In response, he chuckled to himself, muttering something I couldn't hear but was sure I heard the word cute and his favourite word 'fuck' in there somewhere.

But getting ready for bed ended up including ten minutes wasted when in my closet looking for suitable PJ's to wear. This was because most were rather funny, childish, or just plain weird, like the pair Pip bought me once that had the words, 'Cute But Psycho, But Cute' on the front. So, I decided to go with my 'Nerd is code word for genius' PJs seeing as he already knew by being in my room that I was a nerd.

It also had cute shorts that were covered in black rimmed glasses and the top was a white tank style, that admittedly without a bra looked near indecent. Fluffy pink socks, or Bobs as they were now named and a lightweight soft cotton dressing gown in grey with pink stars completed the look. Well, that and my hair up in a messy ponytail and my glasses on, which made me say the moment I walked back in my room,

"Look see, I match" which for some strange reason I combined this with a pose that was anything but sexy. But it didn't matter as what I found when walking back in the room made me shriek in horror. It was also something that made me run straight over to him, tripping as I did, which meant I landed half in his lap and half across the bed. This was because I was diving for the book he had in his hands that made me hiss,

"Don't read my diary!" but he was too quick for me and stood with the book in his hands, that shamefully had Vampire stickers over the cover. This was something Pip had put in my Christmas stocking one year for a joke, knowing early on of the crush I had on Lucius. Of course, this had been before he had broken my heart like the bastard I had believed him to be back then. And, therefore, those stickers had received some choice graffiti after that.

"Why not, I clearly feature in it enough," Lucius said looking down at me as he held it higher when I started to try and climb him like a damn monkey in pyjamas!

"Because it is private! Hell, don't you understand the concept of a sodding diary!" I snapped, as he still wouldn't let me have it but instead due to his height was actually able to continue reading it without me reaching it.

"Arrogant asshole was I…? Too hot for my own big head… oh and wait, what's this…oh, now that is just cruel," he said faking a hurt and shocked tone after reading something else I'd written. But this meant he finally lowered it enough for me to jump on the bed and swipe it from him.

"Gimmie that!"

"Well, I think we know that last one is most definitely not true," he said and suddenly I was letting out a yelp as my legs were pulled out from under me and I was now flat on the bed with him on top of me. Then he pushed his hips forward, grinding his erection against me and said on a growl,

"Does this feel small to you?" I rolled my lips inwards and shook my head to tell him no, knowing now exactly what comment he had read. Especially when he continued,

"And I think by now you know exactly what I can do with it," he added making me nod a yes, again with my lips still held tight so I wouldn't laugh. But then he got even lower and whispered in response to the very last part I'd written at that particular time,

"And how long I can last." After this he kissed me and plucked the diary out of my hands and flung it behind him telling me exactly what he thought about those years we weren't together. And I had to say, I was totally with him in that.

For his kiss eradicated all words,

Past and present.

A little time later I found myself curled up next to Lucius in bed. He had taken off his shoes and his waistcoat and was currently lay back with his ankles crossed, listening to my childhood stories as he played with my hair, after first removing the tie that held it back.

"Wow, look at the time, it's nearly four in the morning, and I have been talking nonstop," I said yawning big after it.

"I like listening to you talk."

"Why, is it a good cure for insomnia?" I joked making him grin down at me where I was tucked under his arm.

"On the contrary, it actually soothes me," he said like a confession.

"Soothes you?" I pushed for more.

"You are familiar with the concept, Sweetheart," he commented dryly making me smirk against his chest as it was worth trying.

"Yeah, well, with what you're doing to my hair, that has the power to put me to sleep even after ten cups of coffee…it feels so good," I confessed making him kiss my forehead and tell me,

"Then go to sleep, Sweetheart."

"I guess I'd better get a few hours in. But you don't have to stay…probably safer if you don't," I said in a disappointed tone at the thought of him leaving.

"I told you, I am not going anywhere," was his stern reply.

"But…"

"But nothing, I gave you my terms in the car and I meant them," he said now being firm.

"But what if someone catches us?" I asked,

"Does your family make a habit of just barging into your

room without knocking?"

"Well, no but…"

"Then I don't see the problem," he said, suddenly getting up and walking away from the bed. Which was when I bolted upright and my slightly panicked voice asked him,

"I thought you weren't leaving?" in a tone and a question that kind of proved how much I wanted him to stay. Something his satisfied grin told me he was pleased about. So, he walked back to me and, placing a hand either side of my hips, leaned in and said,

"I am getting ready for bed, and unless you have any in there for me, then don't expect me to come out of there wearing pyjamas, *my little nerd."* Then he playfully pulled at my top directly over my nipple and at the same time bit my chin to make his point. Then he grinned when I started rubbing my breast and mouthing an exaggerated 'oww'. To which he mouthed back a silent,

'Baby'.

After this Lucius walked into my bathroom and out of sight, making me squirm impatiently for him to hurry up and get back so I could see him without his clothes on. However, when he finally did, I missed the sight. Because I must have fallen asleep as I didn't even stir when he slipped in next to me. Something I knew he had done as when I woke the next morning, not only did I feel as if someone had poured a sandcastle's worth of sand down my throat, I also felt a hot body next to me.

But then I also looked to the side tables connected to my unusual bed, briefly wondering what Lucius had thought about it when climbing in for the night. This was when I saw that there was a glass of water there ready for me to consume and I couldn't help but smile, remembering him telling me to hydrate. I swear I didn't think I could have loved anyone more in that moment.

So, I gently peeled myself off Lucius, who admittedly I had been plastered against and rolled to face the glass so I could gulp most of it down.

"Thirsty this morning, any reason for that, my little drunken sex pest?" Lucius said after rolling into me and hooking me around the waist with his arm pulling me back against his naked body.

"Sex pest?"

"I spent half the night trying to be a gentleman, but with your wandering hands, well let's just say that it made it extremely difficult," he teased.

"I did not!" I cried making him chuckle in my neck and say,

"I very near had to restrain you with one of your pink fluffy Bobs and then punish you by bringing the original Bob out of retirement."

"I thought he was just on sabbatical?" I teased back after giggling. I felt him shrug behind me and say,

"Let's just say that with me here now, well then he's lucky he's not in the fucking bin!" I laughed at that and rolled into him, at the same time loving the feel of his hands as they ran under my tank top and up my bare back.

"Good morning," I muttered softly.

"It is indeed."

"Mmm," I mumbled happily and just as I was basking in that loving morning glow of being in Lucius' arms, despite my obvious hangover, the blissful moment was utterly shattered as the second I heard the knock at the door…

I froze solid.

But this wasn't the worst of it, as the second the person announced who it was, I hissed the words no secret boyfriend in your bed ever wanted to hear…

"Shit, it's my dad!"

CHAPTER SIXTEEN

A FATHER'S MISTAKE

The second my father asked if he could come in I totally panicked and in said panic I ended up pushing Lucius out of bed and off the other side with a thud just as my dad was opening the door, asking what the noise was. I also heard a slight hiss and looked to find my star wars lamp missing from the side Lucius had been pushed off, so I took it as a sign.

"Oh nothing, I just woke up suddenly at your knock and accidentally must have hit my lamp off the table." I then reached across the bed, thanking whoever had made it, that they'd made the bed high. This was because, even as my dad entered the room, he couldn't see the big blonde Vampire I had hiding down by the side of my bed.

I stuck my head over the side and found him staring back up at me with the light sabre part of the lamp in his hand and I had to try everything in me not to react when he handed it to me and mouthed the words,

'Big trouble'.

In turn, I mouthed back a quick,

'I'm sorry' and scooted back on the bed with the lamp in hand, telling my father,

"Got it!" doing so in an overly enthusiastic way as I placed it back where it was kept. Meanwhile, my dad was still stood closer to the doorway looking unsure and uncomfortable. I also quickly surmised that Lucius was hiding his presence from my dad with some small level of mind control. As my dad should have been able to detect another person in the room with me, even if he couldn't see him.

"Erm…why don't you take a seat," I suggested hoping he wouldn't come and sit on the bed as I didn't yet know just how far that mind control thingy would stretch.

He nodded and grabbed a chair, one that was based on the Emperor's throne from Star Wars which had been in front of my Tie fighter desk. He spun it around to face me and I was just glad that it meant he was positioned further way from the bed. Then he sat down filling the seat with his bulk and looking every bit of the King he was.

"How are you feeling?" he asked and with that question alone I knew that he had been told that I had been drinking, so I told him,

"Hungover, but I guess you already knew that would be my answer."

"Well, the empty bottles and a talkative Imp with green hair and a candy tooth kind of gave it away." I laughed at this and added,

"That and mum told you."

"That and your mum told me," he confessed on a laugh of his own.

"So, this is…what exactly…mum sending you to see if I need an Advil or something?" I asked making it clear that by him being in my room it didn't mean that I was letting him off the hook. Even though technically, that would have been the smartest thing right now seeing as I didn't know how long Lucius' 'boyfriend hiding mind mojo' was going to last.

"No, but if you do, then I can just..." he said half getting out of his seat just when I folded my legs on the bed and sighed,

"Just say what you came here to say, Dad," I told him making him release a sigh of his own as he sat back down. Then he said the last thing I expected him to say,

"I'm sorry."

"Erm...come again?" I asked thinking I must have been mistaken...did he just say he was sorry? Because I had been anticipating the lecture on how not to disrespect him in front of his people... blah blardie blah etc.

But an apology, was not what I was expecting.

"I would have come and told you last night, but after I saw you drinking with Sophia and Pip, well, I thought it best left until morning," he told me and I waved a hand around and said,

"No, no, get back to the part where you said sorry and explain that bit...*in detail.*" He flattened his lips in a grim line before releasing a frustrated groan and explaining it...*in detail.*

"I am sorry for what I said to you last night, had I known that was how it sounded, I would never...well, I would never have said what was said and I wish I could take it back."

"You wish you could take it back?" I repeated, still needing to hear it again just to be sure I wasn't dreaming.

"Yes."

"Which part exactly...be specific," I demanded and yes, it seemed as if I was making him jump through hoops but damn it, it was about time he did, for there had been a lot of bloody hoops stacking up over the years.

"I didn't trust you could take care of yourself and now I realise that I have pushed you away at the expense of what I thought was keeping you safe. You deserved better and I failed to act sooner. Failed to see that by protecting you I was actually segregating you from my world and pushing you further and further away until you felt…disconnected."

"Wow," was all I could say at that point, as it was honestly like hearing my own thoughts coming from the one person in the world I wanted to hear them from. To listen, take them in and really understand them. I rubbed the back of my neck and muttered another wow before I had to ask him,

"Is this all mum's doing?"

"Actually no, this came from somewhere else." I frowned, wondering which miracle worker I had to thank, when I didn't have to wonder long.

"Who?"

"It was actually Lucius who argued your point and managed to convince me, quite compellingly at that."

"Convince you of what exactly?" I asked with my heart pounding.

"That you could hold your own and not solely against the trained humans you fought, but also against the rogues you dispatched with great skill." I could barely believe what I was hearing! Lucius had been the one to stand up against my dad and fight for what I would have thought seemed like a small thing to him. However, it wasn't to me and therefore I guess that meant it wasn't to him.

"Well, like I said before, you taught me well," I said as I didn't know what else to say as most of my thoughts were still caught up in a 'Lucius is my hero' bubble.

"Yeah, I taught you well, Amelia, but come on, a sink and a shoe? I didn't teach you that!" I grinned and shrugged my shoulders like it was no big deal yet inside I was buzzing! Lucius had told him everything!

"No, that was all you and I have to tell you, I could not be more proud of you, my dear, for all I can say is that I underestimated you and for that I am most sincerely sorry for it. Lucius was right…"

"About what…what was he right about?" I asked almost desperate to know and trying not to let on by my eager tone.

"That my love for you as a father clouded my judgement, for I already know the strength and courage that comes from being human, as it was that same strength and courage I saw in your mother all those years ago when we first met and that…I should never have forgotten," he said with a shake of his head as if what he spoke of had been a crime he had unknowingly committed.

"I understand, dad… I really do, as your world is much stronger than the human one and you were just doing as you thought best" I said trying to ease his burden now that he had realised his misjudgment, even if it had taken him years to do so.

"But it wasn't, was it?"

"Not really no, because I so badly wanted to be a part of your world but at times…"

"I pushed you away from it, that's why you left home isn't it, it's why you became more…?" He paused this time as he didn't want to cause offence, in case I took it as I had last night.

So, I finished for him,

"Human? I would be lying if I said no, but I would also be lying if I said it was the only reason." I said because I didn't have it in me to pile on all that guilt when he should not be the one to carry it alone. Because yes, I had been pushed into belonging more with my own kind, but I had also embraced it much more as a way of escape from the world that reminded me of nothing but Lucius at the time. And living with a woman who I believed had been the only person he had ever loved, being my mother, well that part hadn't exactly been easy.

So, I had left. And it was a decision at the time that had

been best for us all. A decision done so as the resentment I felt mounting yearly didn't ever get to a point when I just decided that I would turn my back on it all and never set foot inside the doors of Afterlife ever again.

"And that would be…?"

"Something you are going to trust me with as my own business…yes?" I said in return, testing the new waters my father was no doubt only just learning to swim in.

"But of course, it is none of my business." I grinned at that and refrained from going over there and patting him on the back and saying well done.

"Thanks, dad, I know this probably wasn't easy."

"No, but it was most definitely overdue…I see that now," was his sincere reply.

"As a father I will never stop loving you and seeing you as you will always be to me."

"Your little girl," I guessed making him nod with a warm grin as if he could still see his little girl in pigtails bouncing on his knee with a doll in my hand.

"It is a father's way. The need to protect his girl no matter what your age, it is never easy letting go and with that, comes my trust in the decisions you make…I know I have to learn how to respect them but please know, I have never once not been proud of you, Amelia, and it hurts me to know that you believed that by me calling you human, that you thought it left my lips as an insult." I hung my head at this and muttered into my lap,

"I know… I was just hurt is all."

"I love you, Amelia. I always will and being human is who you are and is a part of that love…*you have to know this,*" he told me and after that I could stand it no longer. So, I got up and ran over to him at the same time he stood, seeing the action coming and preparing for it. He took me in his big arms as I hugged him to me for the longest time. And it felt wonderful! It felt more than just a gesture, it felt like a promise for a better future.

"I love you, dad." I told him softly and I felt my head being tilted back so he could look into my eyes.

"I know you do, little one, but then your love for me has never been in question and I hope you will grant me the same in return," he said in that gentle way I had been used to when growing up, making me nod before hugging him to me once again and holding on tight.

"Good, now tomorrow night I have called a meeting for the Table of Kings…"

"I know, and I won't get offended if…" He quickly cut me off,

"I want you there," he told me and my eyes grew wide in question.

"You mean as a witness or something?"

"No, as a place at the table sat beside your mother, as is your right and one you have earned not through blood alone, but now through strength and experience." At this my mouth dropped open as utter shock morphed my features enough to making him chuckle.

"Holy shit…really?!" I asked knowing that this was huge… no, not just huge, it was colossal! My dad chuckled again at my reaction and said,

"Yes, really my daughter." I grinned big up at him and said,

"Well, yeah I mean I will have to check my calendar and such." He laughed fully this time and said,

"Be sure that you do, my clever, busy girl." Then he patted me on my arms before standing back, to look at me,

"Gods, but I still can't believe how you have grown and how…"

"Kick ass I have become?" I added for him, making him grin.

"Yes, kick ass indeed."

"So, Lucius told you it all then, huh?" he nodded with a grim look making me laugh,

"Be honest, you freaked out, didn't you?" At this he raised a brow in a way very much like Lucius did and I had to wonder if it wasn't a king thing.

"I like to think I handled it somewhat better than I usually would but perhaps that was down to Luc being there," he said cryptically.

"What do you mean?" I asked with my heart in my throat.

"There was once a day when Luc was more than just my second, he was a good friend and offered me more than a sound council, he offered me hope, and reason and even at times, strength." Wow, I swallowed hard and asked my next question trying to hold back the shake in my voice I could feel close to breaking up the words,

"And now?" I held my breath whereas my dad let his out on a sigh,

"And now, well I guess old habits die hard for in that moment I still found all of those things mentioned when listening to his words…for as much as he can be a pain in the ass, he is still one of the wisest people I know…although it is not something I would ever confess to him in person…after all, I have my pride and now you have my secret to keep," he said making me gulp as unfortunately no I didn't.

No, *now Lucius did.*

So, I decided to give him something in return because it was only fair after what Lucius now knew.

"How about I tell you one of his in return?" My father grinned big and leaned in, saying secretively,

"Do tell."

"You will be proud to know I managed to put him on his ass in the ring." My father drew back and said in earnest,

"You jest?" I laughed at both his shock and how old fashioned my dad sounded sometimes.

"I swear on the Devil's name," I said making the sign for the Devil and making him laugh in disbelief before asking,

"What were you doing in the ring with him?"

"He was teaching me some defensive moves and I don't know, making sure I wasn't rusty or something, besides I think he wanted to be sure that I could take care of myself," I told him as this was the most logical explanation.

"And you put him on his ass?"

"Yup and he wasn't going easy on me…I mean sure, it was because I took him by surprise but when means must and all that," I told him making him throw his head back and laugh, telling me,

"Oh, how I would have paid good money to see that!" But then I blushed because I knew very well what came after it and well… No. *No, he most definitely would not.*

"Well, I'd better let you get back to your hangover in peace…remember to stay hydrated," my dad said as he walked towards the door.

"Yeah, Lucius said the same thing last night," I said before I thought to stop myself and my dad stopped, just as I mouthed a silent, 'shit' behind his back. Then he turned slowly round to face me and asked in a questioning tone,

"He did?"

"Erm, yeah he helped me to my room and told me to drink plenty of water…why?" I said deciding to be honest about part of it, so he couldn't detect a lie.

"No reason, I just think he seems to really like you." I tensed all over and tried to breathe normally before I said something stupid like, 'Oh, you have no idea' or ' well, he seemed to really like me last night when he was about to get intimate with me and Bob'... but thankfully I just laughed and went for the less murder worthy,

"Yeah, well he would do, seeing as he most likely wants me to keep the fact that I put his ass on the mats a secret." My dad laughed at that and thankfully left still shaking his head as if he couldn't believe it himself. Then, I finally closed the door, put my back to it and released what felt like the biggest sigh of my life.

Then, the second Lucius stood up, I realised just how much I had to thank him for, so without thinking I took off running, and jumped onto my bed. Then, a few large bouncing steps later and I was over it and into his arms, glad that he reacted quickly, taking note to catch me. I then wrapped my arms around him and said,

"Gods, but I fucking love you!" Then I kissed him, embedding my hands into his hair and holding tight as I wrapped my legs around his waist. But just as quickly, he was turning the tables on the kiss and took control as I knew he would. After this battle of the lips he pulled back and said one thing,

"Put me on my ass, did you?"

"I may have exaggerated a little," I admitted in an innocent voice.

"Umm, well it looks like Bob and I are gonna have to teach you a little lesson about lying," he said making me giggle,

"Oooh, sounds kinky," I teased back, making him growl,

"Oh, you have no idea, Pet." Then, just before I had chance for a witty reply, I squealed out loud as he let me go, so as I fell back on to the bed. Then, before I could blink, he was on top of me, with his hands travelling up my top, saying,

"Now it's time for me to put you on your ass, with my coc..."

"Good morning, sleepy head!" I heard Pip calling loudly, along with my aunty Sophia, saying,

"Why are you shouting when we aren't even at her door yet?" Which meant one panicked look at Lucius and he only had time to say one thing before he was once again being pushed off the bed…

"Fuck me, not again!"

CHAPTER SEVENTEEN

PANTIES IN A TWIST

After Lucius was pushed off the bed for the second time that morning and made to hide, Sophia had walked into my room muttering,

"I love you, but you are so strange sometimes." This was directed at Pip who followed her inside and was laughing nervously. Of course, my mum also followed in after that and I swear it was starting to feel like a damn family reunion in here…that or the bus stop used in getting there!

"Gods," I muttered before then asking the obvious,

"Erm, so as much as this hangover isn't joyful enough, I have to ask, what are you all doing here?"

"Well, we thought seeing as we were all together again and it's been ages, that we could all go shopping!" Sophia announced enthusiastically, making both my mum and Pip point a finger at her back and mouth,

'Her idea,' making me now squash down the urge to laugh.

"I thought you only just got back from a shopping trip, just yesterday in fact?" I asked really hoping to get out of this one.

"Yes, but that was with Z…"

"Ziggyzigan…erm, sorry, I swear it's like a habit now," Pip said adding this last part towards my mum after Sophia shot her a death glare. My mum just patted her shoulder and said,

"Don't worry, we will work on it." Which was sweet. But then, that was my mum and also, to some extent my aunty Sophia, because as much as they teased Pip, they were also mindful of her sensitive nature. They also loved her dearly and with that came being incredibly protective over her.

"Okay, well you do get that a hangover cure doesn't usually include shopping?" I said in a way that hopefully didn't sound as though I was trying to get rid of everyone, when in reality… *I really, really, really, was.*

"Or sex…what, just saying…I mean hangovers don't include a lot of things…other than Jellybeans and headless Jelly Babies…seriously, they just wouldn't fit up there with their heads on…what?"

"Eww, Pip," Sophia said making her lift up her hands and shrug,

"What, I am talking about my tooth not my Moomoo," Pip replied making me laugh before realisation hit as to where I had heard it being called that before. Suddenly utter dread filled my veins.

"Your Moomoo, seriously, what are you, like 5 years old?" Sophia commented and before I could stop where I knew this was going, I opened my mouth to try and steer the conversation when my mum said

"Aww, yeah, but don't you remember that's what Fae used to call it, and then it turned into Moocow." At this I actually smacked a hand to my forehead and said,

"Gods, please spare me." Of course I was ignored by both Gods and the female members of my family.

"Oh yeah, Mummy, my Moocow itches…remember that

one at the council table...? Dom's face was a picture as he handed her over to you and said, 'that's your department, my dear'...fucking crackers that one was!" Pip said making me actually groan out loud and with a hand still to my forehead, I then hung my head in shame...one they would never fully understand, seeing as my boyfriend was currently hiding next to the bed no doubt getting a big kick out of this.

"Aww don't worry, Faebear, your secret is safe...oh!" Pip said when I gave her a look that said it all. Then she mouthed a word at me so the others didn't see,

'Where?' So, I motioned towards the bed with my eyes, telling her where Lucius was hiding and listening to this whole conversation. But then my mum began walking towards the bottom of the bed and started to bend to pick up the dress Lucius had thrown on the floor last night.

"Jeez, Fae, I know you were drunk but you really need to be more careful with a dress like..."

"Woohoo Boobies! Look everyone, do you think they are growing, 'cause I think they look bigger, look, look at my breasticles!" Pip shouted in an almost frantic way gaining my mum's attention as she suddenly whipped up her top exposing her little breasts and jumping around trying to make them dance. I swear, the look on both my mum and Sophia's face was an utter picture as they both stopped dead and stared at her in disbelief.

"Uh...Pip, what you doing there, honey?" My mum asked in a concerned tone that said it all. Especially when Pip started stretching all the way over to her side touching her toes whilst saying,

"Oh, just stretching them out a little, giving these little ditties some air and exercise, you know, keeping shit fresh." Meanwhile, I snapped out of my own shock and stepped up to my mum, leaning down myself and grabbing the dress so she wouldn't notice the big Vampire feet by the end of the bed.

"Oh yeah, like they don't get enough exercise," Sophia commented dryly whilst crossing her arms over her plum coloured pencil dress that was cinched in at the waist with a thick black belt. My mum was in her usual jeans and fitted grey cashmere sweater, whilst Pip...well, she was dressed as if she had robbed the children's section at Macy's.

"I don't know what you mean," Pip said now stopping her 'boob flaunting' and pulling down her cropped Sponge Bob knitted sweater that showed off her belly and was one that made me secretly cringe at the name Bob written under the yellow cartoon square. Man, was I ever going to live down the Bob thing?

To this she'd added a gypsy skirt that looked as if it was made up from patches of denim pockets. Which I could see had different packets of candy wrappers sticking out from the stash she was constantly carrying with her these days. This was on account of the tooth she refused to get fixed. It was also one that my mum assured me wouldn't last as once she had tried all the different sweets (as my mum called them) then she would soon get bored of using the same thing twice. Of course, before that happened, mum warned me that Pip would no doubt first get very, very inventive.

"You don't know what I mean...? Yeah right, you had them out last night in front of everyone...remember, when you were smushing them in Adam's face and asking him if there was a headless jelly baby stuck under one...and it was still in between your teeth!" Pip chuckled at the memory and turned to me and said,

"Yeah, I totally did that."

"Alright, well as weird and delightful as this morning meeting between us girls is, can I crawl back into bed yet and let my hangover live out life as it's supposed to?" My mum laughed as I said this, after I first grabbed the top of her arms from behind and steered her towards the door as she still chuckled. This had been because I spotted her heading towards my diary, something else Lucius had thrown to the floor, and she was aiming to pick it up.

"But what about shopping?!" Sophia declared making me groan and give in,

"Alright, shopping."

"Yey! Girly road trip!"

"Erm, hold it there, cowgirl, we aren't going to Vegas," my mum said making Pip pout.

"Well, we won't be going anywhere with me in my PJ's," I declared hoping they finally got the hint.

"Alright girls, I think what Fae is delicately trying to say is we need to leave whilst she gets ready." I released a sigh and said,

"Thanks, mum." But then that sigh was premature when Pip nudged my arm and said,

"Why do you want us to leave, you got a boy hidden under the bed or something?" Then she winked at me a couple of times and I couldn't help it, my mouth actually dropped. My mum laughed and came and patted me on the cheek, saying,

"Not my Fae, she's a good girl…besides, Draven's got weapons." It was my turn to laugh nervously at that, saying a lame,

"Ha, ha, yeah good one."

"Yeah, well, she wasn't a good girl last night!" Pip said sniggering and it was at this point when I was silently asking the Gods *'why'*. This was also when we all looked at her, me especially, in utter horror, then she said,

"What, I meant when drinking…sheesh, tough crowd," was Pip's reply.

"You've got thirty minutes, so go get your cute ass in the shower as I want to spoil my niece," Sophia declared blowing me a kiss and walking to the door. My mum kissed me on the cheek and said,

"Wash good, baby girl, you smell like the upend of a shot glass…oh, and stay hydrated, honey," I groaned and muttered back,

"Yep, so everyone keeps telling me."

"Is it just me or is Pip acting stranger than usual today?" I heard my mum asking Sophia as they both walked out the door, leaving Pip a little behind, as she had started walking backwards. This was so she could punch two thumbs up at me in the air in what she thought was her accomplishment at keeping my secret.

Then, once the door finally closed on this strange picture, I released an exhausted sigh, one that turned into a groan the second I heard Lucius' laughter erupt from the side of the bed. And seeing as he hadn't yet got up, I decided to crawl onto the bed, getting to the other side to find that Lucius could barely contain himself.

"Don't you dare say a word," I threatened and it was one he totally ignored. I knew this the second he raised himself up, got in my face and told me,

"Not one word…*my Moomoo.*"

The rest of the day was spent in a whirlwind of shops, bags and dressing rooms, with a lunch thrown in for good measure. To be honest, I might have been hungover, but it had been a really fun day, reminding me of old times. But then it usually was with us all together, Pip ensuring lots of laughs for sure. However, having to start it by missing out on sex with Lucius was the only thing that didn't make it perfect. Although, the evening certainly wasn't without its…

Sexual Challenges.

Once again that night was spent at my father's table and it felt like take two, only with Lucius' sexual need for me increasing by the minute. Not that this was what most would class as a bad thing. But when I was in front of my family, whom I was trying to hide that fact from, which included the disappearing Lucius act we had entertained this morning… well, let's just say that it was getting harder by the minute.

I didn't know how many times I had tried to remove his hand from my leg, unsuccessfully doing so when I had nearly choked on my drink the second his hand reached so high, he touched my clit. Then he acted like the perfect gentleman asking me what was wrong and patting me on the back as if this was helping, whilst his other hand continued the reason I had been choking in the first place.

I swear that by the time the evening had ended, I had been so turned on I could barely walk without coming. This was because Lucius had decided that once he had gathered up my skirt, he then proceeded to position my panties in such a way they were now acting like a thong up the front of my sex. He had twisted the scrap of material in between his fingers and pulled it up in between the centre of my folds and tugged making me nearly shoot out of my seat, gaining the attention of everyone around the table.

"Sorry, just stubbed my toe." I had no choice but to tell people as he softly chuckled next to me. Then, once the night was through, the second he helped me out of my chair, he whispered down at me,

"It had better still be like that when I come to get you from your bed tonight." Then after this secret order, he had bowed his head respectfully at me whilst purring a sensual,

"Princess," as a way of goodbye. Then I had watched as he had walked away wearing yet another delicious suit. This time one of dark grey, that offered me a toe curling, lip biting view of his behind as he moved his tall and powerful frame across the VIP.

"See something you like?" Pip had asked whilst waggling her green painted eyebrows and grinning whilst showing off the fizzy cola bottle in her tooth, as was today's choice. I ignored her comment with only a look in reply, one that made her giggle and followed suit with everyone else leaving. However, when I left, I had no choice but to do it slow.

In fact, I barely made it back to my bedroom without looking cross legged, and in doing so I fell onto the bed, touched myself barely once and came hard, calling his name.

And as for my panties,

They stayed in place but the only difference was that,

They were soaked and for once in this bed…

There was no help from Bob.

CHAPTER EIGHTEEN

STORIES OF SEX

I don't know what happened after I had found my release by my own fingers, but I must have passed out. Because the next thing I knew I was opening my eyes and finding myself in a place I shouldn't be...*somewhere other than my bed.*

"Sleep walking?" I asked myself when finding that I was in the family library with absolutely no recollection of how I got there. The library was a huge, grand room filled with carved wood, antique furniture and the smell of old books coming from every wall. So, naturally because of these things it was by far my favourite place in the whole of Afterlife. With its tall cathedral style ceilings, and its walls cram packed full of books on three different levels, *it was my version of Heaven.*

Highly polished wooden floors matched those of the ornate and heavily carved twin spiral staircases that mirrored each other at the corners of the room. Both of which led to the upper levels, where shining brass ladders on runners awaited you to climb, in order to discover the treasures on every shelf. Open balconies framed the entire space offering a walkway of ease to every book.

Well, all but one…*the forbidden archive.*

But the rest of the room offered plush and comfortable antique seating areas, with rugs dotted on the floor, velvet tasselled cushions and tables. Tables that also offered, not only a place for books, scrolls and maps to be displayed but also fancy globes and brass statues adding decoration.

However, it was the enormous black fireplace that dominated the room, as it was the first thing your eyes were drawn to. Especially, seeing as it faced the entrance being positioned at the very end of the room. It consisted of two large cast iron statues that stood either side of the grated flames, both of which were holding up the heavy mantle above. They each looked like the guards to the back door into Heaven, for they weren't quite gruesome enough for Hell. And yet, they were a little too menacing for what one would believe to be a grand golden entrance into Heaven.

Two large swords clasped in between their hands stood taller than I did, which spoke of how large the entire fireplace was. But the sight had never intimidated me, as I had grown up quite differently to most. For starters, it had been where I had spent most of my time growing up, with my head buried in some demonic tale of woe, being the huge bookworm that I was.

But then there had been a section kept behind a locked latticed wall of metal that teased me endlessly for as long as I could remember. It was at the very top row that couldn't be reached unless you had wings. Which meant that basically it was the stuff I hadn't ever been allowed to read. But now I was an adult and my father had just discovered this new mentality of trusting his daughter, so who knew?

But none of this made sense as to why I was there?

The only explanation was that I had been sleep walking and if that was the case, then what was Lucius going to think if he found out. Because the last time that had happened it had been because of a witch and I had nearly been eaten by Hellhounds. But then, what else was I going to say, that I just decided to pop in here real quick for some light reading, before he was to show up and make love to me?

Now, if there had been a section on Sci fi porn, then that might have made sense and given me a viable excuse. However, brushing up on my demonology or chronic diseases didn't really cut it. Unfortunately for me, I didn't have much time to decide on what to do as the second the door opened, I panicked and grabbed the first book on the closest table next to me, foolishly not even looking at the cover and hoping to blag my way through the reason why I was there.

The second Lucius saw me I could tell he had been worried, as the deep sigh of relief was one I heard from halfway across the room. Then he stepped fully inside, closing the double doors behind him as he faced me. His face was a calm mask from what I knew he was actually feeling as that dominant nature of his that felt disobeyed was displayed in the way he held himself against the door. All those concealed muscles tensed and forced into action when deciding to now stalk towards me, doing so slowly with each step precise and with purpose.

Then came his words.

"I must say, Sweetheart, I am not a fan of waking up with you gone from my bed, just as much as I am not a fan of turning up expecting to find you in one, only to discover that you are not," Lucius said as he continued to cut the distance between us. So, I lifted the book up without reading its title and shook it a little, telling him,

"I couldn't sleep." But then I wanted to smack myself after he reminded me,

"How strange, for I thought I had made my intentions quite clear on what would happen once I arrived at your bed…one you weren't in like I requested, I might add…" He paused right in front of me and only continued his comment after his gloved hand collared my throat gently and his thumb was then used to press my face up to him. Then he told me firmly,

"…and well, *sleep was the very last thing on my mind.*"

"Well, yeah I know but I…" I tried to say but then my excuse fled me when he pressed his nose into my cheek after using his hold on me to bring me closer to him.

"You?" he prompted against my skin.

"I just thought I would grab a book and read a little while I waited…to keep myself awake," I told him now back tracking and hoping he would let it slide…

Naturally, *he didn't.*

"Now it was to keep you from sleep…*I see."* He hummed this last part to himself and tapped his thumb on my chin twice before taking a firmer hold and turning my face to his so he could suck in my bottom lip, holding it with his teeth in warning. I whimpered at his dominant hold, one that was making me squirm. This, in turn, was making my aching clit throb against the twist of my panties, as that was one order I hadn't disobeyed. But then he let my bottom lip go by first sucking on it to soothe the sting before letting it slip through his own lips. Then he took a step back, dropping his hold on my face for one on my wrist instead. Then he raised up my hand, the one that was holding the book so he could freely read the title, making him ask,

"Umm, now I have to ask, whether this is your idea of some light reading or research, as I will fully admit to hoping for the latter." I looked down at what he was reading and nearly groaned out loud, damning Pip at the same time. Because she was the only suspect in reading a book titled, 'Phallic

Worship'. The naughty little minx was most likely hoping for pictures!

"I must have picked up the wrong one," I muttered trying to save face.

"Interesting, I suppose Hodder M Westropp, has other works that would be more interesting to your personal tastes... Sexual Symbolism perhaps, or maybe the Tao of Love and Sex by Jolan Chang is more to your liking?" he asked smoothly after taking the book from my hand.

"Erm...how do you know about...?"

"You are not the only one who has shared a home with Pip or received her quirky idea of a gift...now the more important question is...*how do you know of the book, one whose sub title is the ancient Chinese way to ecstasy.?*" He asked this last part on a sexual purr, that offered the promise of much more than the title held.

"Oh, Pip...most definitely, Pip," I said making him smirk.

"Ah, so she is going to be a scapegoat for the both of us then?" he asked, taking the time to scan a finger across its pages before throwing it back to the table I had clearly snatched it from.

"How did you know where I was?" I asked changing the subject.

"Power of deduction," he told me in a way that told me he was holding back the real reason he knew he would find me here. Did he somehow know that this had been my favourite place when growing up? Or had I mentioned it in my drunken state last night, when I had tried to talk his ear off?

He stepped into me, pulling at the silk bow that tied around my waist, tightening tonight's dress choice to hug my figure. It was a strappy little number of emerald green satin edged in a darker shade of silk. Its floaty skirt finished inches above the knee and the top half was pleated, creating a thin row of ruffles across my chest. And it was those pleated ruffles he was currently running his fingers across just as he had done with the pages of the book.

"Now, the biggest question of all is if *both my orders* were disobeyed?" he hummed in a dangerously seductive tone that told me of what would happen if I answered incorrectly… pleasure or pain, merging into a mixture of both…I swear my lady parts were weeping in anticipation of the orgasm to come. So, I decided to be brave, gaining height on my tiptoes and whispering in his ear,

"Why not take me back to my room and find out for yourself?"

"Mmm, now that reply tells me that my girl has done well and has pleased me, for I near bet my life on the fact that your pretty pink pussy is still spread and held prisoner against that tight twist of material." I swallowed hard at the sound of his erotic words, knowing there were more to come the second he put his lips to my ear and said boldly,

"I can scent it for myself, but I want to hear you say it. To say you're ready for me, that you're soaking that lace against your abused bundle of nerves…tell me, Pet, *will I find your clit glistening for me?"*

Well, if I wasn't 'glistening' before, then I most certainly was after that! Which was why I took his hand in mine and said,

"I think it's time you find out just how ready I am." Then I boldly started to walked past him, intent on taking him with me. But the second my arm was pulled taut behind me from his resistance I knew it wouldn't be that easy. Something that was confirmed the second he said,

"Oh no, my fuckable cock tease, you're not getting away with it that easy." Then he tugged back suddenly so I had no choice but to stumble into his chest. One that was rock solid under his black dress shirt that he had matched with a dark grey suit this time. But like last night when carrying me back to my bedroom, he was now minus the jacket. His sleeves were rolled as usual and he had forgone the waistcoat for a dark burgundy red tie.

"But I thought I had…"

"*You* still weren't where I told you to be, which means at least one punishment, if not the other," he told me firmly.

"But we can't…we can't do it here, what if someone catches us?" I asked, now panicking about more than just getting spanked. Lucius grinned down at me, enjoying this reaction and the hard outline of his cock beneath his trousers was also telling me he was getting off on it too. Especially when I started to try and escape him by attempting to peel his fingers from their grip on my wrist.

"What's the matter, my little Pet, don't you trust me?" he challenged, now dipping his finger below the top of my dress and skimming the tops of my breasts near to my already hard nipples.

"I just don't think we can chance it," I said trying again to pull back against his hold on me. But then he suddenly yanked me back and growled down at me,

"For you, Sweetheart, I would chance the wrath of Gods!" His eyes then blazed with his fierce words spoken into my cheek before suddenly I was crying out. This was because his arm banded around me at the same time he released his wings and in half a second we were flying straight up. Then, before I could fully get my head around what just happened, we were landing in the one section I had never been in before.

It was the locked section and at the highest point above the double doors and closer to the arched ceiling. It was also the only place not accessible by the staircase and I couldn't help but grip tightly onto him as it was so high, it was making me dizzy being on the small balcony.

"Easy, my little Šemšā" he said at my back with a firm hold on my body, with his arm wrapped tightly around my waist. Then he was pulling me from the edge and walking me back against the grated cage that kept the books locked away from my eager human eyes.

"I wonder, just how many times did your gaze wander up here and wish it could get to what was locked away?" he asked guessing where my thoughts were at.

"A few," I confessed making him scoff as he knew it was a lot more than that.

"And now every time you look up here you will think of something else," he all but promised me and I shuddered at the thought, but asked anyway,

"And what will that be?"

"The first place that I fucked you inside the walls of Afterlife," he told me firmly as he raised my arms above my head and pushed them back against the metal, making it rattle as if to drive his point home. I swallowed hard feeling myself squirming in anticipation, which was only managing to tighten my twisted panties against my clit, making me have to resist the urge to moan.

"Mmm, you feel it, don't you…tell me, Pet, did you come once you got back to your room…did you pull it tighter against your pussy? That sweet burn as it dug deeper, spreading you around the twisted lace?" he asked at the same time he was lifting the skirt of my dress, doing so in a slow and tantalising way that was messing with my senses, allowing me to focus on nothing but his words and his hands.

But my own were in desperate need to touch him, so I pushed against his hold, making him tut down at me. Even his wing feathers ruffled, shadowing us in hues of burnt orange, deep blood reds and darkened yellows. It cut out the rest of the room below and with it, the dizzying heights so all there was, *was Lucius.*

"I see you aren't going to play nicely by abiding to my rules," he commented with a sigh and before I could ask what he meant by this, he was loosening his tie. He started undoing the extra buttons of his shirt, allowing me a glimpse of perfect pale skin over solid muscle whilst tugging the length of silk from the now open collar. It was quite possibly one of the sexiest sights I had ever seen...well, other than Lucius down in his training room, bare chested and pounding the crap out of a punchbag!

His bare skin had been the sight I had unknowingly denied myself last night, getting only moments of it this morning before it was ripped from me by way of family interruptions. But then by focusing on that slight hint of muscle, I had instead not been focusing on the tie he now had wrapped around my wrists. A length of which he was feeding through the holes in the lattice so as to secure my arms above my head. He then tugged sharply making me gasp as the silk tightened, making him say,

"Mm, much better and gives me twice as much fun when playing with you," he said in a dark, masterful tone whilst lifting both his free hands, and I had to confess, that I couldn't help but sexually respond to it all. Because Lucius could be so many things. He could be funny and playful and teasing. He could be caring, loving and at times even sweet. But then he could be possessive, dangerous, dominating and like he was now...*masterful.* And I loved every single one of them! Because I knew that he would never hurt me, not unless it was for sexual pleasure. But cause me real hurt, or pain? *Then no.* Which was why I trusted him.

That was until I heard the door opening below and instead of releasing me, Lucius was covering my mouth to muffle the yelp of surprise and panic at knowing that any second we were going to get caught up here. I felt Lucius' lips at my ear as he told me,

"Now listen to me very carefully, I am masking our presence but whether we get caught or not is up to you and how quiet you can be...do you understand?" I nodded as I wouldn't have been able to speak anyway as he still had his hand covering my mouth. But at least I relaxed knowing that we weren't going to get exposed.

However, this hope died the second I felt Lucius whisper,

"That's my good girl, now try not to scream as I make you come all over my hand." I tensed and pulled on my hands but the second the metal moved slightly I had no choice but to stop. Lucius raised a brow at me with a look that dared me to do it again. Then, when I didn't, he grinned down at me in that knowing way when I held myself still.

I couldn't see who it was down there as his wings were still blocking my view, but just knowing we weren't alone was both making me panic and also turning me on even more. It was terrifying as much as it was exhilarating. It was bad as much as it was oh so good, especially when I felt my skirts being lifted once more and this time it was like he said…

He had both hands to play.

"Just fucking look at you…Gods, you're stunning…so Gods be damned fuckable, I just want to eat you up, my girl," he told me as he sucked and kissed and nipped his way across my chest, before slipping a finger beneath one of the thin straps. Then I felt the sharp tug against it, before it fell off my shoulders all together. This therefore allowing him to free one of my breasts after first yanking hard at my dress. Once he had done that, he lifted it up for his mouth so as he could latch onto my nipple. But just before he did, he paused so as he could tell me,

"Now remember, try not to scream." Then he sucked me in at the same time he gripped the twisted lace and tugged, making my mouth drop on a silent cry the second he clamped down on my aching nipple. By the Gods, it felt incredible as the pain he caused from his teeth connected directly to my clit, the one he was abusing with the material, making me feel like a puppet in the hands of a master pulling my strings.

It didn't take long before I was about to explode but seeing as I didn't trust myself not to scream I suddenly buried my face against his chest and bit his flesh. Doing so hard enough that my teeth went through the fabric and I tasted blood bursting across my tongue. I felt him react, as he hissed a,

"Fuck!" and his hand wrapped around my bound wrists and he pushed me further into the metal wall. He was getting off big time from my bite and before I had even finished coming, he lifted both my legs up, spread me wide and stepped into me. Once there I wrapped my legs around his waist, so he was free to release himself from his trousers. I then felt the sharp tug of my panties, making me moan at the torture against my swollen clit before they were gone.

Then he held himself at my dripping entrance, moving its head up and down in between the folds of my sex and coating his cock in my release before pushing in an inch, doing so agonisingly slow.

"Please…please, Lucius, don't tease me…don't make me wait any longer," I begged and it was something that pushed him over the edge of his own restraint.

"I can't fucking wait!" he snarled and then turned his head and snarled out a demand,

"Take your book and leave…do not come back tonight!" I knew then that this spoken order was said so his mind control would ensure us privacy once more. Because the moment the sound of the door shut, he slammed into me, making me cry out, for nothing in that second would have been able to stop it. *And Lucius knew it.*

"AHHH!" I screamed as the size of him stretching me, made me realise just how, in the few days in between us having sex, it was enough to tighten my core to the intrusion. And I wasn't the only one as Lucius' gaze turned to heated crimson as he growled down at me,

"So, fucking tight...Gods, woman, it is no wonder I find this perfect body of yours so fucking addictive!" I let his words penetrate deep and combined with his actions then he was the one who was the addiction!

He then allowed me this moment to get used to his size before he started to move once more and soon I was crying out my second orgasm to the sound of both my screams and the rattling of the caged door I was still tied to. Lucius had a firm and almost painful grasp on my hips and I couldn't help but hope to find bruises there tomorrow from where his fingertips had dug into my flesh.

I could then press on the marks and feel once more what I was feeling now, reminding me just how this moment of utter sexual bliss felt. I wanted more though, and he knew it the moment I tilted my head to one side, silently begging him to bite me. To feed from me the way I had tried to feed from him. The wet patch on his shirt from the blood that soaked it was proof enough of that.

"Mm, fuck me but such a temptation… how could I resist such sweet nectar…*all fucking mine!*" he snarled as he released his fangs before sinking them into my neck and making me scream louder this time! At first it was the pain and then it was the explosive orgasm that followed from having him bite my neck, one that was always forced upon me in the most erotic way.

"Lucius! Fuck, yes, YES!" I shouted as he began fucking

me even harder and faster telling me that he was nearing the end, doing so now as he sucked even harder at my blood, in a near frenzied way. His hips pounded against me, his hands most definitely bruising my flesh and his cock hammered inside my quivering core. As then we both came the last time together, with his demonic roar of release drowning out my own screams of pleasure.

Even his wings stretched out and shuddered as if they too had felt every bit of his stimulation as he emptied himself inside me, so much of it that I could feel it dripping down my thighs, bursting down around his shaft.

It was so hot and turned me on so much that the walls of my sex continued to shudder around his length, milking him of every last drop. We were both panting hard and the moment Lucius' possessive grip on my hips eased, I knew he was finally coming down from his own high. He placed his forehead to mine, closed his eyes and told me in a firm tone,

"Tonight, I sleep with my cock inside you...do you understand?" I nodded, 'cause the shock of that demand took my words and my breath away, as it was one of the hottest things he had ever said to me.

That and his promised vow, one at the time I had no idea he would be breaking.

"Good, for tonight…

"…There is no escaping me."

CHAPTER NINETEEN

PAST UNDEAD

"*Princess…princess…carrier of blood of Kings.*" The moment I heard these whispered words, I opened my eyes and what I saw this time made even less sense than the first time when finding myself in the library. Because once again I was no longer in my bed where I should be. And the Vampire who had been tucked against me, locking me to his body with his hard length seated inside me was gone.

For history seemed to be repeating itself as his warm touch had once again been replaced by the bitter bite of snow, as I was back in Germany. Back in Lucius' blood rock castle and once more my bare feet were sinking in the snow that coated his rooftop garden. I frowned looking down, as if expecting to see someone else's feet making the steps I didn't ask my body to make. But all I found was my own betrayal, as they not only belonged to me, but they continued to journey away from the safety at my back.

I also took notice that I was no longer as naked as I had once been, covered in soft skin and the hard flesh of my

Vampire no more. No, now I was dressed in simple black and white check cotton pyjama pants, and a thin T shirt of plain white. One that did nothing to ward off the bitter chill that felt more like that of a draughty old building than being in the middle of snow-capped mountains.

I felt myself shaking my head as I tried to recall the memory of me getting up out of bed, putting my glasses on and getting dressed, all without waking Lucius. But then my simple questions faded into one more serious as I started to watch the snow at my feet melting into sand. Then that too evaporated under my feet giving way to stone slabs beneath.

It was like a wave of ages, and with every step taken giving way to the next year for me to pass through. I don't know how I knew this, but it was like being pulled between the fabrics of time. One moment I was on the snowy rooftop being hunted by Hellhounds, then I was being forced to walk in the baking hot sands with the spears of my enemies at my back. Until finally I was somewhere new, being pulled by invisible strings down a deep dark tunnel of stone. But with each new step I took, I did so not alone, for in front of me was a sight I was becoming to know all too well…

The witch.

First, she was in the blood red cloak I had first seen her in, stark and almost glowing against the gleaming white snow. Then the sands would roll in and she was there stood next to a lone tree, one twisted and dead, with bark that peeled back like curls of skin baked from the sun.

She wore a brown cloak of coarse thick material, woven by what I imagined were calloused fingers. It covered her face but her long black hair hung like thin black vines, limp and dead against the slight frame of someone who looked half starved. But then, the last sight of her would appear, now as a broken young girl, flashing at the centre of the end of a tunnel. A darkness swirling around her like snakes of power coiled and ready to pounce. Then a blink later and,

She was gone.

This continued until the seemingly never-ending cycle rotated, each time bringing me closer to the witch, first in the red cloak, with the snow biting at the bare skin of my feet, until they gave way to the burning sands once again.

The hooded girl had been close enough this time for me to see her looking to the thickest branch, the one twisted as if it had been tortured into growing in such a way. She nodded towards it making me look for myself and sucking in a startled breath the moment I saw the noose, hanging all bloody as if used many times before. I pushed back my weight only to feel the sharp spikes of the spear tips at my flesh, telling me it was death either way.

But one gasp later and suddenly I was facing a cell door and it suddenly dawned on me where I was. I had been there only once before. A foolish and childish mistake by sneaking down into the lowest levels of Afterlife. I remembered seeing it the first time. Stepping inside the tomb of souls. A resting place of my father's kind that I'd read about in books. Books I knew would be added to those locked away should anyone find out the truth of what I discovered that day.

However, seeing the tomb in the flesh and I had been in awe yet scared at the same time. But no more so after I continued on, placing my hand inside the monstrous door and feeding the dead vines that covered it, for my blood was both payment and the key.

This was the only way to gain access inside the Temple. It was the place I wanted to go the most, to see it in all its splendour. The painted pictures I had seen in the scriptures had me mesmerised and desperate to see them for myself. Were the pictures of Heaven fighting Hell as beautiful as they were painted on the scrolls or even more so?

I was always a curious child and once fixated on something I was then stubborn beyond all reason until I achieved my goal. Well, being down there had been no different that night. As I held my breath hoping that my blood, even though human, was enough. It was said that my mother's blood had been, and like for her that night, *it opened.* Although, instead of those colossal doors simply opening allowing me straight access inside, all it showed me was the blinding light beyond. So, I took the chance and stepped inside, with hopes of being rewarded for my bravery. However, those mighty castle doors only led into a tunnel of darkness, one where I had fumbled scared and alone until finally reaching the other end.

Yet no Temple greeted me.

No, but my father's prison had.

It was the same prison I now found myself in and once more faced with the cell door I had been drawn to that very night. However, it had been one that remained empty at the time, with the door wide open and most definitely uninviting. But it had been the horrors behind the ones that weren't open that had made me run from the place screaming. Doing so only to find myself in the arms of my uncle Vincent. He never said anything. He never shouted at me or reprimanded me. He also never told anyone that he had found me there that night.

He had simply carried my shaking form, my 10 year old self back to my bedroom before settling me back in my bed. Then he turned on my old night lamp, one I hadn't needed for years, but one he knew I needed that night. Then he told me quietly, without once raising his voice,

'That is not a place for a pure soul such as yours, little one…you won't venture down there again." I had shook my head, telling him without words that I wouldn't and that had been all he had needed. That and my memory of horrors that had welcomed me. And up until this very night I had kept my silent promise.

But as for now, well like that night I was faced once more with the cell that had drawn me to it like a moth to the forbidden flame. But this time,

It wasn't empty.

Because the door was closed and the moment I touched its heavy metal panel was the second the cold penetrated my skin. I recoiled back from it as a blue light started to come from the small arched window above my head. It was one like all the rest in the room, heavy riveted doors of steel and iron, with bars in the small windows to prevent escape but that granted access for jailors to see the prisoners inside. None of them had conventional locks but small flat metal disks that I knew required blood to get the locking mechanisms to work. That was what I had read anyway.

But touching it now seemed to activate a memory of sorts. Yet it was half mine as that ten-year-old girl and the other half belonged to someone else. It was like a wave of time crashing through me and along with the rest of the room of cells that came alive with the sounds of the past. I heard an echoing of banging, high pitched screeching, wails and screams, combined with pounding fists against metal. But then the voices started to form words,

"I smell human sweat upon flesh." A gargled voice spoke like a ghost of the past, whilst another one said in a more guttural tone,

"I smell a ripe fruit ready for plucking…One I would gladly tear apart, skin from flesh, flesh from bone!" But despite the threats, I turned around to find there was nothing but that of eerie silence. It was like being trapped between two worlds, stood at the very edge of an echoing canyon of the past. And then the blue glow started to get brighter until once more it stole my attention as was intended.

"Help me, please." The strained voice of a girl spoke beyond the cell door and I frowned, knowing all too well that things weren't as they seemed. Because yes, I was human, but I was no stranger to my father's world. I was not the naive prey whatever was behind this door had hoped me to be. But with that being said, I was still curious. I had to look inside as right then my present self was compelling me to do so.

So, I reached up on my tiptoes and it was as if I was doing so after first slipping into the ghost of the past soul. The one who had done this once before. But no humans were ever granted access to this place. It had been why I had been so brave to try it myself as a child, never once believing I would get inside. But then again, there was one more human with blood fated by Gods...

My mother.

Was it her past life I was being made to witness by doing as she had once done? This question seeped away with the sight that met me. A girl was stood with her back to me, dressed in a long white gown with long black hair, sobbing quietly at first. But despite her cries, it was as if time had suddenly been suspended, as it waited for me to say next what was needed...*but I refused.*

Like I said, I wasn't the once naïve human my mum had been when she must have first stepped foot down here all those years ago.

"Well...aren't you going to ask me if I am human?" she asked, as if a switch had been flipped and the tears stopped instantly, now being replaced by a hard, bitter tone of someone obviously not getting their way.

"No, because I know you're not," I said boldly, then she

looked down over her shoulder, her blanket of black hair covering her features, as she mocked in a chilling tone,

"Yes, but I am very afraid, will you not help me?" It then became shrill as she laughed, an evil grating sound. She then raised a hand and with a twirling motion of her finger, I was reacting. It was as if she had the power to rewind the past and with it, she was making me her puppet. Because suddenly without being able to stop myself, my mouth was moving and instead of my voice, another innocent desperate one echoed around the room.

"What can I do, I don't know how to open the door?"

"Mum?" I uttered the second my voice was released back to me, because I had been right, this was my mother's memory. The girl started laughing then, telling me,

"I had a mother once, but unlike yours, I was made to watch her burn." It was then that I started to rattle the bars of the window, as if mirroring my mother's once desperate actions of kindness to save her. Only now my own were being used in anger for using her the way she had tried to use me.

"Your mother deserves to burn, just like mine did...*and she will...*"

"Fuck you, witch!" I snarled this time making her turn to face me, coming at the bars quicker than I could have imagined until I was now faced with this bringer of death, the one behind it all. A scarred face of a girl that lay eternally trapped between being that of a girl and a woman. Deep carved scars in her flesh looked almost fresh without the blood of the action whatever blade's tip did this to her. Symbols all crudely cut into her features, morphing what I knew was once the face of a beauty, had it been allowed to develop fully before being mutilated. But despite her obvious past hardships and pain, I growled back in her face with nothing but hatred. For I knew she was the bringer of death to not only an entire race but to the man I loved.

Something confirmed when she finished her sentence,

"...The Vampires that did this to me will pay...they will all pay, for the blood of kings owes us all, for the tree of souls is weeping and nothing you do will stop it!"

"What tree of souls?!" I shouted back but she just grinned, a row of teeth, sharpened into horrifying points, my only sight before she continued with cryptic clues as to what our future held.

"The last leaf will fall, and with it the single crimson rose will wilt and when it finally finds the ground...*death will find you, Chosen One...for your soul did not escape him...the one he stole will die...will die along with its keeper.*" I shook my head trying to make sense of her words and finding nothing but my anger in return as I vowed,

"We will stop you!" But it was a threat she merely laughed at and told me,

"It has already begun. The day of reckoning is upon you and you...*you are the key*...AHHH!" She was quickly cut off by my quick and brutal actions making her scream the second I lashed out at her through the bars. I had scratched down her face, getting her blood under my fingernails as skin had peeled back through the scars on her face. But her reactions to it were more than just a scratch, it was as if my touch had burned and because of it she dropped to the ground in a slump behind the door.

"HEY!" I shouted banging on the door wishing I hadn't cut her off so hastily, now demanding,

"How am I the key?! Tell me!"

But I knew it was pointless when she started laughing once more and slowly, inch by inch, she crawled back into view, only this time it was no longer the witch I had attacked...

"No...no, it can't be...stop it...don't...*Don't do it!*" I shouted desperately as my mother crawled into view. Only it was how I had never seen her before. She was on all fours shaking as she made her way over to a dirty air mattress that suddenly appeared in the cell.

She was in a pitiful state, with her clothes torn and filthy and her once beautiful blonde hair in a knotted mess. Large clumps of it hiding the face of a girl so beaten down it was hard to ever imagine it had been her. No, this couldn't have ever happened…not to my mother, not to one of the strongest beings alive!

But deep down I knew. I knew without the misleading shadows of doubt, ones I wished in that moment would consume me, that what I was seeing now was the horrors once experienced by someone I loved. A knowledge that currently felt as if it were being carved into my soul, for what I was seeing now was my mother's past.

It had once been her, but I knew it had not been in this cell. But this picture wasn't the end of the horror for it was simply the start. Because it continued to play out until I watched in utter dread as she pulled out something hidden in the shadows. Then the delicate sound of music started to play its haunting tune, as if from a child's music box somewhere inside. Then just as I uttered a pleading,

"No," I saw the flash of light and then the reflection of my mother's face in a deadly shard before suddenly I heard her own voice begging from where I stood, splitting this vision of the past into two pieces.

"Please, don't do this!" her own voice pleaded echoing now as a distant cry for help from inside the cell was heard. No, *not help*…but instead, it was her own goodbye to the world,

"There is only one way to save those that I love," she whispered and I saw the barest hint of her lips trembling on the words. Which was when we both screamed at the same time,

"STOP IT!"

"STOP IT!"

I fell backwards after letting go of the horror of truth I'd just learned, doing so now by welcoming the winding of my body as I landed flat on my back gasping for breath. The pain was one I welcomed, as if needing the reminder that I was alive. But then, as I closed my eyes, the same memory I'd had when landing hard in the forest assaulted me.

I had fallen from a tree swing and upon impact panicked when I couldn't breathe. I had looked up at the bright sky, until a shadow blocked out the sun. My father had come to my aid that day after I had called out his name in panic. He calmly bent on a knee next to me and after helping me to sit up, he told me to breathe slowly through my mouth, while pushing my stomach out. Then to suck it back in on an exhale to stretch out my diaphragm that was tightening up and preventing me from breathing.

Then he told me, when I started to cry, that pain as scary as it can be, is our body's way of telling you it still breathes life and there are times when we should be grateful for the reminder. Well, I had never forgotten that lesson and did as he had taught me. Doing so by sitting up and breathing the way he showed me. Of course, since that day I had experienced having the wind knocked out of me a few times in the training room and like that day, my dad had been there reminding me of the lesson, adding to it the order for me to shake off my knock down and get back to my feet.

For a Draven never stays down.

And he was right. So, despite feeling the forest floor beneath me, before I then felt the sand and then the snow, I got up just as all memories flashed before me,

My mother's. Mine as a child. Lucius as a man. And lastly it was me in the snow on that silent and deadly garden. It was all our lives coming full circle and all I needed to do now…

Was get up and run.

Which was why I quickly flipped to my feet and started running, not knowing where I was going, just knowing that it had to lead me out of here! Meaning that I continued on even as all the memories continued to merge as one. But it was one that only stopped the second I threw myself against a door. I then slid back the heavy latch that kept it locked from the outside and hoped that the reason for this wasn't one that could kill me.

I pushed on the hammered metal and wood, feeling it scrape along the stone floor and squeak as if the hinges hadn't been used in quite some time. I took this as a good sign as I stepped inside and slammed the door closed behind me. Then, with my forehead to the frame, panting through my fright, I felt something. I looked down at my hand the second I felt the blood of the witch still there tingling, making the skin beneath pulsate as if humming with power.

After this I braved looking at the rest of the room and found myself stuck in yet another vision. Only this time, it felt different. It felt like one I was intruding on instead of being made to witness. As if I had turned the tables of time myself and by coming in this room with the witch's blood on my hand, I had activated something she hadn't intended me to see.

The room was oval in shape and kept changing in between what I imagined it most likely was now and how it had been when my mother had foolishly made her way down here. Into what was quickly becoming my private Hell as it had been for her.

Fading in and out of new and old, richly furnished and totally dilapidated. The walls were stripped bare brick and then they were covered in torn shredded wallpaper. Thick and once regal paper of royal blue and gold fleur de lis, covered the walls, only the past offered it in pieces. With long claw marks slashed through the plaster and beyond it, even down to the brick peeking through. It looked as though it had once been some lavish cell for a raving beast.

The broken furniture, splinters of wood from the aftermath of destruction said as much. Along with the fourposter bed that was tilted on broken legs with a mattress slashed beyond all use. All of which was framed by the creepy shreds of what curtains remained. And like the paper, had no doubt once been luxurious blue velvet that now hung limp like the matted hair of my mother in the cell. It had once been a grand room and even when flickering into the present day, it still wasn't what it had once been.

It had once been a room of opulence and grandeur, but for whom I had no idea. But now it seemed more like a room used for people to wait in, with a simple seating area around a small table. One with bare brick and nothing more. But this wasn't the most startling difference as the very second it flashed back to the ravaged room once more, it then showed me what I had been missing.

"No...no...*it...it couldn't be,*" I stammered the second I saw her, my biggest enemy in the war and the one that had tried to kill me for little more than the sake of jealously,

"Layla."

The second I hissed her name the image of her on her knees appeared with her back to me, scratching her bloody fingers into the wall. She seemed totally insane! Her mind lost completely to the madness that consumed her. And the source of that insanity was easy to see as my eyes left her ragged form and took in what she had done to the room.

Decorating the walls with more than claw marks in paper.

But one name written in the blood of the insane...

"Lucius."

CHAPTER TWENTY

MADNESS OF SOULS

"*Lucius,*" I uttered in revulsion the second I saw his name clawed into the walls over and over and over again like some crazy mantra that needed to be seen all around her. I wanted to gag, not just at the sight of what she had done to every one of her fingers, but also to the numerous bloody fingernails I found embedded in the scratched lines of his name. Other than the sight moments ago featuring my mother, it was one of the most haunting sights I had ever been made to witness.

"Mine!" she snarled at me, snapping her head around to face me from the floor, looking like some wild creature, gone far beyond the woman that had faced me with a gun. Her face looked beaten and bloody, and teeth marks in her bottom lip told me she had done it to herself. Had she been running into the walls?

"Why? Why this madness?" I couldn't help but ask the ghost of her past image, when she suddenly rose from her knees in one creepy fluid move that put her once again at my level. But I stood my ground despite the pounding in my heart, telling myself this was nothing more than a vision. She couldn't hurt me. For starters, she didn't have a gun this time and her claws were now embedded in the name of my Chosen One.

"But you still have those, I see," I muttered as her fangs grew dangerously, now dripping with saliva like some hunger starved hound. Eyes of burning hatred and bleeding crimson tears,

"This madness is his…this is what he does…what he is capable of, but you will see, for you will be next…" She hit her own chest, pounding it hard enough that she rocked back on her feet,

"He will destroy you…your heart will crumble to dust at his feet…he will take and take and take until there is no more." Her voice was a shadow of what it usually was, broken and hoarse from hours and hours of what I knew was screaming his name.

"No, it won't happen," I told her, not for her sake but for my own. As I needed to hear the words right then like a balm to soothe the ragged edges of my soul, one the sight of this room had done to me.

"But it's already started…for he already owns that part of your soul, the part he stole…he fucking owns you and with his death, yours will follow!" She screamed the best she could and the second she lunged for me I fell backwards, tripping on a broken chair. But she was gone, and all that was left were her crimson tears now running down the walls!

A bloody river flooding the walls and soaking beneath the wallpaper I knew was no longer there.

"It's not real…it's not fucking real!" I told myself over and over again, closing my eyes.

"No, but it will be," the voice of the witch told me, whispering it in my ear and I screamed opening my eyes now

back to the past. Only this time, I wasn't a part of it. I was just a stolen witness to it.

Layla was now slumped to the floor with her back to the broken bed with her head in her hands. She was speaking in low tones, hushed and quiet as I had never heard her before. Her head was so low it nearly touched the floor, with her body being near bent over double. She sounded scared and almost to the point where she was sobbing.

Who was she speaking with?

"I can't, not to him...*I love him,*" she uttered on a desperate plea. But then I saw another person in the room, someone who was stepping from the shadows in a cloak...*one of blood red.*

It was the witch. But what was she doing here at this point in time? Well, my answer soon played out in front of me, as it didn't take me long to see that she was trying to get Layla to do something for her and clearly, it was something she didn't want to do.

I watched as she knelt next to Layla's crying form,

"But I will help you. Just let him come for you and when the time is right, you will be rewarded."

"Rewarded how?" Layla asked, now raising her head, bloody tears streaming down her face. I had never seen a Vampire cry tears of blood before...was this because she had been lost to madness or something the witch was responsible for?

"I will reward you with the gift of time," she told Layla.

"With time? But what good will time do me?" she argued but then whimpered and tried to scramble back from the witch when she touched her shoulder. She gripped it tight, making bluish light come from beneath the palm as if her touch burned like the blue part of a flame.

"Time is everything," the witch hissed angrily as if needing to teach her this lesson.

"Time will grant you the chance to finally have what you want," she continued making Layla and I both utter the same name, one in hope and the other in fear.

"Lucius."

"Lucius."

"Time will give you chance to kill the bitch he loves, but patience will be needed." I sucked in a painful breath at this, hearing her speaking of the love she believed he had for my mother. As my mum was the only one back then she tried to kill, many times in fact. Those had been Lucius' own words when speaking with the rogues and trying to convince them to release me. Layla had snarled venomously at the mention of my mother and it simply caused me an unspeakable amount of pain.

"Lots and lots of patience, for your time will come…the blood of the kings is due to us all and soon the tree of souls will weep with the venom of God," she said once again, making me frown at the significance of it all and remembering those words. They stuck with me like puzzle pieces that started to show the centre image instead of just the edges we had only to start with.

"Now, I will take your place, for my time in this vessel has come to its end, for you know what we must make them believe," the witch said and I shook my head trying to piece this together once more…was what I was seeing now in reverse? Was she talking about putting herself in the cell as I had seen her…as my mother had found her all those years ago?

"But what if he doesn't come for me?" Layla asked in a desperate tone. At this I saw the hood fall back on the same girl I had seen in the cell, telling me it was her…she was the one pulling all the strings. She was also dressed in white, with that same face of just a young girl, yet this time, there were no scars in sight! She also looked no more than fifteen years old. Yet, despite her age, Layla seemed equally terrified of her as she was transfixed. The girl stroked back Layla's matted hair, and hushed her like you would a crying child, and told her,

"Ssshh now, for he will come for you...the blood king always comes for one of his own." Then she was walking away, but before she could disappear from the vision completely, Layla reached out to her, speaking her name for the very first time,

"Vetala, wait!" The girl looked back at her, no longer with pity in her gaze, but now with a hard stone cold look of indifference. One that told me that Layla had been nothing but a tool to use and no doubt still was deluded into believing she was more. Although, I could see what she couldn't, as my mind wasn't lost to madness as hers was.

"I am Vetala no more, for your work is done for now, you served me well. But I will be reborn when the time is right... and you will serve me once again, Lahash. Serve me as the next Queen of Blood, for my name will be one all Kings will soon find eternity kneeling to...*the name of Daiva, I shall become.*" After this declaration she left the next vision completely, leaving only Layla in its place. I tried to think back on her words, replaying them in my head but before I could make sense of her plans, the past changed again. As Layla was no longer sat slumped by the bed, but instead waiting in front of a torn tapestry and she was clearly waiting for something.

No, not something...

Someone.

The second she heard whoever she must have been waiting for, she started to weep again, her bloody hand slapping against the fabric in desperate relief. I shook my head, trying to drown out her sobs and concentrate on the voice she listened to. It was male...a male voice I knew well. I frowned, finally gaining my feet once more but never taking my eyes off her, waiting to see which face would emerge from behind the curtain of fabric. As she faced a tapestry and I knew from experience that in this place, there was usually a door to be found behind them. But then I heard the locks turn and knew this was someone here to free her.

It was someone here to…

"NO!" I screamed the second he stepped inside the room, and I couldn't help but scream his name. The same name that surrounded me now, in blood and madness…

"Lucius!"

This was when I staggered back against the wall and the second I touched it, everything suddenly vanished. The image of the past evaporated and all that was left was a broken girl in a once broken room…*me.*

Because there was no denying it, Lucius had been the one to break her out of Afterlife. He had broken her out even after she had wanted to kill my mother! I felt sickened by the sight of him helping her, despite it being the past.

I was also mentally drained and confused as to what it all meant! The witch, she had a plan all those years ago, this hadn't just happened, this had been set into motion over thirty years in the past!

"Gods, no," I whispered as the sight of him disappearing came back to me, making me become the one to crumble back to the floor. But then I looked down at my hands as they started to tingle once more and the witch's blood under my nails that had once been there, started to fade just as the scene in front of me did.

Was I right, had this really been something I was never meant to see? Had scratching her in the cell not been a part of her plan and had reversed her power somehow, because surely this was something that she wouldn't have wanted me to know?

I decided to get up and get the hell out of this place as there was only one person that would know what was going on and she was the one who had been here during that time...*my mother*. So, I ran from the room, with no choice but to go through the same door that Lucius had stepped through. But once inside I quickly realised I wasn't just back inside the prison, but a different area of it. And one look around the walls, and I knew exactly what part this was...*it was a torture chamber.*

I cried out in shock, covering my mouth with my hands as I realised what the true purpose of that opulent room was. As there was only one reason for it to be next to such a place. It was simply another form of torture. Only one not so much of the flesh, but of the mind. It was one that prisoners were taken to, to await torture and then being thrown back into such luxury after a night of agony and pain was just another form of it.

To be given the choice to talk and tell my father what he wanted to know in order to stay in the room with its nice paper on the walls, its comfortable bed, no doubt with hot hearty food waiting. I couldn't imagine many not breaking from such a method.

But then my father was King. A King that ruled with the hand of the Gods both in Heaven and in Hell...Hell being the operative word here. He was in charge of ruling over some of the most powerful and brutal supernatural beings that all realms had birthed.

So, it stood to reason that a King like him needed such a place to keep such beings. Just like Lucius would no doubt have his own in the bowels of Blood Rock. And as for Layla, well she had found herself tortured for the crimes against my mother. Because no one tried to take my father's Chosen One from him and lived to speak of it...all but one...the one Lucius had help slip through his fingers. And now, through that mistake, she was back and this time it wasn't my mother she wanted to kill...

It was me.

I walked through the brutal place and the darker side of my father's world that up until now I had been sheltered against. Because what the witch had wanted me to see had backfired, as bringing me down here may have been part of her plan but what happened next hadn't been.

So, I started running, past the row of iron maidens, past the chains and hooks embedded in the walls. Past the body stretchers and wall of spikes, I passed it all, until soon I found myself faced with a row of cells again.

"She knows…the girl knows too much!" A voice stopped me in my tracks, and I couldn't help but be drawn over to it. And I did as I had done before, raising myself up to the window, using the bars to steady me. What I found was a dirty white padded room that looked like any you would have found in a mental hospital back in the 1800's. Only this one had twenty-foot ceilings.

But as I peered inside, I found an Angel with his torn and bloody wings pinned to the high ceiling above him. The remains of where they once were on his back now nothing more than broken, snapped bones protruding from his back. Blood staining the bandages were all he wore around his torso. White trousers covered in strips of material all hung like a skirt. But I couldn't see his face as he was sat facing a step ladder that rose all the way to the ceiling. However, it was one that was missing all but the top two rungs. It was like a symbolic reminder of how close he was to getting his wings and had the broken means never to do so. It was another form of torture.

"You work with the witch?" I demanded and his head turned to look at me, a face of years of pain and suffering making what once would have been handsome into something sad and pitiful. His skin looked grey as if decades without the sun had transformed it into solid ash. Hair white that could have once been golden and only his beautiful amber eyes remained what they were, although the glow of life had been drained long ago.

"No one works with the witch," he told me in dull tone as if I bored him.

"And you are nothing but a spider dangling in a web of his lies," he said making me shout out in anger,

"You know nothing!"

"I know enough and so does she…" He then nodded to a window that showed the moon and made me realise this part of the prison must have been on the cliffside. But that darkness outside showing the night was quickly flooding the cell with moonlight as it parted from the clouds. But the warming glow of night wasn't the only thing it brought with it as soon shadowed hands started to emerge from the frame of the high window, as if dragging itself inside.

I narrowed my gaze as they continued to grow inside, stretching along the floor and towards me, until the hands went from my view behind the door. I was just about to take a step back when I suddenly screamed the second the hands reached me, shooting through the bars and grabbing onto my wrists in a vice like hold. I screamed again, the second a blue light emerged from beneath them just as it had done to Layla with the witch's touch. It started to burn the second it glowed brighter making me scream in pain.

Then it let go and I fell backwards, continuing to do so until I reached the wall opposite. I rubbed one of my burning wrists before switching to do the same with the other, taking a premature sigh of relief that I was safe.

However, this nightmare wasn't done with me quite yet as this too turned out to be a grave mistake. Because I was now being grabbed again, only this time by what felt like hundreds of hands all behind me!

"NO! NO GET OFF ME!" I screamed again, trying to twist

out of their hold and managing it only enough to find myself side on now facing the horror of what had hold of me. It looked like a giant wall of skin stretched thin and almost see through when the faces of tortured souls were pressing themselves up against it. Doing so now in an attempt at biting me, with demonic teeth trying to pierce their way through trying to get to my exposed flesh. One that made me vulnerable not only with the hands that held my limbs pinned, but also at the clothes they tore at, trying now to get to skin beneath.

"GET OFF ME!" I screamed again, only when their hold turned painfully tight, I had no choice but to scream the one and only name I could think of. It was the only one who had a connection great enough that would hear my cries and feel it in our blood connection. The one I knew who would come and save me.

After all, it had worked before.

"LUCIUS, HELP ME!" I screamed one last time.

This was just before the face closest to me had forced all others out of the way. Hands, elbows and any other body parts in between me and it, disappeared and now the one hungry enough to get to me was just about to lunge.

But it never happened.

As just as it was about to bite at my face, a flaming serrated sword of purple appeared inches from my eye. It speared through the skin wall and into the demonic face, making the whole wall howl in agony. Then, all at once, every hand let go. I was taken into someone's grasp and yanked backwards, landing into a large chest, one big enough that at first, I thought it belonged to my father.

But then I watched the glowing blade still embedded in the wall and followed it, as it retracted back into the wrist of the being it had come from. Its deadly jagged edges were unlike any blade I had ever seen, for the ones belonging to my father were smooth with a deadly razor edge.

Meaning only one thing.

So, I looked up and said in a shocked tone,

"Brother?"

CHAPTER TWENTY-ONE

OH BROTHER

"Hello, little sister," Theo said in that smooth voice of his, one that had only managed to deepen with age, along with other more obvious changes, I thought when looking him up and down.

"Erm, technically we were born on the same day," I said with exasperation making him smirk and lean down a little so as to comment in a smug tone,

"I wasn't referring to age, little lost girl." This was his nickname for me and had been since we had first met a little over ten years ago. This was because the first time I saw him I had been climbing out of a window at the time. I had been sneaking out and about to get onto a bus with the rest of my school friends on a trip to London. Much to my parents' annoyance at the time and why my grounding included not just putting me in my room for a week but sending me off to Scotland. (for my safety of course) But since then, I had been 'little lost girl'.

Of course, being one of triplets and never meeting either of my brothers until we were sixteen years old, well… having at the time not even knowing they existed was a big blow to a teenager…to all three of us actually.

But it had been the will of the Fates that the two souls that were both born without a human body as I was, had no choice but to wait until their destined vessels were ready to merge with the supernatural element of their souls. It was around that age that I was informed our home was being turned into a school for a group of young Demons and Angels. A new generation of supernatural power that needed guidance, for they were the first of their kind. However, what nobody ever told me was that one of them would be my brother. No, this was something I had found out the night I had run away and was caught by non-other than Lucius. The Vampire King, who had been charged with hunting me down by my father and mother, who at the time had been frantic.

That was the day we first met.

It was also the first time in my life I had been attacked and he had saved me. And both my brothers had witnessed the whole thing, seeing as the two of them battling it out had caused my reaction to begin with. As let's just say that finding out the way I did hadn't been easy and wasn't a time I looked back on with fond memories. Hence, the tiniest bit of a chip on each shoulder I might have held on to for far too long, one named Theo and one named Thane.

But then I wasn't the only one in that department seeing as Thane held the biggest chip of all. Of course, it was also said that he was the one who suffered the most with the change, seeing as his demon was unpredictable and had been battling him ever since for supremacy. But Thane had also been unwilling to learn from Lucius how to contain his Demon in the way that he should. It seems there had been three groups of teens inheriting their souls all in the same day and the fifteen boys and girls had been split into three. One group with my father, the second with Lucius and the third with King Cerberus, who was the King of Hellbeasts. Oh, and also just so happened to be fated to my human cousin Ella. Someone who also met her Chosen One on that same fateful night I met Lucius.

Although, like I had said, she had fled for reasons I didn't know exactly, and the King of Hellbeasts was waiting for something before he could claim her. I didn't know what exactly as it certainly wasn't age, seeing as she was a few years older than me. Saying that, if he was anything like the other Kings, then once whatever it was that stood in his way was over, Ella would find herself running no more. For once he was finally free to claim her, then I knew from experience, there would be no amount of hiding that Ella could do to stop him from finding her and making her his. And Jared Cerberus was a bad ass biker and known as one of the most brutal and ruthless Kings at the table.

Although to me, who he had known since I was a baby, like all the other Kings, he had simply been like another Uncle that wasn't one of blood. But Ella was utterly terrified of him. This was after seeing him in his other form, which had unfortunately been her introduction into her uncle's world. A secret she had sworn on her soul to keep that night, as it had been my fault in the first place. We had gone on the school trip to London together with her as a Senior and me as a Sophomore.

But then my reasons for going weren't solely for a good time with my friends and cousin, but because I had heard about the infamous fight club, the Devil's Ring. This was owned by Jared and it was after sneaking in, that I realised I had been followed by my poor cousin, Ella. A redheaded, almost nineteen-year-old beauty, who got more than she bargained for that night.

And speaking of Fates, as for Theo, he had found his soul

mate and unfortunately lost her due to what I heard was an impossible choice he had to make at the end of the Blood Wars. A time I had spent safely locked away in my father's Scottish castle, playing the little helpless and reprimanded princess. This was while Theo got to lead an army into battle and become the Hero to all. Hence my own nickname back,

"Whatever, Golden Balls." This made him chuckle before patting me on the top of the head in a patronising way and say, after nodding at the wall,

"Oh, and you're welcome, little sister." I growled at his back when he walked over to the moaning skin of creatures swarming beneath it and leant down to pick up my glasses that I hadn't released I'd lost until then. Then, as one snarled out at him, he twisted his large torso and punched a meaty fist into the wall, making it ripple with the power that emerged from his combined souls.

My brother was like my father in most ways, other than looks. No, he looked more like our mother in that department, with a slightly darker shade of blonde hair that most of the time looked unruly. He also had her shade of eyes, that seemed to change with his mood, being their usual grey/blue at the moment.

But flecks of green and navy blue were there in the mix just like they were with our mother. Although flames of purple was also the colour that came through when his mood took him down a darker path and that part of him, well that was all Dad.

Now, as for his smile, then that really was killer! He was full of easy smiles and handsome grins, with perfectly shaped lips that seemed naturally tinted into looking soft. It was a grin that transformed the good looking into stunning. Lighting up his eyes in a way that often took a girl's breath away. In fact, I knew without a shadow of a doubt that if Wendy ever met him, then she would have passed out in some dramatic fashion just so he could catch her. But then, she had a big thing for Thor... like most of the female population did.

But he had my father's chiselled features, with a strong jawline and cheekbones, artist's would go apeshit for. But what differed between our father and Theo was his easy-going nature. Even though at times that natural born confidence of his morphed unknowingly into that of a born leader. Yet admittedly, this was done without arrogance but more out of a sense of duty. He was born wanting to do the right thing and had a conscience the size of Texas!

He kind of reminded me of Thor even more in that way, with that righteous 'defend the kingdom and world' thing, combined with his looks and sheer size of him. The God of Thunder was a good nickname and one I might start calling him instead of Golden Balls. Because now I was older, well, it kind of felt a bit mean.

But then there was also that raw side of him that was all my father. The demon half of him that he kept a tight and firm hold of, whereas my brother Thane never had. However, no matter how much they fought and reigned in that side of their natures, there were always the times it managed to rise to the surface and when it did with Theo, then look out world, because he was one scary bad ass!

"Jeez Theo, did you eat a wrestler on the way here or something?" I asked, playfully punching his arm after calling me little sister again. He chuckled and said,

"What was a guy to do, he tried to eat me first." At this I stopped dead and stared at him. He then looked back at me and,

"Jeez, Fae, did you lose your sense of humour on the way here or something?" he mocked making me roll my eyes.

"No, but by being here I did!" I commented looking back at the wall with a shiver. My brother followed my eyes and frowned before telling me,

"It's called the wall of Souls."

"Original," I commented dryly making him grin down at me as we started to walk from the cells, with him naturally leading the way.

"It's another form of prison for those that can't be contained the conventional way," he informed me, nodding to the metal doors as we passed.

"How do you know that?" I asked pushing my glasses up my nose after first giving them a clean with my torn and now tattered T-shirt.

He shrugged his big shoulders and told me with a wink,

"You're not the only one that reads, little Miss Bookworm." I thought back to what mustn't have been that long ago and couldn't help but try to hide my blush.

"Ah, but of course, you have wings," I commented trying not to sound bitter about it, although he didn't help that process when he added,

"That and a key."

"Yeah, yeah, no need to rub it in," I said sarcastically. Then I felt him nudge my arm and say,

"It was said as an offer, Fae...not as anything more." I grinned up at him big and said in a hopeful tone,

"Really?"

"Yeah, although I am not sure you need it now." I frowned in question and before I could ask, he beat me to it.

"Any reason you called out the big Vamp's name over any other?" Shit, shit, shit! Okay, so this was bad!

"Well, I ...I didn't think it best to give dad a heart attack... you know and well, there is mum too, she would worry and..."

"Huh, uh sure, sure," he said folding his arms making his faded Led-Zeppelin T-shirt tighten around his arms. This was his usual attire, never being one to fall in line with the whole suited and booted side of being royalty. Nope, it was usually just jeans and a Tee for my brother. Now as for Thane, it was usually the black suit of an assassin. In that way he kind of reminded me of John Wick on the few occasions I had ever seen him. He was all darkness and quiet rage that one.

"What are you trying to get at Theo, me and Lucius are just…"

"Each other's Chosen Ones, yeah I know." At this my mouth dropped open in shock.

"Uh, no we're not," I said hoping my tone of astonishment was taken more from the idea of what he said and not the fact he knew.

"Oh, so you're just fucking then?" he asked making me jerk back and say,

"No and I don't appreciate…"

"It was me who walked into the library last night, Fae."

"Fuck!" I hissed making him chuckle.

"It was?"

"Wow, you break really easily," he said after whistling and at this my entire face dropped.

"What?!" I hissed making him chuckle.

"I mean, you could have at least challenged me a little."

"You must have been there, otherwise how did you know about the library?" I challenged making him tell me,

"Oh, come on, if there was ever a place you would take a secret boyfriend then of course it would be the library!" he said laughing but then he obviously took pity on me and nudged my arm again, telling me,

"I'm teasing you, little lost girl." Then he winked at me making me release a huge sigh of relief, well that was until I still had something to panic about, seeing as this still meant that he knew about me and Lucius.

"You are so mean!" I complained making him chuckle again before shrugging his shoulders and saying,

"What do you expect...half demon remember?" At this I laughed and informed him,

"Now you sound like Dad!" he scoffed at that, but his easy smile told me that he didn't take the comparison as a bad thing. He and my Dad were really close and just as they said that I was my mother's daughter, then with Theo, well, he was most definitely his father's son.

"So, you were really there, huh?" I asked, now tiptoeing around the subject and trying to gauge the level of shitstorm the forecast was predicting coming our way.

"Yup and I have to say, the Vamp is good at keeping your dignity intact, I will give him that but he wasn't strong enough for me not to know that you were both up there...although, commanding me to leave was a nice touch," he told me as he held out an arm telling me to proceed him through a tunnel and one that looked to lead back into the Tomb of Souls.

"Oh Gods, I am so screwed," I muttered which only managed to echo in the large space anyway.

"Why?"

"Because you know and now your gonna tell dad and then there will be blood and..."

"Why would I tell dad...I haven't yet, have I?" he pointed out but I didn't give in to hope just yet, making a point of saying,

"But you only just caught us and..." His laughter cut me off, that and the shaking of his head, making him need to run a hand back through his floppy hair.

"Fae, honey, I have known for years, just always wondered when you two would stop dickin' around and make it official." Okay, so if I thought my mouth had dropped before, well now it was of the catching flies variety.

"But how...and when and well, how again?" He smirked and said,

"Let's just say I am way more perceptive than Mum and Dad."

"Okay, I am not seeing this as a good thing here, bro." He chuckled and said,

"Most people couldn't see it, but I knew something had happened when you came back from Germany. You weren't the same after that." I cringed at that and couldn't stop from asking,

"What gave it away?"

"I don't know, it was just like a light had gone out or something…don't take this the wrong way but you just seemed a little…*broken*. Besides, it takes one to know one I guess," he said with a shrug of his shoulders and I swear my heart ached. Gods, I had no idea how selfish I had been. Which was why I grabbed his beefy arm to stop him and before he could say anything I threw myself into his torso and hugged him tight.

"Whoa!" he chuckled, before asking me,

"Erm, as nice as this is, Sis, I gotta ask, whatcha doing, honey?" I chuckled before telling him,

"What's it look like I'm doing, bad ass, giving you a hug!"

"Yeah, got that part, Fae, I meant what's it for?" he asked now patting my back like he was uncomfortable, but trying to make the effort all the same.

"Because I am sorry I was sometimes a bitter bitch to you and I am sorry that I was in so much pain that I didn't recognise your own and because…well, I am sorry Janie left you." I said making him tense with the last thing I said. Then I pulled back and said,

"Plus, I think if I tried to do this to Thane, he might kill me." I joked making Theo scoff because well, hate wasn't really a strong enough word for how they felt towards each other.

"Yeah, well, don't talk to me about that demonic shit stain!" he commented dryly.

"Wow, that's harsh even for you," I commented making him

grunt and reply,

"Bastard deserves far worse from me. But in regards to the hug, and the reasons behind it…I get it and never blamed you. Hell, I was even tempted to go to Germany and kick a Vamp's ass." I laughed at this and asked,

"What stopped you?"

"Well, other than the fact the guy is one hard fucker to kill, I think the most obvious reason not to even try is the same reason Dad can't and won't do shit." I grinned big at this and then asked,

"So, you're really not going to tell him?"

"Haven't yet, not going to now."

"Can I ask why?" I was curious to know and just hoped that by asking I wasn't pushing my luck.

"You mean can you ask *Golden balls* why?" he commented giving me that look.

"Mainly, because it isn't any of his fucking business, you're an adult, Fae and you know what you're doing…he needs to learn how to respect that."

"Oh my Gods." I muttered stopping dead.

"What?" he stopped and looked around as if he was missing something.

"I think I am going to hug you again!" He chuckled, held up his hands and said,

"Uh, that's okay, let's just keep that one for Christmas …yeah?"

"Deal…and if it's any help, I am thinking of changing Golden Balls to Thor anyway," I told him with a grin, one that got even bigger when he said in an exasperated way,

"Please don't."

"Thor, it is!" I declared with my hand in the air and his groan of frustration was my only answer.

We made our way back to the other side of the tomb and I

stopped dead yet again the second realisation seemed to slam right into me.

"Hey, are you alright?" Theo asked seeing as I was no longer next to him. Then I slapped a hand to my forehead and shouted,

"Gods, I am such an idiot!"

"Bit harsh but alright, I will play." I frowned at him making him chuckle,

"I am so blind! It was what that Angel said back there…All this time we thought the witch was working for someone… Gods, how could I have missed it?!" I complained to myself with my eyes going everywhere as if it was all written out for me to see.

"Erm, I get that you're the smart one of the group here, Fae, but your gonna have to give me…"

"The witch! We all thought that she was working for someone in control of it all, another rogue we didn't yet know the name of." I told him quickly.

"Yeah, Dad mentioned what's been going on… but wait, you think what exactly, that she was the one…"

"The one pulling the strings, you bet your Thor ass I do!" I said making him frown,

"You really are going to start calling me that, aren't you?" I clapped my hands and shot him a pointed finger from it and said,

"Yes, yes I am!"

"Alright, fine, whatever, get back to the witch," he told me with a shake of his head.

"Think about it, it's the perfect cover. She creates this rogue in charge, that way she can just be classed as the 'power' to prevent Lucius from controlling his enemies, but what if its more?" I started to point out the facts making him naturally ask questions.

"Like what…I mean, why would she?"

"I don't know, 'cause she's a woman, a witch and not a Vampire. Maybe she needs the persona of a master who is a vamp to get others to follow her in her cause. So she can just use them to get to Lucius. That way she could watch unseen…"

"I don't know," he said in a sceptical tone, so I told him,

"What's the one thing dad always taught us…"

"Keep your friends close and your enemies closer," he answered making me nod,

"Exactly, she hates all Vamps, that much is clear, so who better than to create an army of rogues she can simply kill off later on."

"Collateral damage she cares two shits about," Theo added, looking thoughtful.

"The Angel, he said it, he said that no one works with the witch…what he was really saying is that you only ever work *for her.*"

"But why, what's her motivation in all this…what's her great beef with Vamps?" I bit a lip in thought and eventually admitted,

"I don't know but what if it's only *one* vampire she has a problem with."

"Yeah, but come on, kill an entire race just to kill one, it doesn't make sense?" he argued making a point which ended up with me discovering my own…and it was a fucking big one!

"She's not…she's…*fuck!*" I said before I took off running with Theo now having to catch up, running behind me,

"What? She's not what?" So, I turned my head looking back at him and the second I reached the door back into Afterlife, I paused before opening it so I could give him my answer,

"She's not just killing an entire race…"

"She's killing an entire army."

CHAPTER TWENTY-TWO

PINNED WITH LIES

After running through half of Afterlife, I ended up bursting into my parents' chambers having little clue on the time but knowing that it was already morning. My dad noticed the second I did, especially when I shouted frantically,

"Is everyone here?!" My dad had been sat reading the paper dressed and ready for the day and it looked to be one of all business as the black suit he wore said as much. He dropped the paper with a look of concern.

"Amelia…what happened?" His gaze travelled the length of me and I knew what he would find…I was a mess and unless my bed had attacked me, then I think it was obvious something had happened. But there was no time to explain. Not yet anyway.

"The Kings for the meeting, are they here already?" I asked again making my dad look to Theo who appeared at my back.

"Theo, what is going on?"

"We will explain later, just answer her," he said sounding as impatient as I did.

"Yes, they arrived a short while ago, why what has happened?" I then looked around the room and asked,

"Where's mum?" Because she was going to be very much included in this conversation, as she may be able to fill in some of the blanks.

"She's with Lucius helping him with locating some of his people...why?" I had to say that it hurt, seeing as I had needed him. But then to know that he had left my bed in search of my mum was something I couldn't afford to think about right then. Nor could I afford to think about him being the one who helped Layla escape. In fact, there was a lot of things I couldn't afford to think about that all centred around Lucius.

"Never mind, just call a meeting!" I said making my dad frown,

"What, now? Can't it wait until tonight, they've only just got here."

"No, it can't." I said and Theo quickly backed me up and told him,

"Call the Kings, we don't have time to wait." My dad looked first to Theo and then to me, before nodding, accepting our demands and finally conceded,

"Alright, Theo go and inform them the meeting is in thirty minutes, that should give everyone enough time." Theo nodded once then looked down at me and said,

"I hope you're wrong about this, little sister." Then he left just as my mum and Lucius arrived, making her ask,

"Wrong about what?" Then she continued to walk to my dad who was ready to curl her to his side. Meanwhile, Lucius looked down at me with nothing but far too many questions in his gaze, especially when I made a point of giving him the cold shoulder.

Because it wasn't just the fact that he hadn't come for me when I had needed him, or the fact that he had been with my mother at that time. It wasn't even what I had learned when down in the prison about the past. Or even the fact that he made it clear to me how we would be spending the night and at some point he had slipped out of bed right along with slipping out of me. No, it wasn't just one of these things...

It was all of them combined.

"Fae, what happened, are you alright...your clothes?" My mum asked now taking in my appearance and well, she wasn't the only one.

"What happened?" Lucius demanded.

"I will explain at the meeting," I told them both. One who was definitely frowning more than the other and it was no guess who out of the two, was looking more pissed off by the second.

"But I thought that was tonight?" My mum asked looking up at my dad.

"Amelia has discovered something that can't wait," my dad replied and it was Lucius who asked in a stern tone,

"Where were you?" Now it was my turn to frown, because come on, could he be a little less obvious.

"Not that it's any of your concern," I stated hoping to make a point and making him state right back,

"It is the concern of all of us if you were to get taken, for your ransom would be held against us all."

"You think someone could take her from here?" my mum asked sounding horrified at the idea.

"From the looks of things, I would say they have already tried," was his reply and he looked murderous at the idea of his own words.

"What!?" my mum shrieked, outraged.

"Mum, I'm fine."

"Then how did you get those marks on your wrists?" Lucius

snapped nodding down to my hands and looking beyond furious. He also looked far too close to the edge and any minute I knew he was going to find his limit on keeping our relationship a secret. So, I decided to tread carefully.

"A lapse of my judgement." Obviously, this wasn't enough for him as he was just about to snap something else when my dad beat him to it. He was suddenly in front of me with my hands in his and looking down for himself at the red handprints around my wrists.

"What happened, who did this to you, I want their name immediately, for they will be…!"

"Fucking dead, that is what they will be!" Lucius finished off for him on a deadly growl.

"Look, I will explain when…"

"No! Explain now!"

"You will explain now!" Both of these demands came from the two men in the room who were both close to losing their shit and neither seemed to want to back down. But it was about time they understood that they couldn't bully me by demanding things of me. And if I said that they would have to wait, then damn it they were going to wait!

"No, I will explain when I said I was going to and both of you are going to respect that because, Lucius, you are a guest in our home and not someone who is here to throw his weight around…" He growled at this, but I ignored him and turned back to face my dad and told him,

"…And dad, you have recently discovered this new, less controlling and more trusting side of yourself with regards to your daughter, so with that being said, I am going to go get changed, whilst you both go practice waiting for me to be ready to talk about it…Mum, see you at the table." I said finishing this by looking at my mum who was smirking big and looking as though she couldn't have been prouder of me for putting these two in their place. And I had to admit, I, too, was feeling pretty good about it.

Well, that was until I left, made it all the way to my door and was just stepping inside when I quickly found Lucius at my back stepping us both inside and slamming my door behind us. I tried to step away only to find two hands at my hips making me moan. Because my wish had come true...I had his fingerprints bruised on my skin and the second I felt the slight ache, I couldn't help but think of last night. Then those hands travelled further up and crossed over my torso so he was holding me fully from behind.

"That was cute in there, Pet, but you don't get to tell me when and where to throw my anything around, for you are mine and therefore that means when I ask you who fucking hurt you, then guess what...*you fucking tell me!*" he snapped and I tensed in his hold but then relaxed before telling him,

"Yes well..." I paused so I could grab his hand in a hook hold before slipping my weight down at the same time, ducking under his arm whilst bringing it back up with me. This ended with me pushing him face first into the door, pinning him there with the lock I had on his arm behind his back. Which was when I chose to finish my sentence,

"...maybe if you hadn't left me in the night, then perhaps I would have remained in your arms instead of waking up down in my father's prison!" I snapped and far quicker than the move I had done, he used his free hand to put extra weight down on my lock so he could straighten his elbow. Which meant that I had no choice but lose my pin on keeping his elbow bent and his arm up his back. Meaning that before I could counteract the move, he was putting a bend into his turn and was soon hooking me around the back of my neck. Doing so now with what had been his free arm, putting me in a head lock with startling ease.

This put me at the disadvantage of being bent over with my head tucked against his side.

"Now, do you want to say that again?" he asked down at me and stepping out of my way at trying to free myself when I tried to stomp on his foot. So, using my Wing Chun training, by bringing my arm up over his shoulder and pointing my fingers down to the ground, I then tried to grab his face. Ideally, this was by aiming for his nose so I could push up and be ready to stand up straight the second I got his head pulled back. However, he was too quick for me yet again, and after grabbing my top with his free hand, he fisted the material. Then he positioned his leg so when he pulled me over his thigh he could then drop me to the floor with ease. Once I found myself there, I tried to roll but again, his actions were lightning fast. Terrifyingly so, as before I knew it, he was holding me down with a hand around my throat. Then, once pinned to the floor, he simply snarled down at me,

"Yield." But I was too angry and besides, he wasn't hurting me, so I tried to hook his wrist. I did this by making sure not to grab it with my thumb separated from the rest of my fingers so he could slip out easier or potentially hurt my thumb as he fought for escape. But knowing this and with his free hand, he knocked my elbow up so I lost the hold. Then, so I couldn't try it again, he quickly dropped to his knees over me and pinned my other hand over my head making sure not to hold onto the burn. This was when he had really had enough and snarled down in my face,

"I said fucking yield!"

"Fuck you!" I shouted back making him growl this time and tell me,

"Uncurl your claws, kitten, and just fucking yield before you hurt yourself!" That cocky bastard comment only made me want to fight even harder but with his hold on me, I knew that he was right. To try and get out of his pin now and I was only in danger of hurting myself. But then I wasn't going to make it easy on him either. So I told him,

"You left me."

"What hurts you most, Sweetheart, that I left or that when you found me again, I wasn't alone?" At this I screamed in his face, hating that he was right,

"Ah! Get the fuck off me!"

"No," he snapped and then sighed, before informing me,

"Not until you have heard what I have to say."

"Fine, then just fucking say it!" I snapped back.

"I left because I had no choice. I still have a responsibility to my people and as much as I want nothing more than to be buried inside this delectable, hot little body all night, one that I own…" His hand moved from my pinned arm so he could emphasise his words with his touch. Something that started when he ran his fingers down the side of my breast to my waist and further. Something I stopped when I hit out at his chest, making him pin me again, to stop the fight from continuing,

"…My people needed my swift decision, one that was far too difficult to make and not one that I would have held my people responsible for." I closed my eyes at this and asked,

"Which was?"

"The mass execution of the two hundred and fifty six rogues they collected from the streets," he told me, making me suck in a quick breath. Because he was right, that was a shitty decision he had to make and being king meant he didn't want that hanging over anyone else. Meaning that as far as reasons went, it was a pretty good one…*damn him!*

"Get off me, Lucius," I said in a small voice, one he simply growled at,

"No fucking way." Then he growled low and menacing.

"Lucius, I said…"

"I know what you said. I am not fucking deaf, just as I know that you are not, which means you will hear me perfectly fine when I say that I am not letting you go anywhere until I have had my own answers out of you," he told me sternly and it was a tone I knew not to argue with.

"Fine, then can we at least have this conversation off the floor?!"

"No," he stated firmly.

"No?"

"You're not deaf." This was snapped, making me roll my eyes at him, only this turned out to be a mistake. I felt the sharp sting to my ass before I even knew he had moved his hand and rolled me to the side so he could access it. That was when I knew that he had been holding back all those times, as his speed was one I could never hope to win against.

"AH!"

"Count yourself fucking lucky it was only one, now if you want more, continue your fucking attitude and see where it gets you!"

"I am not a fucking child, I am your girlfriend!" I retorted back, ending it on another cry as I was spanked again...*twice this time.*

"You learning yet?!"

"Fuck you!" I shouted making him spank me yet again, this time...it was three.

"AHHH!"

"Shall I make it a fourth?" he asked doing so more calmly this time and wisely, I held my tongue.

"Good to know you can learn," he said, infuriating me enough to say again in a quieter tone this time,

"Like I said, I am not a child, I am your girlfriend."

"You're acting like a child and no, Amelia, you are not my girlfriend." At this I sucked in a harsh and ragged breath, but my face must had said it all...*hurt.* Because the next minute the spanking stopped, and he was lowering himself down over me. His face was then in my neck, where he whispered,

"You are so much fucking more...*you are my Chosen One... which makes you mine to play with whenever I choose."* This time, at the end of his words, I didn't have time to suck in a breath because his lips were there over mine stealing it, tasting it for himself. A kiss that quickly became heavy and soon I found myself no longer being pinned down but wrapping my limbs around him. I found my hands curling into fists at the back of his head, with his soft hair held prisoner, just as my body was his.

His hands were everywhere, in some frantic need to have me, to feel me, to touch every inch of me, which was when I realised what else he was doing...checking to see if I was alright. He wanted to check for any other injuries, and I had to say, the fact made me melt. So, I whispered in his ear,

"I'm fine."

"I heard you calling for me...*I felt your fear,"* he told me, looking down at me and I tried to turn away from the intensity of it all.

"Theo saved me," I told him, still avoiding his gaze.

"It should have been me," he admitted against my cheek in a pained voice that spoke of his guilt.

"Why wasn't it?" I asked in a small way that said it all.

"Because I couldn't find you." Now this shocked me.

"You were looking for me?"

"Of course, I fucking was!" he snapped furiously before telling me,

"You think I hear my girl screaming for me and I what? Just calmly finish my meeting and make you wait?!" Oh yeah, he was back to being angry, even as his hands were running down my sides in the softest way.

"Don't get shitty with me, I called your name for a fucking reason and don't you dare spank me for that!" I snapped back getting angry myself, making him smirk at my sass for some unknown reason.

"I found your room empty and by the time I tracked you to the lower levels I caught a fresh scent of you making your way back to your father's room." I narrowed my eyes at this and asked,

"And my mother?" He too narrowed his eyes down at me in return and snapped,

"She was on her way back to your father also." Hearing this and I couldn't help it when I reacted to the lie I knew it was. Because my father had already told me that they had left together, meaning that what he said now was lies. The biggest question of all, was why?

"Right," I muttered making him snap,

"And what the fuck is that supposed to mean?!"

"It means this conversation is over."

"The fuck it is!"

"Lucius, please, I am just trying to make sense of everything that happened myself and seeing as being scared isn't an emotion I experience much in my own home, I just need a minute to sort my head out and would appreciate you giving it to me and not on the fucking floor!" I said trying to make a point and looking like I was finally starting to get through to him.

"May I remind you that I didn't start this, Pet," he said looking down to our current position and referring to me pinning him against the door.

"Yes, well count this as me finishing it." He frowned down at me for that and the second he started growling I added,

"The fight, Lucius, this is me ending the fight."

"That's better!" he snapped before suddenly his weight was

gone and the moment I started to sit up, I found myself being plucked off the floor and back to standing.

"Now you can tell me what happened," he said and I refrained from rolling my eyes even though he caught the start of it and challenged me to finish with just a look.

"I have to get changed, they will all be waiting."

"Let them fucking wait!" I swear my eyes nearly bulged,

"We can't make them wait, Lucius, it's the Table of Kings, it's not exactly like being fashionably late to a party!" I argued.

"Kings, Queens…Hell, there could be the whole damn royal court of Heaven sat waiting for all I fucking care, we are not leaving this room until you have told me exactly what happened to you!" he bit out furiously, making me release an exasperated sigh and run a frustrated hand through my hair.

"I have to get dressed."

"Last time I checked, you don't need your mouth for that, my Khuba" he said dryly, even though he ended it by calling me his love. So, I did as I thought was best and explained to him what had happened, leaving out half of it because I knew if I didn't, then we would never have left this room. So, I explained a little and when he asked me why I had called this meeting, I told him the only thing in that moment that I knew would end with us leaving,

"Because this isn't the first time the Witch has been in Afterlife, that's why." At this Lucius looked to be giving this some thought. Which then allowed me time to kick my feet into a pair of flat black ballet shoes, that completed the simple look of dark blue jeans and a light grey knitted sweater. One that fit tight with a large ribbed V neck that needed the white vest top worn under it so it wasn't indecent. Then, I had brushed my hair into a high ponytail and opted for my contacts. A simple bit of makeup and lip gloss and I was done.

"Why do I get the feeling that you are holding back on

telling me everything?" he asked as we walked down the hallways of my home, heading towards the room that held the meeting. But it was only when I reached for the door that I said back to him,

"I don't know, Lucius…" I paused and just as I opened the door whispered back over my shoulder,

"Why did you lie to me about being with my mother?"

CHAPTER TWENTY-THREE

TABLE OF KINGS

I ignored the growl at my back as I walked into the room that's sole purpose was to hold a table and eight chairs… only today, for the first time in twenty-seven years, it held nine. This was for seven Kings, one Queen and now,

A Princess.

It was also a room that I had never been in before whilst others occupied its space. No, I had only ever sneaked inside when it had been empty. As even the ten-foot doors told a story before you even entered through them, with each panel carved in what many classed as the War of all Wars.

It had been the end of days that had been stopped before I was born and the very reason the Table of Kings was created not long after. It was the one single most important event to happen that brought everyone in high power to the table and made them fight as brothers at arms, no longer as Kings against each other. And the one who had accomplished the impossible had been none other than my mother.

Apparently, she had done what no-one had ever done

before, as it was their combined admiration for her that had brought them all together to fight by her side. Which was why, through all of the carvings, there was one my eyes always went to…a lone figure amongst all the chaos.

It was simply beautiful.

My mother in a beautiful gown with hair flowing and face turned downwards as she looked at a small blade in her hand, whilst all others fought the onslaught of beasts, creatures and demons as they were nearly consumed. It was a beautiful piece and it was there to remind everyone who stepped through these doors why they did so.

Once inside it held nothing more than a huge table and chairs for its purpose was clear. But the table itself was also a reminder of that day, for it was a long rectangle of carved damaged wood about ten feet wide and at least fifteen feet long. Sections of it were also charred black with a massive split down the centre. In fact, it looked as though it had taken a lot of powerful blows from each of the Kings in this room, but I could only be sure about one.

The whole thing had been covered in clear resin to preserve the damaged door that it once was, being the very one the four horsemen had been unleashed through. And it was easy to see how, before that destruction, it was once magnificent, despite what it represented. Meaning that even though broken now, the door itself had once been a thing of haunting beauty, the haunting part being the end of the world.

It was sectioned into four panels that each held one of the horsemen that threatened to pass through its gate into this world. One white, one red, one light grey and one black, could barely be seen now of course, as now most of the wood was charred black and ash, where it had been set alight by my father's own flames. This had been done after the war to symbolise the end. I also imagined that the many slashes in each of the panels could have come from Jared's own claws. Most likely when in the form of his beast causing the giant splits in the wood. But like I said, I only knew of one with certainty to cause the damage and that had been my father... looking at it now though, well... *I knew better.*

Along the sides were the seven locks that had once contained the horsemen. Three ran down each side of the door and the seventh from above, were all connected to a metal scroll at the heart of the door. Of course, now all locks were broken, snapped and bent upwards as if damaged when someone had ripped the door clean off in anger. These were the only parts of the door that protruded up through the resin like seven spikes, each representing a seat for the Kings around the table.

The door, that had been transformed into a tabletop, had been mounted on a more elaborate piece of carved Chinese rosewood. And it was one that continued the theme. The legs were large carved horses charging into battle, each with a deathly rider sat upon the steed,

The four horsemen of the apocalypse.

I remembered reading about them after learning pieces of what happened during the start of the Blood Wars, something that started with my mother and only truly ended with Theo.

The white Horseman was Disease and the paintings in my book showed him as a rotting figure of a man. His horse also looked infected as its flesh hung from dark twisted bones. The red Horseman was said to be the Master of War and his entire body, along with that of his own steed, was bathed in the blood of the lives he massacred.

The Black Horseman was said to bring famine to the land, sucking all life from deep within the soil with every step he took. His skin was like parchment left to bake in the hot sands of Persia and his horse would pant, with dust expelled from its nostrils as it seemingly always struggled to breathe. The last of course was

Death. The Grey Horseman and whose colour choice came from the ghostly figure that sat upon the steed of bones and shadows. He wore a cloak, barely concealing the souls he collected, and naturally he was usually the last horseman to follow his brothers.

I remember reading about them and then sneaking in here and finding it fascinating that this had been the exact door they had come through. It made me wonder what was now in its place.

Of course, there was little time to wonder about such things now as each seat around the table had someone sat in it other than three empty spaces, one for me, one for Lucius and one for my uncle Vincent who was still missing in action.

As I entered, everyone stood and after granting each a shy grin in silent greeting, I walked towards my mother. Her chair was situated next to my father's at the top of the table. To her right was an empty space and what I could see now had been recently added. But seeing that chair now awaiting me and well, I couldn't help but take pause just before taking my seat. The significance of this moment I couldn't help but feel it down to the core of my soul.

But then Lucius took a longer way around to his own seat, doing so now so he could pull out the heavy chair for me, making me quickly sit down.

"Erm…thanks," I muttered, unable to stop heat invading my cheeks and as he pushed the arched throne style seat back in, he replied,

"You're welcome, Princess." This now making it clear what I represented when in this room. After this he continued to his own seat that was directly opposite my father at the other end of the table. But then, as he walked past, the man sat next down from me was the King of the Ouroboros. Sigurd, who couldn't help but comment in an amused tone,

"Fuck me, the Vampire King can be a gentleman...who knew?" he said laughing, making his huge frame shake at his own amusement. To describe Sigurd in only two words would be huge and Viking, for he was also Ragnar's son. Of course, there were other words you could have thrown in the mix, like blonde, handsome, rugged, gorgeous, laid back, oh and breathtakingly hot!

"Fuck off, Snake Eye," Lucius snarled as he took his seat, still making the massive blonde Viking grin. He was the biggest one in the room, being close to the same height as his father. But whereas Ragnar had the bulk of a tree, Sigurd's muscle, although still bulky was also more toned and defined. He was also known as Snake Eye due to the small serpent eating its own tail that circled one eye. Although, as per usual, he wore a hooded jacket covering half of his handsome face, snake eye included.

Sigurd also sat on my side along with another King, known as the feared King of Death. You wouldn't have thought it to look at him, but his power was almost beyond measure. Although, out of all the men at the table he was the smallest in the bulky muscle department. This being said he also looked like a Dior model, with his handsome, angular bone structure. Ash blonde hair was in some messy style that barely seemed tameable but worked for him and his Gothic style. He was still tall but had more of a slim build that was made for stealth, speed and strength.

His Chosen One had also been human once and was a good friend of my mother, which is how they met. She, like him, was more alternative in style and every time I saw her, she had a different hair colour. But like the rest of the Kings, no Chosen One sat at the table other than my mother, so she, like many others, was not present.

"Where is Vincent?" I asked my mum quietly at the same time nodding to the only empty chair left.

"Oh, your father sent him to Germany shortly before you left to see what he could discover." Hearing this and I swallowed down the 'oh shit lump' that had formed, making me nearly choke on it. My panicked eyes automatically went to Lucius, who tried to tell me with his eyes that it would be okay. Although, how he could be sure of that I had no clue!

Because Theo might be cool with knowing about my secret relationship with Lucius, but Vincent? Well, let's just say that I couldn't imagine my uncle being quite so, how should I say...*less murderous*. Besides, he and my father were as close as brothers could get, so I couldn't see him letting this mountain sized discovery slip by unsaid.

My only saving grace in all this was that at least he wasn't here right now, or this first meeting of mine might end in more destruction to this table and I wasn't exactly sure it would survive it a second time round. Next to this thankfully empty seat and across from Seth was Jared Cerberus. Someone who looked every bit of a bad ass biker but not a single shred of a King who ruled a Kingdom in Hell.

He was also, like the rest, insanely handsome but in a more raw and rugged way. His hair was an unusual charcoal colour that wasn't turned this way from age. It was thick, coarse and wiry and all of it was currently pulled back from his face and tied with a leather band in a sexy manbun. However, his shaped and pointed beard was black and framed a full pair of lips.

But these weren't the only strong features he possessed as he had a wide nose that suited the hard bone structure, and eyebrows that were arched slightly. One of which had a thick scar running through it that continued down his face to his jawline before disappearing behind his ear.

But the most startling part of Jared was his silver grey irises ringed in black, bleeding into the whites of his almond shaped eyes. Even the skin around them seemed darker and more dangerous when finally braving a look into their molten depths.

His attire was one I had never seen him in anything but, with a leather jacket that had seen more years than I had. Black denim jeans, heavy studded biker boots, large belt buckle and a leather cut over a black T shirt was his armour of choice. Along with heavy silver rings on scarred and thick callused fingers. Like I said,

He was beautifully raw.

He was also someone that my human aunt Libby and Uncle Frank would have heart failure over should poor Ella ever find herself in a position to introduce him to the family. That is if Ella ever saw past the scary, bad ass biker/ Hellbeast thing and the two of them ever got it together.

And speaking of smooth bikers, Jared was smirking at me before commenting,

"I must say, Dom, your daughter's beauty grows each time I see her, and I speak for us all in welcoming her to the table." I grinned at that and so did my father, who opened his mouth to reply when Lucius got there first.

"Yes indeed, now can we get the fuck on with this meeting before the rest of my people die or would you like to talk about her pretty hair, Hellbeast!" Lucius snapped in answer making my dad narrow his eyes at him. In fact, he was just about to open his mouth to comment when my mum placed a hand over his forearm and mouthed a silent,

'Leave it, Dom.'

Then my mum went back to looking at Lucius in a questioning way, as if she was trying to get a read on him or speaking with him in secret, directing it through their link. One I knew we would never have due to me being human. The only person that laughed was my brother Theo. Of course, this was because he knew what had made Lucius snap.

Although, Lucius wasn't exactly helping our awkward situation either as he currently looked as though he wanted to go a few rounds with a Hellbeast. Jared looked at Lucius and gave him a smirk before shrugging his shoulders and saying,

"I didn't call this meeting, so it makes no odds to me who the fuck starts…and you're right, she does have pretty hair." Then just as Lucius snarled, Jared unleashed a wicked and deadly looking claw and used it to curl back a line of resin in the table…the warning not to fuck with him was clear.

But then Lucius, as blunt and as rude as he sounded, was right. I had called this meeting early and now was the time to explain why. So, I took a deep breath and looked at each of the Kings, and my mother who right now couldn't have looked any more proud of me. She even gave me a little thumbs up under the table so no one could see and mouthed,

'Good luck…take no shit'

I couldn't help but grin back at her before facing the rest of the room. Then, out of respect, I looked to my father who nodded for me to start. So, I took another breath and stood, feeling as if I was facing a jury on the stand.

"As you most likely already know the reasons you're here I am going to get straight to the point." I looked then to Lucius who was watching me in a way that was close to being too bloody obvious…or was it just obvious to me after our argument?

"We first believed that there was someone behind the rogues, who was pulling all the strings and using a witch merely to prevent Lucius from having control over what were once his sired."

"I take it by your tone we no longer believe that?" Jared asked making me nod,

"No, I don't and soon, neither will you." Lucius narrowed his eyes at this, because he was starting to see that I had left something out of our talk, my suspicions included.

"I believe the witch is the one behind it all." At this the Kings reacted and Lucius, although silent, looked murderous and clenched his fists, warning me with a single word,

"Explain."

"Since Germany she has been trying to control me, only managing this mainly when I am asleep, as I guess this is when she thinks I am most vulnerable," I said making my mum gasp.

"Controlling you how?" my father asked in a hard tone.

"She makes me sleepwalk, shows me images of the past, and takes me to places where I eventually awaken," I told him making my dad growl before a question was forced from clenched teeth.

"And last night?"

"I woke inside your prison, dad," I admitted, making him hiss a foreign curse in Persian. My mum put a hand on his forearm as if to offer him strength this time. Then she told him quietly,

"We will fight this, we will protect her."

"What images of the past?" Lucius asked in a dangerous tone breaking through this family moment of discovery, as this was another thing I had kept from him.

"Mainly, yours and my mothers," I said making him flinch as if I had struck him.

"Mine?!" My mother asked now horrified. So, I turned to face her and whispered,

"I'm sorry, mum…I am sorry for what she put you through." She frowned in question, jerking back a little as she said my name as a question,

"Amelia?"

"This witch, she has deceived everyone and this deception

spans back thirty years ago." I then went on to explain what had happened when being faced with the cell and what I had seen, stopping before I spoke about my mother's part in the vision. But from one look at her now, *she knew*. Her hands flew to her mouth and I got a glimpse of the scars on her wrists she used to keep hidden. The ones I had always wondered about.

"Oh my God...Oh God no," she uttered getting out of her seat and my father quickly did the same before gathering her in his arms. This was because she knew what I had seen.

"The girl in the cell, all those years ago...Draven? Is she...I thought she was dead...that you...?"

"As did I." My father ground out with a bite of anger.

"It was all part of her plan. Even back then. She wanted you to believe that she broke Layla out, and was captured in the process but what you didn't know was that she wanted to be there," I told them before going on to explain when I struck her face and therefore turned the tables on the visions she showed me, seeing far more than she ever intended.

"I found the room Layla had been kept in and saw their exchange," I said looking to Lucius who was now looked livid and also...*concerned.*

"She spoke about her hatred for Vampires, and the day all Kings would kneel to her." Sigurd snorted at that and said,

"Then she's bat shit crazy if she believes that will ever happen!"

"Oh, she's definitely got a screw loose, but combine that with a thirty year old plan, the means to carry it out and a grudge that spans time, then that also makes her a dangerous witch with a screw loose," I commented in return.

"I see your point, little one," he replied with a nod of his head, making his hood slip slightly.

"This black heart of hers...what level of witch is she, to hold so much power?" Seth asked in that velvet tone of his that held an edge of insanity to it also. Although, as the King of Death, then I guess you had to be slightly insane to accept that role!

"That we know of, at least a level six but after this…most likely more," Lucius replied, surprising me with this knowledge. A level six was near totally unheard of, so if it was more…well then, we were all screwed!

"If it was more, then that would make her the most powerful yet." Theo said making Lucius nod, saying a strained,

"Indeed."

"But I still don't understand, I saw her death, I was there… she died on that altar by your father's hand," my mother argued, still holding on to that memory in her mind, so I told her,

"I think we both know that in our world, death doesn't always mean the end." At this she released a heavy sigh and looked up at my dad who still held her to him.

"Sweetheart, come now…come sit back down," he told her whilst leading her back to the table after her emotional outburst, one that it was clear, still affected her and after seeing what I had of her past, then I wasn't surprised, for she wasn't the only one it clung to.

"What else was said when the witch was speaking with Lahash?" Lucius asked and I knew this was her demonic name he usually used. But then I knew that look also, as he was trying to judge just how much I knew about this time. Because of course…*it included him.*

"She said that the blood of kings is due to them all and that soon the tree of souls will weep with…"

"With?!" he snapped when I took pause and I couldn't do it. So, I muttered,

"That part was whispered, and I didn't catch it." His face said it all.

"Are you sure?" he all but snapped at me and it was clear my father didn't like his tone.

"Lucius." He said his name in warning making Lucius tear his gaze from me because he knew...*he knew I was lying.* But what he didn't know was that it was done so to protect him. Because mentioning the Venom of God she spoke of would only make Lucius seem responsible for it all. And he may have been the one to free Layla all those years ago, but he did so thinking she was one of his own and not knowing what the future held. I had to hold on to those reasons as being the truth.

"Go on, my daughter, continue," my dad said nodding for me to do so.

"She planned for you to kill her, as she told Layla that her time in her vessel had come to an end and that it was time that she made you believe it was a death solely by your hands," I said looking towards my dad before looking to the other Kings.

"But why?" I thought about my father's question and before I could answer, someone else did and unfortunately for me, it was the last person I hoped to see at this table today,

As an Angel burst into the room and answered...

"Because she needed to get into Hell."

CHAPTER TWENTY-FOUR

ANGELIC THOUGHTS

The moment my Uncle Vincent appeared through the door I sucked in a quick breath that no one heard on account of everyone all acknowledging his sudden arrival. My Uncle looked every single inch the powerful Angelic King he was, and I swear sometimes it even looked as if the sun found him wherever he was and made aspects of him glow. He also looked absolutely nothing like my father and they were like polar opposites. Whereas my father was considered the tall, dark and broody type, Vincent was all light, pale and tightly controlled emotion.

He wasn't far off my father's height being only a few inches shorter. He had light golden hair of tight curls that were tamed back and touching the top of his spine. His sapphire blue eyes shone with intelligence and his pale skin sometimes looked as if dusted with gold. He, like my father and all other Kings, was built with the body of a God. He was also utterly ruthless in battle, according to my father's accounts of history. I could barely believe it seeing as my uncle was one of the calmest people I knew. But then, my father would often warn me not to be fooled by such a calm exterior, for they often turn out the most deadly.

Of course, none of this boded well for me and Lucius seeing as with one look alone at both him and then me…*he knew.* Which was why I silently pleaded with him when no-one was looking, telling him with my eyes to do this for me. To keep my secret and not tell my father.

His emotions, as usual, were hard to read, but then he took in the sight of me nervously biting my fingertips after sitting back down and he must have made his decision.

He nodded.

Obviously, my look of sheer dread must have helped as I let out a quiet whoosh of breath that only my mother heard from being so close. She patted my hand in a comforting way, no doubt thinking that this was all a lot for me to handle. Of course, she had no idea just how hard my uncle's appearance had just made it.

I looked at Lucius to see that he had been watching the exchange with interest and in that moment I couldn't believe it but he actually looked annoyed at my Uncle's choice of silence!

"But wait, I thought she was an Angel?" my mum asked bringing me back to what my uncle had said the second he had walked into the room. This question from my mum had been directed at my dad who looked like his mind was where my mother's was…*firmly locked in their past.*

This was when he admitted to her,

"I did not explain everything that night." My mum frowned at this and after crossing her arms she said,

"Then I suggest you start now by erasing that thirty-year-old lie," she snapped.

"I did not lie either…*not completely.*" Ah, so one of those half-truths then, the ones kings seemed so fond of, I wanted to say due to my own experience… but wisely, I refrained.

"The girl, the one in the cell and who I believed was Marked to be punished was discovered to be more than what was first claimed," he told her making her frown back at him in question after first wrinkling her nose, something she did when displeased.

"What do you mean?" I asked this time, making my dad look uncomfortable for a moment before admitting,

"We killed the wrong girl." My mum sucked in a startled breath and the rest of the Kings exchanged uneasy looks.

"Draven how could…?"

"It was not known until after her vessel had been reclaimed that Potnia, who was the one in line to claim it, had started having visions."

"Visions of what?" my mum asked,

"Not now, Keira," my dad said making her forgo the frown and simply narrow her eyes at him in a dangerous look before demanding,

"No, *now Draven.*" He released a sigh and told her,

"Shortly after Potnia regained consciousness, she had visions of you…" My dad cut himself off and rubbed a hand on the back of his neck like Theo often did when their frustrations showed.

"Of me what?!" my mum snapped, getting impatient. My dad shot a brief annoyed look to Lucius before telling her,

"Becoming a Vampire." My mum sucked in a quick breath and my gaze, like my mother's, shot to Lucius who too looked affected by the news, ignoring me and looking instead at my mum. Of course, none of us expected the next confession to come from my mum, least of all my dad.

"That morning I…"

"You what?" he asked, his concern easy to see as the purple

in his eyes started to seep through the darkness. My mum put her hands to her face as if she was remembering something she had seen on herself and said,

"The next day, I used the bathroom and when I looked in the mirror, I saw…I saw the same thing," she admitted making my dad now be the one to narrow his eyes at her.

"Then it looks like I was not the only one holding back on the truth, for I remember that morning also Keira, and if memory serves me right, then I recall you screaming out and convincing me you merely stubbed your toe." At this my mum shrugged her shoulders and said in a sheepish tone,

"Then I guess lucky for you we are even." At this he leaned in close and whispered with promise,

"Hardly."

"Uh, as entertaining as this is, as I hate to break up any good domestic here, but can we get back to how this bitch is going to kill an entire race?" Jared said making my father growl down at my mother as way of a promise before telling her,

"This discussion isn't over, Vixen."

"Right back at you, muffin tops," she hissed back, making me chuckle, especially when my dad muttered,

"I believe this morning it was muscle tops, and should you continue your sass, little one, I will explain why that is," he warned making Theo release a sigh and grasp the top of his nose in a hold that said it all.

"Fuck me."

"Oi, language!" my mum reprimanded making me grin. But it was Lucius who'd had enough, and this was blindingly obvious when he suddenly hammered a fist down on the table and roared,

"ENOUGH!"

My father stood at the same time Lucius did, meaning they were now just facing each other with the table of the past between them. Vincent narrowed his eyes at Lucius and then looked at me, seeing my panic. One that doubled when my father warned,

"Take care, old friend, for your actions will stretch only too far in sight of your circumstances." This made Lucius snarl back,

"Last I checked it was my people fucking dying, Dom, and if you didn't realise already, one of them is…" This was when I intervened knowing that if he finished that sentence, then my dad would lose his shit. So, I stood and banged my own hand on the table, mouthing a little 'oww' which made the Kings all smirk back at me.

"Just stop it! Arguing right now won't help anything and Lucius is right, we need to make a plan of action against whatever move this bitch is planning next!" Lucius took a deep breath and I nodded for him to sit his ass back down, and when he did, I turned my attention to my dad, who mirrored his old friend.

"Then what of the box, your father said you managed to get it open?" Jared asked making me release a sigh and start explaining about the box and the useless map. Then five seconds later Adam knocked on the door, entered without a word and left again after first placing a pile of papers on the table. Lucius nodded down at the pile and told everyone to take a copy and make of it what they will. I also took a copy, despite already secretly having one, after swiping one off Lucius' desk when I ran back inside for my sweater.

But he didn't know about that one.

"Fuck me, vague much?" Sigurd said making Jared throw his back on the table in frustration and by the time it had floated to the table he snarled,

"Fucking useless is what it is!"

"I have to agree, although without all the F words," my

mum agreed. But it was my brother who said,

"It looks like it's missing something."

"Yeah, like GPS coordinates, or Hell, even a fucking village name I would take," Sigurd commented dryly. I ignored the comment and asked,

"What are you thinking, Thor...I mean Theo?"

"Thor?" Vincent asked with a grin and Theo shot me a look whilst answering him,

"Golden Balls expired." I tried not to smirk at this, even if my uncle did.

"Can we get back to the fucking map already?" Lucius snapped again, this time making me shoot him a look that said, 'What is your fucking problem?'. Obviously, it was ignored.

"Well, everything else about this fu...erm, box has been smoke and mirrors, so stands to reason the map found inside it would be too," he said making me refrain from chuckling when he was about to swear, but one look at our mother stopped him. Good one, Thor, I thought with a secret chuckle.

"We are asking the wrong questions," Seth said bringing his hands together on the table and his long sleeves slipped back to show paint stained fingertips and black nails.

"Oh yeah, then have at it, buddy boy," Sigurd said motioning with his hand for Seth to explain.

"If we discover what she wants with the box, then we will discover what weapon we potentially hold at her throat."

"Genius," Sigurd uttered under his breath making Seth shoot him a death glare side on, one that had the power to do just that. Although, it would have to be directed at someone less powerful than Sigurd, as he could more than hold his own. The living shadows swirling in irritation under his hood right now became testament to that.

"Seth is right, because at this point, we know she wants the box not the map, one she might even not know about," I said trying to bring down the level of testosterone in the group. This was when Lucius spoke up,

"She knows."

"Why do you say that?" my mum asked before I could.

"Just trust me on this, Keira girl, she does," This was his reply and I hated the nickname he had for her, making me try and hold back my reaction, which instead came out as a snap,

"We need information shared here, Lucius, not simply to trust that someone has it." He looked to me and snapped back in challenge,

"Agreed, information is key…in the right hands." This was obviously referring to me keeping most of what I had said at this table from him.

"Where is the box now?" Jared asked moving on and my father nodded to Lucius for him to answer,

"It is being kept in Dom's vault until we know more about it."

"Why?" I couldn't help but ask. He raised a brow at me, shocked I had asked this question myself.

"So it is only his blood that can access it." Now I was the one surprised to hear this and almost questioned why again. But then I stopped myself as I quickly started to understand why and I had to say, the reason hurt.

"You don't trust yourself?" Theo asked in my place and Lucius didn't make it quite so obvious when he spoke next, doing so without looking directly at me but only doing so once he had finished,

"I don't trust whoever may have gained access to my blood, for it was what opened the box to begin with."

"But I thought Amelia opened it?" my father asked with his features now set in stone and his eyes narrowed suspiciously. Vincent also looked as though he was about to say something, but Lucius got in there first.

"She did, with my help of course, seeing as it was her idea for me to slit a vein," he replied in a calm yet, 'don't fuck with me and what I say' tone.

"You failed to mention that," my dad said with annoyance, making me swallow hard.

"Probably because I didn't see the relevance or importance enough to waste time in going into detail, as I don't now," he stated firmly.

"I see the fucking relevance, Luc."

"Why, did you want to know if she enjoyed the act?" Lucius replied making me snap,

"Lucius!" This was at the same time my father's demon growled in challenge and I swear if this meeting didn't end soon, then I was going to end up screaming the bloody truth! But Lucius looked completely unaffected, and his hard, unyielding gaze only softened when my mum said,

"Luc, that's not helping."

No, it wasn't and neither was making me feel like shit because I shared his blood and was considered a weak link or a risk to it getting in the wrong hands.

But then, the more I thought about it, could I really blame him for thinking this way? I guess looking at it without the emotions of our relationship, then it kind of made sense. Especially seeing as he had found me once before with the box in my hand. And like that night lost in his silent garden, my blood had obviously been used as a key to get it the first time... or should I say, *his blood inside me*.

I swallowed the reasons like I was swallowing something bitter and looked down at the table, noticing the way Theo looked at me as I did this.

"So basically, let's see if I have this right, this witch, someone who should have died thirty years ago, only did so because she needed Draven to send her to Hell so she could become stronger and then wait until the time was right for something we don't know, but get this box for something she thinks will kill all Vampires...do I have that right?" my mum asked making me say,

"Yeah, pretty much."

"We are missing something," Lucius said to himself as if the floor to his side held all the answers he was searching for. Because it was obvious when hearing my mum lay it all out like that it was making him see a bigger picture...or at least know there was one somewhere.

"I agree," my mum said making me frown and it wasn't solely down to the fact that it meant, *I had missed something.*

"And this is when you share with the rest of the class," Sigurd said with a roll of his tattooed hand.

"It doesn't add up, if rogues have already started dying, then why does she still need the box, why the high jacking attempt if Vampires are already falling, because that can't be her only gain in this?" my mum said making a good point.

"Fae thinks that she is trying to get rid of Luc's army, by using one of her own," Theo said after our earlier discussion.

"You do?" Lucius asked, making me sigh and lift my hands up before admitting,

"At this point, I feel like I don't know anything but speculation."

"But you did, only an hour ago in fact?" Lucius asked again making me say,

"It makes more sense...she hates vampires, yet she is using them against you. So, what if the era of Vampires you turned, she has targeted for a reason?"

"Explain," he said sharply.

"Okay, so she makes up this fake leader who is a vampire, doing this so she knows others will follow, as let's face it, there would be little reason they would follow a witch with nothing but a grudge," I said making few nod and Lucius tell me more calmly this time,

"Go on."

"So, like I said, under this fake persona, she recruits as many Vampires that you sired in one era, one that would not be too long ago…"

"Why?" he asked cutting in, so I raised a finger and said,

"Ah, but I'm getting to that." This made his lips twitch in amusement.

"My apologises, please continue, Princess," was his smooth reply, one I tried to get my lady bits to ignore.

"She does this so as to leave it as long as possible before this curse or whatever it is, simply wipes them all out for her, after of course she has got my use out of them."

"And what uses would those be exactly?" Lucius asked motioning with a hand for me to answer and I had to ask myself when this had become a conversation with just the two of us?

"Attack you and your army on the promise of an eternal life not linked to yours and therefore to live without the threat of a master. I mean, it's not like she hasn't used them enough already and besides, like we said, she still wants this box for some reason," I said, this time making a point of looking at the others and not just at Lucius, who had been leading most of these questions.

"Then why wouldn't she just get herself a flight to Cuba, sit her ass on a beach somewhere with a cocktail and sit pretty until this curse wipes them all out…why is she still trying to get the box?" my mum asked making me now ask myself the same thing.

"She still needs to use her power to prevent me from taking control of her rogues and stop me using them for my own gain, for that she needs to be present," Lucius pointed out and I nodded, but again it was like my mum said, she could have simply set the cogs into motion and then disappeared to let the inevitable happen. Because for this curse, she didn't exactly need an army. However, to get the box she did.

"Perhaps," I replied quietly, deep in thought.

"It's a shame we can't just grab one of the rogue fuckers and interrogate them, as I will gladly offer my services," Sigurd said making my dad respond dryly,

"As helpful as that is, Viking, it has already been tried and has already failed...*many times over.*"

"Yeah, and what a fucking mess that was!" Theo said before shooting my mum an apologetic grin for swearing.

"Sounds like fun," Jared said making Sigurd grin.

"They have all been branded with a death hex," Lucius said making both Kings look disgusted before Jared admitted,

"I take that back then."

"Yeah, try getting that shit out of your jeans...not fu...*fun,*" Theo said pausing and turning the 'fucking fun' into just 'fun', making my mum smirk and wink at him, which caused him to roll his eyes.

"So, there you go, reason enough for her to stick around then...right?" Sigurd asked making Vincent reply,

"Her being around for that isn't necessary, as once the hex is cast, it is permanent."

"No top up required," my mum said with a snort and then mumbled a quiet,

"Sorry, bad joke." My dad granted her a soft look before turning his attention back to Lucius,

"In the meantime, what do you need from us?" Lucius went on to talk about the plan to contain the outbreak of vampires that had turned rogue and each of the Kings to put together a kind of taskforce to hunt them down in the different areas they ruled and resided. Each accepted but it was Seth who pointed out,

"And once we have hunted them…what did you want us to do with the infected?"

"Kill them." Lucius said in a firm tone and my mum sucked in a startled breath.

"But can nothing be done? Is there no hope of one day turning them back?" Lucius released a sigh and looked at my mother in a way I couldn't describe, maybe it was sadness or regret…but then it also looked so much more.

"No, Keira, nothing can be done," he admitted in a softer tone.

"Do you still intend to leave after this meeting?" my dad asked but this knowledge shot straight to my heart like a bullet and manifested into me suddenly giving myself away by shouting,

"What?!" Theo shot me a look as if to say, 'smooth' and my Uncle Vincent granted me a look that said it all, that if I carried on with those type of reactions then he wouldn't need to tell my father anything, as I already would have. Although now, he wasn't the only one as everyone was. All except Lucius, who was outright smirking behind a few fingers he had held by his chin as if deep in thought.

"What I mean is…is it really wise you choosing now to leave, after everything we still don't know?" I asked trying to smooth over my mistake.

"He had always planned to leave shortly after bringing you home and once this meeting was concluded, so I see no reason why not," my dad informed me, and unbeknown to him, that knowledge hurt me more than I was allowed to show. So, I looked away from Lucius, too afraid that if I did then the disappointment and devastation would show in my eyes. I also started biting at my fingertips just to stop myself from screaming at him! He had always known he would leave me here and yet he said nothing!

"Amelia," he said my name to gain my attention despite how odd it looked, so before he could do anymore damage, both in keeping our relationship private and also to the pain I felt, I said,

"The only person that may not have a Hex is Layla, as it seems that she is the only one who has been part of the planning of this from the start, so perhaps it would be wise to see if capturing her wouldn't be our next move."

"Oh, now I like this plan!" my mum said enthusiastically clapping her hands.

"What? Everyone does remember how many times this bitch has tried to kill me…right?" my mum added when everyone stopped to look at her. Sigurd chuckled and Jared commented,

"Way I remember it, there were a few, Kitten." My mum growled a little and said,

"Hey, how's that jacket still holding out, Jared, you manage to get out the rubble dust yet?" This must have been a private inside joke as I didn't get it. But whatever it was, it made Jared throw his head back and start laughing anyway, so it looked like the joke was on him.

"You mentioned the vision of her in that room, if it wasn't the witch that helped her escape, then did you see who it was?" my father asked me, as if now giving it some thought. But this time I couldn't help it, my gaze travelled to Lucius to find he was staring at me. He also held his body tense and rigid, with his palms flat to the table to prevent them from turning into fists. His look almost as if daring me to tell the truth.

However, my love for him conquered all else and I found myself saying quickly,

"No…I didn't see who helped her escape."

CHAPTER TWENTY-FIVE

LEAVING AND LIES

"*Amelia...Amelia, wait would you!*" Lucius hissed trying to catch up with me after the meeting and his growls of frustration at not being able to just grab me in front of everyone was obviously pushing at his restraint. The meeting had ended, and I should have felt great about it, especially when my dad came up to me and told me how proud he was of me. But all words had become a blur of noise that I couldn't concentrate making sense of any of them.

I had embraced my Uncle and heard him whisper something in my ear as I did but again, I couldn't focus. I just needed to get out of there! I felt as if I couldn't breathe, like the room was closing in on me and at the centre of that gravity was the cause of it all. Lucius, who had been speaking with my mother at the time the panic hit, felt it and his head snapped toward me. And with a single questioning frown, he knew I was close to losing it.

Gods, but why was this happening now?

In the end it had been Theo who had recognised this and

made a show of asking me if he could speak with me privately about something. It was at that moment when Lucius was being forced to watch me leave that he made his move, determined to speak with me as he tried to reach us. But then Theo walked me out of the door and told me,

"Go...go get some air and let me deal with him." I nodded glancing over his shoulder as I saw Lucius reach the door, telling my brother to get the fuck out of his way. Well, at least he did so quietly enough not to draw attention to what was going on. So, trusting that Theo could keep Lucius busy, at least long enough so I could make it outside,

I ran.

I ran and I ran, and I ran some more. I ran until finally my legs had taken me to a staircase. One I knew would lead up to some rooftop garden that my Aunt Sophia would have had some garden designer make fabulous. I often used to question my aunt's choice at not wanting a seat at the Table of Kings, but now I was starting to understand it. Because she once said to me that,

'Great leaders don't tell you what to do, they show you how it's done' and then she went on to say,

'And I don't need seven kings to show me how to bake a cake'.

Well, just then I didn't need seven Kings telling me how to bake a cake either...no, I just needed the one to stay and eat the one I'd made with me. But Lucius was leaving and with that decision, one made without even telling me, well, I couldn't help but feel utterly betrayed. Just like having him lie to me about not being with my mother, when I knew from my father that he had. Why lie if you had nothing to hide? But despite feeling this way, I still couldn't bring myself to tell everyone that it was Lucius who freed Layla that day.

The moment I made it up to the very last step and burst

through the door, I bent over double and tried to drag in my breaths. Being outside definitely made it easier to breathe, that was for sure. Well, that was until I heard my name being called from back inside the staircase.

So, I slammed the door, making a point and stormed over to the pretty stone seating area that was facing the stunning views of the national park. It also just so happened to put my back to the door that I could hear bursting open as an angry Vampire emerged. I heard him take pause at the sight of me and release a heavy sigh.

I continued to take in deep breaths and tried to focus on the sound of the wind, or that of the small water feature that was trickling softly from one rock to another. I tried to focus on the smell of roses, that climbed up over the arched wall that surrounded the roof on one side. I even took in the vast green beauty before me, before looking up at the clouds and asking myself how long I had before the rain came. But then Lucius stepped up behind me and I could do nothing to block out his touch, to block out his scent or the sound of his voice when he told me softly,

"I was going to tell you."

I closed my eyes at this as a single tear fell and the second they snapped back open, I found my anger. So, I tore myself out of his arms and stood facing him, now wiping away that tear in frustration.

"When? Huh, by fucking text when you landed at wherever the Hell it is you're going?!" I snapped in anger seeing now that Lucius was panting hard himself.

"Of course not."

"Then when?!" He released a sigh and admitted with a rake of his hand going through his hair,

"After the meeting."

"Yet you knew days ago?!" I asked or more like accused.

"Yes," he admitted, making me close my eyes in pain before asking him,

"Then why, Lucius…why does it feel like I was the last one to know?"

"Because you were the hardest one to tell," he replied immediately and as nice as the sentiment was, I couldn't hold back from snapping,

"Not good enough!" He groaned and told me,

"Can we at least talk about this so I can explain without you throwing attitude my way?"

"Oh, I am sorry, is my reaction to you lying to me not convenient for you?" I asked sarcastically.

"I didn't lie," he stated firmly and my eyes widened in disbelief.

"Oh yes you fucking did!" I threw back making him start to get angry.

"Then if that is what you believe lying to be, I suggest you re-educate yourself on the term, for keeping knowledge from a person isn't lying," he told me making me want to slap him. But seeing as that always ended up with us kissing, then I decided to hold my palm in check…for now.

"No, no Lucius, you kept from me about leaving, but you lied about something else," I told him making him frown and start to say,

"And what did I lie about, exactly?" he asked folding his arms across a dark red T shirt that he had turned up to the meeting wearing. And let's just say that jeans and a T-shirt was not exactly his usual attire to wear to a meeting with the Kings. I also bet my life that it was the first time ever. But then he had been a little preoccupied before it, too busy arguing with me and hey look, here we were again, I thought with bitterness!

"You told me you found my mother walking back to their room when you were looking for me." I reminded him.

"And?"

"And that was your lie."

"And you know this how, exactly?" he asked in that arrogant tone of his, one he portrayed so well.

"Because my father told me that the two of you had left together for some reason or another." Lucius heard this and took a deep and calming breath before saying a short,

"I see." I frowned at this and waited to see if he would give me more but he simply took a seat and said nothing, making me snap,

"And?!"

"And what?" At this my mouth actually dropped before I said,

"Do you deny it?!"

"I have no need to deny it, as it happened," he told me making me cry out in frustration before I snapped,

"Goodbye, Lucius, enjoy your flight won't you!" Then I walked past him and stomped all the way to the door, only to find that it was now locked up shut and no matter how hard I tried, I couldn't get it open.

"Open the fucking door!" I demanded making him, stretch an arm out over the back of the stone bench and look back at me over his shoulder.

"Not until you come back here, sit down with me and we discuss this in a calm and rational manner," he ordered in a firm tone that was no longer angry and why should he be, he was the one who got caught out. I didn't move from the door but instead remained staring at it not knowing what to do.

But I jumped when his hand came to the wooden frame next to my head. Then he said at my back,

"Or you could just fight me again and see where that gets you." I closed my eyes against his playful words, ones that I knew he was using to try and entice me into doing as he wanted. So, he tried harder, by getting closer and this time his teasing words were whispered seductively in my ear,

"I might even let you throw me against the door again, if that is what it takes." I released a sigh and told him truthfully,

"You hurt me, Lucius." At this I heard him release a sigh and place his forehead at the back of my head as he whispered,

"I should have told you sooner."

At this I turned around, pushing back at him so as he gave me the room to do so. Thankfully, he got the hint and didn't make it harder for me. Then, when I was facing him, I said,

"The problem with that, Lucius, is it now makes me question what else you, *should have told me sooner?"* After mocking his own words back at him I then watched as an array of emotions played out over his face, one that stood out more than the rest…*it was guilt.*

That was when the true horror of what I witnessed struck me,

"Oh Gods, there's more isn't there?!" I asked now taking a step back and my back hit the door.

"What?"

"There is more you're keeping from me," I argued making him frown before suddenly anger replaced the guilt in his eyes and he tore himself from the door and put his back to me.

"How…how much more?" I asked unable to hold back the tremble in my voice. But he didn't answer me. No, instead he asked me,

"Why did you tell your parents that you never saw me when you fled from Germany?" This was totally out of the blue and instead of answering him I wanted to know what brought this question on. But in the end, that wasn't the question I asked,

"How do you know that I didn't?" He turned around to face me this time. His face was a mask of unreadable emotions.

"Because your father asked me if I had seen you whilst you

were there and if so, did I know of any reason why you would be upset," he told me making me wince.

"I don't know why." I said looking away from him, because I didn't want to admit why.

"That's not an answer and you know it!" he snapped.

"No, then maybe it's the only one you are going to get!" I bit back angrily, because really what the Hell did this question have to do with him lying to me or not telling me that he was leaving? Was this just his way of deflecting? I stormed past him seeing as I couldn't get out the door, determined to at least put space between us. But then he grabbed my arm and spun me to face him,

"Don't toy with me, Pet, just fucking tell me…why didn't you tell them about seeing me?!"

"Because I didn't want you to get into trouble, alright!"

"In trouble…in trouble by who, I am not a fucking child!?" I growled at this and tried to pull out of his hold but he held on tight.

"I didn't want to cause problems for you with my father, okay. He was pissed enough when he found out I'd decided to leave the first time, and I didn't want him blaming you for me leaving a second time." Hearing this his gaze softened slightly and he closed his eyes for a brief moment and asked,

"And tonight?" I knew what he asked but I wanted to hear him say it anyway,

"And what…be specific, as there is a lot I am keeping from my parents," I said making him sigh before saying,

"Yes, and done so through your own choice… now answer me…why did you lie when you know that it was me who freed Layla?" Ah, so there it was, he finally said it. So, I told him the truth,

"Because no matter how pissed off I am with you for lying to me, I still love y…" I never got chance to finish as he suddenly crushed his lips to mine and consumed all my anger in a kiss. Taking it away until it evaporated into nothing but his touch. His hands gripping onto my sweater, his tongue dueling with mine, his lips soft yet demanding…it was no wonder I was left with nothing more to do but cling to him as if any moment I would fall.

But then strangely it hit me what this was…

It was goodbye.

I knew it the moment it finished, and he placed his forehead to mine before telling me,

"I needed to hear you say that, just as I needed that kiss before…"

"Before you go and leave!" I accused, pulling myself from his grasp and this time, he let me.

"Yes, before I leave you," he said in a pained tone and his words cut me deep. So, I turned away from him and tried to swallow back my tears.

"Amelia, please try and understand, being here is the best place for you, you will be safe," he said trying to get me to understand.

"You knew even before we left Germany that you were going to just drop me off and leave…*didn't you?*" I guessed and his deep sigh told me that I was right.

"Sweetheart, please…" I felt his hands come to embrace me from behind, but I shrugged out of his hold and repeated again,

"Didn't you? Say the words, Lucius!"

"Does it even matter, for the outcome is still the same." I guess what he said was true but to me, yes it still mattered. But I didn't tell him this. No, instead I asked him,

"Lucius, can you do something for me now."

"That depends," he responded in a wary tone.

"Unlock the door."

"What, so you can just run away again before we have

sorted this out?" The pain in that statement was easy to detect. He didn't want to leave things this way before he left.

"You're the one who said what does it matter, as the outcome will still be the same. Besides, you had your 'I love you' and your 'last kiss' so consider it a win on your account and by unlocking that door I will consider it a win on mine," I told him making him growl behind me before I was quickly spun around to face him and he was once again demanding more,

"Stubborn girl!" he snapped before he was crushing his lips to mine again, this time pushing me back against the door, and pinning me there whilst he ravaged my mouth. Then I heard the door unlock and he tore himself off me so quickly it made my head spin.

Then he snarled one word,

"Go!"

I had to say, it wasn't the goodbye I was hoping for after that kiss but then, what else could I expect, seeing as it had been what I had asked for. But still, I felt the guilt in my gut at just leaving.

"Lucius, I…"

"I said GO!" he roared suddenly, and it was so shocking that I stumbled back, until I found myself grabbing hold of the handle and pulling it down. Then, just as I slipped through the open door, I told him,

"I guess me telling you that I loved you wasn't enough." Then I shut the door to the sound of my name being whispered from his lips, missing the part when he said…

"No, it's the reason I leave."

CHAPTER TWENTY-SIX

BLOODY TRUST

After running from the rooftop, I did what any normal heartbroken girl would do, I ran to my bedroom, threw myself on the bed and spent a good portion of the day feeling sorry for myself. I also spent this time arguing with myself on ifs, buts and whys.

Because, despite how upset I was that he hadn't told me he was leaving, I knew that I was more upset with the fact that he was and less concerned with the telling me part.

Simply put, I just didn't want Lucius to go. But then I also knew that by acting this way I wasn't being fair on him either. I couldn't guilt him into staying and to be honest, he deserved better than having me even try to. Because he was a King and I knew that the only two reasons he left now was to ensure my safety and to also be responsible for his people.

Meaning he had to do something to try and stop this curse from spreading as the lives of his people depended on him. Which also meant that every moment he spent here with me, lying in my bed with me curled up next to him in a naive and blissful state, he had been doing so with a heavy weight on his mind. For what was to become of his people?

I knew in that moment that my actions today weren't those of a queen. But those of a selfish person in love. Which meant that three hours later when I finally realised that I had been in the wrong and if I let Lucius just leave now, thinking of me as selfish, then I knew I wouldn't forgive myself. I would stew on it for I don't know how long, convincing myself that he may not even want to come back to me. Gods, but I had just walked away and left without even knowing when I would see him next or if he would even be able to call me.

No, I wasn't going to let that happen! I was going to find him and tell him that I was sorry. Then we were going to talk things out calmly like he had wanted to in the first place, before I had pushed him into his anger.

So, with this firmly in my mind, I got up and decided to go and look for him. I had no idea where he would be but thought the best place to start would be the library. It made some sense, seeing as it was possible that should he want to find me too, then he knew that it was a good bet I'd be there. Although, saying this, when I was halfway there I also asked myself, if he wanted to see me, then wouldn't he have just tried my room first?

These uncertain questions continued all the way until I was pushing open the massive set of doors that led into my favourite place. One I was thankful was empty as I didn't exactly feel like making small talk, whilst inside I was a bag of nerves. What if I was too late? What if he had left already? I continuously plagued myself with these questions until I growled in annoyance making my own frustration echo around the room.

I paced the floor wearing new tread marks in the thread of the Persian rugs of rich reds, creams and blues which I used to sit on as a child and trace the patterns with my little fingers whilst reading my stories. Fairy tales of Princes saving their Princesses before declarations of love were made. But those stories never contained the raw truth about what that love would make you do. How it would make you shout, scream, twist the truth and believe the lies. It didn't speak about the pain or innocence or naivety. It didn't mention how dangerous giving your heart to someone could be, when trusting another to keep it safe and not break it.

No, real love wasn't flowers, sing song sentiments and sunset walks. It was red raw, tears flowing, heart achingly brutal. It burned. It terrified. It hurt beyond all else. And then, when finally it was yours, it twisted all of these things into something so profound, so real, that you asked yourself how you ever survived without it.

That was what true love was.

It was the reason I looked up to the one place I had been avoiding looking at since I first walked inside. Quickly discovering that Lucius had been right. Every time I looked up there all I saw was that night. All I saw were my hands tied above my head with his tie, as he made me cry out his name in more pleasure than I even believed my body capable of accepting without first being ripped apart.

And it was that true love that made me lash out, swiping all the books on the table closest to me onto the floor, before I collapsed back into a seat and cried. Because something was telling me in the back of my mind what I didn't want to fully accept,

I had already lost him.

I don't know at what point I had fallen asleep but the second I felt a hand cupping my cheek, I opened my eyes.

"Lucius?" My groggy voice said his name the moment I saw him down on one knee next to my chair.

"It's me," he said, his voice smooth and void of any anger or frustration it had held earlier. So, I suddenly threw myself into his arms, clinging on to him as I buried my head in his neck where I told him,

"I thought you had left without saying goodbye. I thought…"

"Ssshh now, I am here, and that is all that matters," he told me, hushing my emotional outburst whilst holding the back of my head to him and smoothing back my hair.

"You're not leaving?" I asked in a hopeful tone and he shook his head, telling me that he wasn't. But then that guilt started to niggle in the back of my mind where I knew I couldn't be selfish. Lucius needed to be with his people, he needed to do what he could to help them and by being here with me now, then I knew that wasn't happening.

It wasn't being the King I knew he wanted to be.

The King I knew he was.

"Lucius, I am sorry. I should never have…"

"Amelia, I have something to show you," he said making me take pause and before I could ask, he grasped my hand in his and stood, before pulling me up with him.

"What is it?"

"Come, I must show you," he told me and started to lead me over to the fireplace making me frown at it in question.

"What are you…?"

"Has your father ever taken you into the Janus Temple before?" His question cut me off and I sucked in a startled breath at the mention of it.

"No, and I hear that the only way inside is through one of the gates and my father's personal entrance is on one of his

English estates at Witley Court," I said making Lucius grin at me.

"Then he lied for that isn't the only entrance." Lucius then looked back at the fireplace and I followed his gaze as he ran a hand over the front of it, extinguishing the flames instantly and making something click into place. Then a large section at the back of the fire opened, which was when I realised it was in fact a door.

"What, here?!" I squealed in shock making Lucius look to the door of the library and narrow his eyes before telling me,

"Ssshh." I looked back also, wondering who it could be that was about to enter.

"Do you wish to see it?" he asked in that seductive tone that lured me in. So, I nodded enthusiastically, as it was always something I had dreamed of seeing one day.

"Then quickly, follow me before we are caught," he said opening it fully and stepping inside the darkness beyond. But I laughed and said,

"I didn't think you ever cared about being caught?"

"Give me your hand, Amelia," he ordered without responding to the comment and I looked back one last time at the library door. Because something felt off with Lucius. He was never normally worried about anyone, let alone someone catching us in the library together.

"Last chance, are you with me or not?" he asked this time in a slightly stern tone. So, knowing that this was a once in a lifetime chance, I nodded. As what harm could it do when Lucius was with me? I swallowed down my worry and placed my hand in his, letting him pull me inside.

"Gods, it's...it's incredible," I said in utter awe moments later after the door was closed behind us, giving way to the colossal space beyond. The temple wasn't like any temple you would have encountered. It was more like a series of vast and huge hallways that were tall and wide enough that thirty-foot giants could have roamed with ease. In fact, the ceilings were so tall you couldn't actually make out the details.

I looked down one way and couldn't actually see an end. Then I looked the other and could see a larger space that could have acted as a lobby, as I could see even more of the same hallways branching off from it.

But it was the walls that fascinated me the most, for they were covered in nothing but doors. Doors of every type imaginable and ones that barely even resembled the word. Wood of every type and carved in every way. Whether smooth, highly polished or battered and worn. Then there were ones made of glass, etched, frosted and even cracked to almost completely shattered. Gods, but there was even one that looked like a whole tree trunk had been used with a door carved inside it.

There were more modern materials used too, like plastic moulded and cast into shape as well as one that looked like melted wax. And metal was a theme throughout also, whether it be hammered and crude shapes or forged gleaming steel. There were hundreds of them, all around us on this level and ones above where, like in the library I had just come from, walkways offered access to each one.

I couldn't help but turn around and look at what my father's door had been and smiled when I saw that it was a bookshelf.

"Cute," I muttered making Lucius look back at me for a second as if he too was preoccupied and had just remembered that I hadn't been here. But then he closed the door, and the sound of it closing echoed in such a way, it almost rippled like skimming stones on water.

"So, this was where the battle of the Blood War started?" I asked after Lucius told me to follow him. He looked down the hallway to the larger space and nodded towards it.

"Most of it happened there."

"And we aren't going that way?" I asked as it was obvious that I was eager to.

"Not yet, but maybe after I have what I need," he said making me ask,

"What is it you want here anyway?"

"Do you always ask this many questions?" he asked back over his shoulder at me, finding me still taking in the space with awe on my face. I chuckled once, another sound that danced along the walls,

"You know I do." He scoffed once and said,

"That you do, Princess."

I continued to follow him, taking note of the doors we passed and the keystones above each one.

"The symbols, are they names of the realms the gateways take you to?" I asked nodding to the etched stone above almost all the doors.

"They are," he replied and it was clear by his short answers that he was most definitely preoccupied. So, I caught up with him and after hearing the echoing of our steps, it made me wonder about the battle they had fought in. How it would have been at the time, with these halls being flooded with demonic creatures brought forth by Cronus himself. The harrowing echo of the hooves from the four horsemen as they approached the battle. It must have been terrifying.

"What was it like?"

"What was what like?" he asked looking down at me over the side of his shoulder.

"The battle?" I nodded to the large space that we seemed to be walking further away from.

"I will show you after if you like."

"Why, we going to re-enact it or something, 'cause you

should have brought your sword in that case?" I asked on a chuckle.

"I think I would need a lot more than a sword for that, but you're right, battling with you would be fun," he said winking and before I could ask what he meant by that, he stopped at a door.

"Where does this one lead?" I asked, being faced with a huge stone door, one that held a hole in the middle edged with a ring of symbols. The rest of the door showed one big picture of my family crest, telling me this was another door that belonged to my father. It had no handle and looked to have no way of opening the door either.

"It is your father's vault." I shot him a look of confusion, wondering why he'd brought me to this door...especially after what he had said in the meeting.

"But why?" Lucius released a sigh of frustration but, unlike he usually did, he didn't run a hand through his hair this time. No, this time he said the very last words I wanted to hear,

"Your father knows." I sucked in a jolt of shock, which turned into covering my mouth and muttering a muffled cry of dismay,

"No."

"But how?" I then asked after Lucius nodded.

"We don't have much time, but from what I can gather, he was told."

"Vincent." I uttered my uncle's name making Lucius nod looking dire.

"Yes, that was my guess as well," he told me and he looked...*upset?*

"But why do you look so worried, you were the one who wanted him to know and now you have your wish?" Lucius looked uncomfortable for a moment before admitting,

"I am worried for you, your father...I didn't expect him to

react the way he has. He is threatening to have you sent away, Amelia." Hearing this and I automatically thought back to my days in that castle knowing these were the natural reactions of my paranoid father. So this was why Lucius had been acting weird and distant since coming in here.

"But he can't do that!" I argued.

"No, he can't, which is why we are going to take the box and leave."

"We are?" I asked sounding hopeful.

"Yes," he stated firmly before continuing on to say,

"But we don't have much time as he will know something is wrong when he can't find either of us. And bringing you in here is the quickest way for us to leave together. He has forbidden us from seeing each other and I can't allow that…I can't chance anyone taking you from me…which is why we need to hurry!" he told me nodding to the door and making me do the same.

"I can't believe this," I said making Lucius grip my arm in annoyance and snap,

"What part don't you believe as I saw his rage with my own eyes!" I could see that he was upset as I knew it would be bad, but I didn't think either of us expected this…banished from seeing each other…I mean that was outrageous! He seemed to get a handle on himself after looking at his own hand around my arm and he forced himself to relax.

"Amelia, please…time is not on our side here," he said looking back the way we had come as if expecting to see an army he would need to fight. So, I took a deep breath and told him,

"Alright, what do we need to do."

"I just need you to bleed," he said making me frown in question. Then, before I could say more, he grabbed my hand and placed it in the hole, gripping my wrist and holding me there until I felt something clamping my fingers.

"Hey!" I yelled at the shock of suddenly being forced but he just looked down at me with pleading eyes asking me to trust him. So, I nodded and allowed whatever was supposed to happen…well, *happen.*

"I thought my blood wouldn't be able to open it?"

"There is still the blood of a Draven in you…it just might need a little more than usual," he said just before it happened. Meaning I was soon crying out in pain. Lucius looked as if he was struggling with making me do this, at least that was what I got from the hard lines in his face and the tense look in his jaw.

"Ahhh! Lucius, it hurts!" I shouted as I felt the razor points piercing into my flesh in what felt was over and over again.

"I know it does, Honey…just a little longer," he told me making me frown and the second I could bear it no longer I tried to pull my hand out, but when his hand clamped tighter, my reactions kicked in.

"No, that's enough!" I shouted as I threw my weight into his side to knock him out of the way and therefore making his hand slip from my wrist. I then yanked out my bleeding hand and cradled it to me, making sure to try and not get blood on my sweater.

"What the Hell?!" I shouted but Lucius just looked to the door as it started to open, the image of our family crest now sinking into the door, making it flush with the stone behind, before it split down the centre and suddenly opened.

"I'm sorry, we have no choice, come on," he told me now pulling me inside and I followed him. But then once inside it wasn't as I thought it would be. Another long stone hallway faced us as if we had just walked into the entrance to another temple or something.

"This doesn't look like a vault," I commented as I faced a long line of stone columns, each with concaved lines and topped with curled ram's horns. They ran the full length of the wide hall on my left-hand side and a jagged stone wall was on the other. Down the centre were large stone slabs placed down in a random way that looked as if they had been laid an age ago. At the very end was a large, open doorway with smaller pillars either side and a large stone tablet above that showed some kind of carved story, one I was too far away to make out.

"This is only the entrance…come," he told me from ahead where he had started to walk without me, meaning I had no choice but to catch up. Now running alongside the pillars and seeing the pool of clear water beyond it. It was as though it had come up through the rocks as it seemed naturally formed and had I not been rushing, I would have walked over to it and run my injured hand through the water to rinse off the blood. But Lucius was near the end by the opening and the second I saw a light glowing from beyond it, I had to shield my eyes.

"Lucius?" I asked as I could barely see him and I shrieked as I felt my hand being grasped by a glove of leather and pulled through the doorway. It was then that the light dimmed, and I could see that we were faced with a cavernous space the second Lucius clicked his fingers and one by one flaming torches ignited.

"Oh…my…Gods," I said in disbelief as this was obviously where my dad's vault was, as the treasures it held were beyond measure. It was like an Aladdin's cave of wonder. Artefacts and relics were hung, held or mounted along with artwork of every kind and era.

It wasn't pots, overflowing bags or pyramids of gold and jewels but organised chaos of history. Great statues dotted the inside of what looked like a mountain, along with seating areas surrounded by shelving filled with the rarest of books and other treasures. Closest to us was even an old statue of my father that must have been from when he had been King of Persia. I wanted to examine it, to try and date it when something else caught my eye.

Because there seemed to be a section dedicated to my mother, where her paintings and pictures of her were displayed as you would a gallery. Only these were hung on freestanding stone walls you could walk around. A maze of them in fact, with shelving too that housed what looked like pieces of her life, or the life they shared together. Even clothing, a lot of which seemed to be dresses and most of them torn in some way. There was even a punk style tie that had even been given its own glass box and held around a jewellery style, velvet holder as if it was the crown of the kingdom.

One hand flew to my mouth as I sucked in a shuddered breath when I realised what this was...my father's private obsession with my mother.

"Gods, Lucius," I uttered, but when I received no reply I looked around and saw him walking towards a glass case the box was sat in.

"Amelia," he called me over and I knew then his own obsession was getting that box and getting the hell out of here. So, I walked over to him, still cradling my hand as my blood continued to drip along the floor.

"Can't we take a minute for you to heal me...kind of hurting here?" I said making him glance down at me. Then I felt a hand cupping my cheek before he told me,

"Just try and be brave for me a little longer...yeah?" I nodded, taking a deep breath and said,

"Alright." But then I noticed the box didn't have a lock so I wondered why he wouldn't just take the time to heal me, as it wasn't as if he needed my blood anymore. I looked down at my hand as a memory started to seep into the moment.

It was something Lucius had said to me once in his office,

'There is no reason in this world to ever take a fucking

blade to this skin,' he had said, being so angry at me for cutting myself and opening that box. But then why wasn't he now?

So, I asked him,

"It's a bit like that time in your office isn't it, you were so proud of me when I opened that box." At this he grinned down at me and, running the back of his fingers down my cheek, he told me,

"Yes, Honey… it's just like that." I swallowed hard and told him in a cold and emotionless voice,

"You never said that, and you never call me Honey."

At this I pulled back in horror as I realised that none of this was real. Then, as if some spell had just been broken, I looked to the case the box was in and what I saw sickened me.

It wasn't Lucius in its reflection at all.

But the blood cloaked figure of a scarred and twisted,

"Witch."

CHAPTER TWENTY-FIVE

CRIMSON WALLS

"NO!" I screamed the second I saw the witch in the reflection of the glass and when I did, she reacted before I could. And she did this by grabbing my head and slamming it into the glass case, smashing it around me. I felt the pain explode at the side of my head, along with the glass that shattered around me. The impact felt as if it had rattled my skull before I dropped to my knees and fell forward, hunched over in pain before I collapsed fully to the floor.

"You should have continued to play along, Princess, it was more fun that way…although, I admit, this is fun too," the witch snarled down at me as my world started to blur. In fact, I knew I was only seconds away from passing out and the second I tried to shake it off the pain simply intensified.

"Now it's time to get what I came for," she said and I heard more glass break and fall, dancing on the stone floor and telling me that she was removing the box.

"No…no, you…you…" I couldn't end it as it all hurt too much. But then, the realization of what she was doing next took

hold as I felt my bloody hand being taken and placed on top of the box.

"Ah, Blood of Kings…I am so glad he feeds you as he fucks you," she told me on a venomous hiss before she dropped my hand to the floor with a slap. I lifted my head up trying to ignore the pain of doing so, only to see her walking away, her crimson cloak flapping wildly around her as if it were alive under an ocean of power I couldn't see.

"Until next time…*Princess,*" she said with a cackle of laughter I sneered at. I was in so much pain that all I wanted to do in that moment was pass out and hope that someone eventually found me. But then I knew what would happen should she be allowed to walk away with that box. So, despite how my body wanted to give up, my mind fought it. Because everything in me was screaming for me to move, to get up and fight! My father's words coming back to me,

'A Draven never stays down.'

"Too fucking right they don't…so get your ass up, Fae," I said to myself pushing my hands under me and forcing myself to get up. I fell sideways the second I made it to my feet and put my hand out to stop myself. This landed on a statue of my father as a symbol of strength that felt in that moment like a sign from the Gods. A Persian King who, unknowingly, would be one day holding up his daughter so she could fight the enemy.

"Time to make you proud, daddy." I said before taking a deep breath so I could find it in me to take off running.

And I did.

I ran with everything I had. With every last ounce of adrenaline, I could now feel pounding like a war drum in my veins. I let my anger flow through me like a wave crashing against the rocks, untamed and without restraint. Meaning that I burst through the glow of light like some avenging Angel without wings!

Then I saw her still walking down the hallway just as she was opening the box and lifting the lid. Which was when I couldn't help but call out,

"Hey, bitch...we aren't done here!" Then I took off running once more to the sight of her utter shock at seeing me on my feet, let alone running towards her as if I wasn't the size I was, but like I was a fucking bull from Hell.

Then I said to her,

"You want blood, then here, fucking have it!" I shouted just before I swung a fist and hit her dead on her face, her nose bursting and splitting at the break upon impact. Then, before she could start to defend herself with any of her magic, I tackled her to the ground. The box flew from her hands with the top opening and the map rolling along the floor.

"I will kill you!" she bellowed up at me the second I managed to get on top of her, her bloody, scarred face not covered enough for me as suddenly all I could think about was blood. It was as if I was being taken over and if it had to be given a name then it was simple...

Bloodlust.

I suddenly wanted the bitch to drown in it! I wanted to hold her head under and watch as she had no choice but to breathe it in and choke on it!

"Not if I fucking kill you first!" I snarled down at her, pounding my fist into her face again. She turned her head to the side and spat the blood from her mouth before she started to chant, and that was when I heard the rock wall start cracking. The floors too and then over head as she was willing to destroy the room just to bury us both under its destruction.

Gods, but I was so angry! I had never felt this kind of rage before. Not even when fighting all I had in the past few weeks. Not even when I had hit Layla. No, this was something utterly different and in fact, it felt more like it was being fueled by Hell itself! I even tore my eyes away from her, looking up to the ceiling as if needing to find clarity as if I was being overwhelmed by such raw emotion I couldn't cope! Rivers and rivers of blood were pounding through me, consuming my every thought.

Choke

Drown

Die

"No! It's...It's impossible!" she snarled looking up at me in grave astonishment. But wait...no, she wasn't looking at me... she was looking past me. And the second I looked back over my shoulder I started to see what she saw. A red glow started to come from beyond the columns, filling the room crimson. The rumbling of the walls suddenly stopped and the dust from the cracks stopped raining down all around us as she paused her power.

"You are...no, you're human...you...!" she stopped the second we both heard the sound of an ocean of rushing water and I looked back over my shoulder to see a huge wall of blood now rising up from the pool of water behind the columns. It rose higher and higher and my mouth dropped the second I realised it had been in my vision. But then, as I closed my eyes and muttered a breathy,

"Fuck," it suddenly came crashing down, through the stone supports. Then suddenly the witch's fist connected with my face and I was knocked off her. She scrambled up the second I too scrambled for the box. She missed this by an inch but instead grabbed the map. Then we both started running with a river of blood chasing us. I looked behind me to see it was getting closer, now crashing up the walls in a wave that folded back on itself. I turned my head back to the exit ahead and forced myself

to go faster, just as the witch did the same. Only she had an exit plan that didn't include any door. As seconds later she threw up a hand making a portal suddenly appear on the wall in front of her.

"You might not be human, but you will still drown in your own blood!" she said before slipping through the gateway she'd made, making off with the map. I looked back to see she was right, if I didn't get out of there and quickly, then I was going to drown in blood and from the sounds of it, a river of crimson she thought I had created!

So, with this threat holding my life in the balance, I did the only thing I could do…*I ran faster than I ever had before.* I felt it getting closer, the walls now soaked crimson and pretty soon, a body would be added to that. But then I finally made it to the doors and pushed through just in time before turning quickly and slamming them shut on the river of blood. A crimson spray burst through the sides in squirts at the cracks before it eased into long bloody drips down the pale stone door. I scrambled backwards, not taking my eyes off it after falling on my ass back in the Temple of Janus.

I could barely believe that I not only managed to escape, but also doing so with the box still in my grasp. Alright, so the map was gone but I knew something she didn't…*it was useless.* It told us nothing. Still, I needed to get back to Afterlife and let the others know what had just happened. Now, how I was going to do that without letting everyone know about me and Lucius, I didn't yet know.

But at least I still had the box, I thought looking down at it in my still bloody hand. But then, as it started to shake just as it had that day, I had to ask myself what had been the point of the box at all, if the only thing it held was a map to nowhere?

This question still lingered, along with what the witch could have even wanted with it in the first place? It was the question everyone around the table wanted to know. The curse was already happening, and nobody could do anything...

"Wait a second," I muttered as I lifted the box in my still bloody hand, feeling the vibrations getting more powerful at the continued connection. But then, as I put it in my other hand to calm it down, I reached across the open section to close the lid. This was when some of my blood dripped inside and that was when the sides of the box started to split before slamming closed again.

"What the Hell?!" I shouted as I dropped the box. Now, I was asking myself if I had just seen what I had? I then lowered to my knees before it and look down at my injured hand. Then I said,

"Here goes nothing." I held it over the inside of the box, at the same time making a fist, squeezing as hard as I could and wincing at the pain from the pressure I was putting against all my cuts. I even cried out, my agony echoing in the temple as I dug my nails in, pressing them into the open flesh. Then I watched as it started to work, and a stream of my blood started to drip down and fill the centre of the box. Then, it suddenly clattered on the floor, bouncing as if coming alive before it started to unravel before my very eyes.

"Holy shit," I muttered as it moved in such a way that it started to unfold like a flower blooming before it was soon flat and...

"Map sized," I said, now using my not so bloody hand to pull the copy of the map from my back pocket. The one I had taken from the meeting and folded up at the end to slip back there.

"I really hope that you don't need the original," I said down at it before placing the map flat against the box. Then I held my breath and waited, staring down at it now and praying for something more. It didn't disappoint. As soon the lines and grooves I had been able to explain inside the box all now started to fill with my blood and the second I saw it start to seep through the paper, I gasped.

It was showing me a road and not only that...*but a name.*

"I can't believe it," I uttered, knowing that it was a place I had seen before, all the small details now coming through. Well, I had seen it in a painting once before. A painting that hung over a fireplace.

The question of where had been seconds from my lips before my father's phone call. A picture of a mountain range in Lucius' office.

And now I had a name start to appear in my blood,

"Queriot, Mount Hebron."

CHAPTER TWENTY-EIGHT

LUCIUS

OLD MISTAKES

I don't know how long it was that I sat on this Gods forsaken rooftop. But in that time, it had rained, stopped and rained again with more promised, if the ominous clouds darkening the skies in the distance were any indication. And yet I hadn't felt compelled to move. Of course, I had wanted to find her, force her to listen to my words and try and understand the root of them…but then, that was half my problem…

The roots of them were poison.

"I know you're there, Keira girl, you're not exactly stealthy… *even as a Vampire.*" I muttered this last part under my breath, even if I knew it was pointless doing so, as she heard it all the same.

"One third vampire, actually," she corrected on a chuckle, making me want to respond with how I hoped that would be enough to save her. However, I refrained, as what was the point, she already worried enough about the future of our people, her daughter above all.

"You know you're not exactly helping yourself by punching Theo in the face in front of a room full of Kings...*his mother and father included,*" she commented dryly before coming to sit next to me and say,

"Hell, I should punch you in the face for that one." I released a pained breath and told her,

"The way I am feeling, I might just let you."

"Umm, that bad, huh?" A look was all she needed before I told her,

"I am sure your son is fine."

"Oh, I know he is, but I already have one family member on my hands to try and stop from killing you, I don't need two, Lucius...*or three.*" Of course, the first two would be Vincent and Theo, her son, who I suspected had known for some time. The third she referred to was Dom. I sighed in frustration before telling her,

"Would it make me a bad friend right now if I said I don't give a fuck."

"Erm, yeah, pretty much."

"Then I will just lie instead and say I am sorry," I told her as I continued to stare out into the vast green space that was starting to blur, I had been doing it for that long.

"Well, if I didn't already know that the reason for your pissed off mood was because of my daughter, then I would have told you to get over it."

"Of that I have no doubt," I responded dryly almost at that point of asking her to leave so I could wallow a little longer on my own. Her presence was only a reminder of why I wasn't free to do as I pleased in the first place.

"I hate to say I told you so here, but…" I growled stopping her and snapped,

"Then I would exercise that hate and please spare me, Keira, I am not in the fucking mood!"

"Yes, well, whether you are or not, her finding out you're leaving that way was bound to hurt her," she said making me rise to my feet in frustration and wishing in that moment I could just command her to stop fucking speaking and leave already!

"You think I don't fucking know that!" I retorted before deciding that I couldn't wait any longer, *I had to see her.* I had to make this right. To let her know that her own mother knew about us and I had been keeping it from her. I knew it would hurt her but having Amelia thinking something was going on between us was far fucking worse! My actions made Keira release a deep breath before slapping her hands to her knees and asking in exasperation,

"Luc, where are you going?"

"To find her and tell her the truth…to tell everyone the fucking truth, like I should have done years ago!" I snapped making her start to follow me.

"You really think that is wise?" she asked, knowing what this would really mean for her family.

"You really think continuing to lie to her is?!" I snapped back. Then I walked through the door I had locked and tried to prevent Amelia from leaving through.

"Lucius, wait!" Keira shouted but I wouldn't. I was sick of this fucking charade, playing happy families when it was built on mistrust and lies. Dom needed to know that his daughter was mine! All the fucking Kings needed to know!

Gods, but I had wanted to rip that fucking Hellbeast to pieces for his comment on her beauty! I didn't care how innocent a comment it seemed to everyone else at the time, it didn't matter to my demon who was trying to tear up my insides just to get at him quicker.

In fact, it was all my demon ever wanted to do these days. It was yet another reason I was leaving when I intended to, knowing it had been for the best. Because I was so close to erupting with the truth, I knew the damage that would cause.

I was trying to spare her the pain.

But now, what was the point of that when she was already in pain? Gods, but seeing those tears she tried to hold back, it was a bittersweet trophy I felt cheated into winning. I loved her tears as much as I hated them!

"Lucius, please just think about this!" Keira's voice caught up to me and her own panic was easy to detect. Once upon a time I think I would have done anything for her. But those days were long gone, as I snarled back at her,

"I have thought of nothing else!" I continued down the hallway, no longer giving a shit about who heard our conversation. Not as I had been only earlier this morning when speaking with Keira in secret. Speaking with her when I should have been in bed with my girl, still seated and buried balls deep inside her warmth.

No, instead, I left when hearing Keira in my head asking me to meet with her. That was when she started pleading with me not to tell Dom, as I had threatened to do only the night before. She wanted to be the one to ease the knowledge of our relationship to him, when I knew it would be pointless. His reaction would be the same regardless.

I had just been about to tell her this at the time, when Clay had contacted me. I hadn't lied when telling Amelia about the decision I had no choice to make and knowing that my time here was coming to an end after making it.

So, with this in mind, I had agreed, telling Keira that she had until I returned to claim my girl to tell Dom, or I would be doing it the very second I stepped foot back inside the building. When she had thanked me, I told her for the first time,

"I am not doing it for you, Keira." Her face said it all, for she knew that and yet she was still grateful. But that had been before the argument. It had also been before Amelia had woken up inside a fucking prison being burned by the power of a fucking witch I was looking forward to murdering with my bare hands!

I had heard her calling my name, felt her fear and took off running the second I did. I had torn through the halls of Afterlife, near mindless in my panic. Many of which experienced this when I would just stop and roar,

"FUCK!" in the middle of yet another room she wasn't in. I tried to concentrate on her scent, one I had no choice but to mask since first stepping foot out of the car that brought us here. Doing so foolishly, so no-one knew that she belonged to me. The pain for doing so now sending me into a rage, for it had been masked for so long, it was even taking *me* longer to find it!

That had been until I caught it heading down into the lower levels, when my fear of her being hurt tripled! I had found the quickest way down and instead of wasting time with the twisted staircase, I simply vaulted over the top banister. I had then dropped down the centre as I had done back in Transfusion when I found out she had been taken. It was like fucking history repeating itself all over again!

Once on the ground, I had followed her scent all the way inside the prison, realising now that she had made this journey asleep as there were no traces of real time when tracing her. *Meaning she was being controlled once more.*

Forced to sleepwalk.

Well, the knowledge enraged me as, had I not been the one to leave her bed, then it would have never happened. Something she had pointed out bitterly when I confronted her in her room after the fact.

I continued to trace her movements and I knew, when faced with an old cell, that was when her scent came alive. She had woken up and fear coated her essence like a veil of blood. It was why I had been so furious when finally following it back up to her home. I had found Keira on the way, who told me she had seen Theo and Amelia making their way to her and Dom's room.

By which point I had been ready to walk into there and tell him everything, but one look at Amelia and I swallowed the urge down like bitter pills I nearly fucking choked on.

Because she hadn't needed that stress right after it had happened.

She had experienced enough through my mistakes.

Mistakes I just seemed to keep making.

"You love her," Keira stated and I snapped, before going into the library I knew she was most likely to go at some point,

"Of course I do, she's my Chosen One!"

"She's also my daughter, Luc." Keira replied with love shining in her eyes, telling me the tears would soon come. Tears right then I cared little for.

"I know that, you don't think I fucking know that, after everything we have been through. Gods, Keira…I have held her at arm's length for far too fucking long and for what, so she could potentially get harmed because I am not free to fucking claim what is rightfully mine in this house!"

"I know that…look, not out here, okay… let's go inside where it is more private," Keira said after looking around to check that we hadn't been overheard. So, we both walked inside, or more like she walked, and I stormed inside, near feeling the floor cracking I was that furious. I could focus on little else in that moment, so I told her,

"I just can't do this anymore, keeping up this fucking pretence!"

"I know, but just for a little longer, alright?" Keira replied, one said in a calming voice that was trying to get me to do the same thing. But this felt impossible when her words were the very thing causing my rage.

"Why, why do we have to fucking wait?! Don't you think I have waited long enough?!" I snapped knowing that I had.

"I have done everything you asked, Keira, I have waited…"

"Yes, beyond the time I said was right, Luc, don't forget that, as it's not like you didn't have your chances back then!" Keira snapped back referring to when Amelia had come to Germany and I had fucked up the first time. But she didn't know what I knew. About discovering what I had taken from Amelia back before anyone could comprehend such a time.

"Yes, well the limits to my patience should be understandable then, shouldn't they?" I said making her release a deep and heavy sigh before reminding me of the only reason I had waited.

"And what about Amelia, huh, you need to think of her, to say anything now would only hurt her." I cut her off with a growl before telling her in a hard voice,

"She too needs her own family to know the truth before she can then move on from the pain."

"But now, really?" she challenged as it was true, the timing wasn't ideal. But when was it ever? Which was why I snapped back,

"Yes, now!"

"And Draven, what do you think will happen…? Don't you realise how many will get hurt if you tell people now, if you tell people what we have hidden from them for so many years?" Oh, I knew alright. I knew and the worst of it wasn't what Dom would try and do to me, it was what Keira could do to her daughter. For I didn't know what would become of their relationship after, hence Keira's guilt trip. Not that I blamed her, as I understood that she didn't want to lose her daughter in the process but really, what did she think would happen?

This had all been inevitable.

Which was why I reminded her,

"Out of my respect and care for you, I have kept quiet, Keira."

"I know, Luc…I know," Keira said coming up to me and putting a hand on my own, one concealed under leather. It was also one that only Amelia had seen the true horror of. I closed my eyes and covered her hand in my own and told her in a calmer tone this time,

"Amelia needs to know, and I can't keep pretending anymore, especially here, *it's fucking killing me, Keira"* This was said as I lowered my head and I felt her palm on my cheek offering me the comfort she knew my ravaged soul needed. She was a good friend, but my loyalty was to my heart and the one who held it wrapped in their soul.

It was to Amelia.

"We can't do it, not yet, we can't tell Draven," she told me and her comfort shattered as I pulled myself from her grasp and told her,

"Well, you may not, but I can!"

"I still don't think this is the right time," she argued further so I told her,

"Keira, you know my feelings towards you, you have known for a long time. How much I respected you for your own decisions, but you also have known my own and the reasons behind them. Now I have waited, a very long time…"

"I know but…" I cut her off,

"…and I have done so patiently upon your request out of respect for your husband. I have done everything you asked, I have protected Amelia in every way I could, as you begged me to do. But now it is my turn to act, for I will not hold back my feelings any longer…Keira, now is the time to tell your husband what really has been going on between your dau…" I was suddenly cut off when I heard the clattering of books landing on the floor. Then, as I turned around to take in the room, I let my clouded senses clear and pushed my mind into searching the space. A feeling of dread lay like a ball of lead in my stomach and for good reason.

For it was a dread that turned into cold hard fear the moment I smelled my blood.

Mine and…

"Amelia?"

CHAPTER TWENTY-NINE

AMELIA

MAP OF SORROWS

The second I read that name on the map I knew it had something to do with Lucius' past life. I also knew that this was the break we had finally been looking for!

So, naturally, I had scrambled to my feet after first folding up the map, one now stained with my blood, and putting it back into my pocket. Then I closed the lid on the box and with it firmly in my grip, I raced through the Temple with only one mission in mind...

I had to reach Lucius!

I had to tell him what I had learned as soon as possible, it was too important. Now all I could hope for was that Lucius would take me with him as it was starting to look like he would need me. Because whatever had happened back in my father's vault, there was one thing that remained clear, I had just managed to kick her ass! Now I don't know exactly how I had just done that, but I knew one thing, that river of blood had been my doing, *not hers.* Which meant I needed to find out why or how I had managed to do that and I had a feeling those answers were only to be found by using this map.

So, I ran until I found the bookcase door I knew led back into the library, only I didn't account for it not having a door handle. I lifted my hand, getting ready to knock but then looked for a space to even do that.

"Great! Just fuc...wait a minute." I stopped myself mid-rant when I noticed one book on the shelf of classics stood out from all the rest.

"But of course," I said as I grasped the spine of Jane Eyre by Charlotte Bronte, knowing that it was my mother's favourite book. Then I pulled on it and the second I heard the lock click before opening, I grinned big, feeling pretty good about myself right then!

So, I slipped back inside the library and rushed towards the door, ready to scream Lucius' name from the rooftops if need be. Of course, the second I heard his voice, I grinned again, thinking, 'boy that was easy'. But then I also heard my mother's voice straight after it and it was one that strangely... *sounded panicked.*

So, despite knowing it was wrong, I got closer to the door and heard the tail end of a sentence,

"...because I am not free to fucking claim what is rightfully mine in this house!" Lucius shouted and I sucked in a staggered breath, asking myself if he had been saying that about me or about her?

Oh Gods, I wanted to open the door and put a stop to it all. To take the chance and trust him that it was about me. But after today and knowing that he had lied about being with her...well then, I found myself running back into the room. Then I quickly hid in the same place I used to as a child when it was time for bed. It was the gap at the back of the spiral staircase, that was thick enough wood that it hid all of me.

Of course, there had been more room back there when I had been a child without breasts. But with the bookcase at my back and barely a crack in the wood to see through, I remained as still as I could, which wasn't hard considering the little space I had. But then they both walked through the doors and after a brief glance to find it empty, Lucius stormed further inside in long, irritated steps, making me question what they were arguing about?

Was it about me?

Well, unfortunately for me, I was about to find out. Starting with Lucius admitting,

"I just can't do this anymore, keeping up this fucking pretence!" He seemed so angry and I still had to question if it was about me, and if so, then how did my mother find out about us…had it been Vincent?

"I know, but just for a little longer, alright?" my mum said in return and it was done so in a way that could only mean one thing…

She hadn't just found out at all…*she fucking knew*.

"Why, why do we have to fucking wait?! Don't you think I have waited long enough?!" Lucius almost growled the words at her, and I could barely believe what I was hearing but then trying to make sense of it wasn't happening like I wanted it too!

"I have done everything you asked, Keira, I have waited…" Lucius then continued to say, which was when the true horror of my mother's part in this came to light,

"Yes, beyond the time I said was right, Luc, don't forget that, as it's not like you didn't have your chances back then!" I swear but forcing myself not to react to this was more painful than the cuts in my hand! One that I wanted to ball into a fist and I would have done just that had I not been too afraid of crying out in pain and giving myself away. Although, the sound of my utter heartbreak was close to doing that for me!

Because I knew then that what I was witnessing wasn't about me and Lucius being lovers, it was about...

Their affair.

I swear the knowledge almost brought me to my fucking knees!

"Yes, well the limits to my patience should be understandable then, shouldn't they?" This was Lucius' sharp reply, making her release a deep sigh before my name was then mentioned, cutting me even deeper by the utter betrayal I felt by the two of them.

"And what about Amelia, huh, you need to think of her, to say anything now would only hurt her." Too fucking late for that, mother!

"She too needs her own family to know the truth before she can then move on from the pain," Lucius replied, thinking that I ever would be able to move on from such a thing...*was he fucking insane!?*

"But now, really?" Was my mother's argument and I had to say that my thoughts also went to my dad, who had no idea the level of deceit that awaited him.

"Yes, now!" Lucius shouted back close to losing his shit, a sight I had seen all before.

"And Draven, what do you think will happen...? Don't you realise how many will get hurt if you tell people now, if you tell people what we have hidden from them for so many years?" Oh Gods, but it was getting worse! My poor, poor father! How could my mother do this to him! I thought they fucking adored each other, or maybe after stepping inside that vault, then it was only ever one sided?

"Out of my respect and care for you, I have kept quiet, Keira." Lucius said in a stern tone,

"I know, Luc…I know," my mother said before going to him, and I swear I couldn't fucking breathe seeing it, as it was no longer just words but actions adding to the pain of them. I couldn't see it completely as he had his back to me, but I could see her hand on his gloved one, and instead of removing it like he always did with me, he covered it with his own hand keeping it there.

"Amelia needs to know, and I can't keep pretending anymore, especially here, *it's fucking killing me, Keira,*" he said and this was when my tears of agony finally broke free and started streaming down my face as I put my bloody hand to my mouth. Doing so as a fist now relishing the pain. Because the torture I felt now was far worse than opening up a wound.

So, I cried silently, and when I saw his head lower ready to kiss her, I finally tore my eyes from the sight when I saw her cupping his cheek ready to receive it.

Their kiss being the last piece of my heart being ripped to shreds by their betrayal. But as I sobbed as silently as I could, I also couldn't stop my whole body from shaking.

"We can't do it, not yet, we can't tell Draven." I heard her say and watched then as a quick action drew my attention back as Lucius had pulled from her embrace.

"Well, you may not, but I can!" he snapped, and I shook my head asking myself what madness had overtaken him…

My father would kill him, despite what that could do.

"I still don't think this is the right time," she argued further and had I not still been utterly devastated I would have scoffed at this, if she believed there was ever such a time.

"Keira, you know my feelings towards you, you have known for a long time. How much I respected you for your own decisions, but you also have known my own and the reasons behind them. Now I have waited, a very long time..." Lucius told her needing to cut her off when she said,

"I know but..."

"...and I have done so patiently upon your request out of respect for your husband. I have done everything you asked, I have protected Amelia in every way I could, as you begged me to do. But now it is my turn to act, for I will not hold back my feelings any longer..." As he paused this was when I couldn't stop the uncontrollable shaking and I took a step back thinking there would be room to do so when there wasn't. But no, there was nothing behind me but empty words and promises of fairy tales. I knew that when books all started to fall to the floor making me look down and in that moment I saw my childhood book at my feet.

It was cruelly opened on a page at the end where the Prince was kissing his Princess with those fateful words written so elegantly underneath the lovers. To three words that were nothing but lies!

I also watched strangely fascinated for a moment as my blood dripped down onto the page, landing over the couple kissing. It felt in that moment so symbolic that at first my mind had a job to recall the last sentence he said before calling my name.

"Keira, now is the time to tell your husband what really has been going on between your dau...Amelia?" I swallowed down the pain of hearing him saying my name for what I knew would be the last time.

I fucking vowed it!

For I stepped out from behind the staircase, stepping on the pages of my childhood dreams, letting the moment become an emblematic reminder that fairy tales were a fucking lie and those three words, that fucking 'happy ever after' didn't happen!

And Lucius knew. He knew the moment I stepped out from my hiding place that with one look at me…

He knew he had broken me for the last time.

"Oh Gods, Fae! I…we…didn't mean for you find out this way…we didn't know you…" I had to hold myself back from snarling at her as I let my pain rip through me and peel away the layers of agony until they found the anger that I needed to get the fuck out of here.

"Oh, I know you didn't!" I snapped and Lucius looked me up and down, focusing on my injured hand and then at the box in the other. I could see him now trying to piece it all together. But it was when coming to the streaming black track marks of my tears I knew would be there due to the mistake of using mascara that day.

"It is not what you think it is, my Khu…"

"NO!" I shouted, no, not shouted but fucking roared! I had roared so loud, I swear I thought I heard the whole fucking building groan!

"You don't EVER, ever get to call me that again!" I screamed at him making him flinch, but still he held himself in place before raising his hands slowly as if dealing with a wild animal about to lash out at him. But my mum was muttering, asking him what was going on? What was going on…? *Was she fucking insane!?*

"Alright now, Pet, let's just take a breath and calm things…"

"Calm things down…are you fucking serious right now!?" I snapped before getting in his face pushing the box to his chest and screaming in his face,

"YOU'RE FUCKING MY MOTHER!" Then I ignored everything that happened next. My mother's horrified cry, Lucius' roar of anger as I suddenly ran from the room. My mum trying to reach for me whilst I did snarl at her this time,

"Don't fucking touch me! I never want to see you again! Neither of you…you are both…*lost to me!*" I said unable to say the words I had wanted to say but my heart wouldn't let me.

To say that they were both dead to me.

Then I ran from the room, tears flooding my vision to the sound of Lucius' rage, one I knew would find me should I stay here. But then after this, that was never going to be an option.

I had to leave!

I had to go and this time I wasn't sure if I was ever coming back.

That thought caused me pain but not nearly enough as what I just witnessed. I looked back over my shoulder to hear a door being torn open and my mother arguing with him, no doubt trying to get him to calm down. But then she could only do so much, and I knew in that moment it was Lucius trying to chase after me!

I just didn't understand why he would even bother!

But then, when doing this, I also bumped into the only person that could save me right now.

"Dad!"

"Amelia, what's wrong! What happened?!" he said taking me in his arms and for merely a second I allowed his arms to comfort me as I sobbed. But then, when looking up at him, I knew he too needed to know the truth. Because, despite what I thought before, he wouldn't kill Lucius, he wouldn't because that would mean harming his Chosen One. Someone I knew he would love despite her betrayal.

"Dad, I have to leave… I have to get out of here, please!" I begged as I tore myself from his arms and the second he tried to reach for me, I told him,

"I'm so sorry, dad…I…"

"What is it Amelia, tell me?!"

"I am so sorry, I just…" I took a deep breath, heard the last of Lucius' roars and committed to the decision to tell him,

"…I just caught Lucius kissing mum!" I told him and this time it wasn't Lucius' roars of rage I heard…

No, now it was my father's.

I then knew that as much as it pained me to see my dad's face turn murderous and seeping into his demon side, I knew it would also give me the time needed to escape.

And I did.

For I ran and ran and ran.

And in doing so, I not only escaped Afterlife.

I escaped My Chosen One,

My Vampire King,

My Lucius.

For all I had left now was a Map…

Of Sorrows.

ABOUT THE AUTHOR

Stephanie Hudson has dreamed of being a writer ever since her obsession with reading books at an early age. What first became a quest to overcome the boundaries set against her in the form of dyslexia has turned into a life's dream. She first started writing in the form of poetry and soon found a taste for horror and romance. Afterlife is her first book in the series of twelve, with the story of Keira and Draven becoming ever more complicated in a world that sets them miles apart.

When not writing, Stephanie enjoys spending time with her loving family and friends, chatting for hours with her biggest fan, her sister Cathy who is utterly obsessed with one gorgeous Dominic Draven. And of course, spending as much time with her supportive partner and personal muse, Blake who is there for her no matter what.

Author's words.

My love and devotion is to all my wonderful fans that keep me going into the wee hours of the night but foremost to my wonderful daughter Ava...who yes, is named after a cool, kick-ass, Demonic bird and my sons, Jack, who is a little hero and Baby Halen, who yes, keeps me up at night but it's okay because he is named after a Guitar legend!

Keep updated with all new release news & more on my website

www.afterlifesaga.com
Never miss out, sign up to the
mailing list at the website.

Also, please feel free to join myself and other Dravenites on my Facebook group
Afterlife Saga Official Fan
Interact with me and other fans. Can't wait to see you there!

facebook.com/AfterlifeSaga
twitter.com/afterlifesaga
instagram.com/theafterlifesaga

ACKNOWLEDGEMENTS

Well first and foremost my love goes out to all the people who deserve the most thanks and are the wonderful people that keep me going day to day. But most importantly they are the ones that allow me to continue living out my dreams and keep writing my stories for the world to hopefully enjoy… These people are of course YOU! Words will never be able to express the full amount of love I have for you guys. Your support is never ending. Your trust in me and the story is never failing. But more than that, your love for me and all who you consider your 'Afterlife family' is to be commended, treasured and admired. Thank you just doesn't seem enough, so one day I hope to meet you all and buy you all a drink! ;)

To my family… To my amazing mother, who has believed in me from the very beginning and doesn't believe that something great should be hidden from the world. I would like to thank you for all the hard work you put into my books and the endless hours spent caring about my words and making sure it is the best it can be for everyone to enjoy. You make Afterlife shine. To my wonderful crazy father who is and always has been my hero in life. Your strength astonishes me, even to this day and the love and care you hold for your family is a gift you give to the Hudson name. And last but not least, to the man that I consider my soul mate. The man who taught me about real love and makes me not only want to be a better person but makes me feel I am too. The amount of support you have given me since we met has been incredible and the greatest feeling was finding out you wanted to spend the rest of your life with me when you asked me to marry you.

All my love to my dear husband and my own personal Draven… Mr Blake Hudson.

Another personal thank you goes to my dear friend Caroline Fairbairn and her wonderful family that have embraced my brand of crazy into their lives and given it a hug when most needed.

For their friendship I will forever be eternally grateful.

I would also like to mention Claire Boyle my wonderful PA, who without a doubt, keeps me sane and constantly smiling through all the chaos which is my life ;) And a loving mention goes to Lisa Jane for always giving me a giggle and scaring me to death with all her count down pictures lol ;)

Thank you for all your hard work and devotion to the saga and myself. And always going that extra mile, pushing Afterlife into the spotlight you think it deserves. Basically helping me achieve my secret goal of world domination one day…evil laugh time… Mwahaha! Joking of course ;)

As before, a big shout has to go to all my wonderful fans who make it their mission to spread the Afterlife word and always go the extra mile. I love you all x

ALSO BY STEPHANIE HUDSON

Afterlife Saga

A Brooding King, A Girl running from her past. What happens when the two collide?

Book 1 - Afterlife

Book 2 - The Two Kings

Book 3 - The Triple Goddess

Book 4 - The Quarter Moon

Book 5 - The Pentagram Child /Part 1

Book 6 - The Pentagram Child /Part 2

Book 7 - The Cult of the Hexad

Book 8 - Sacrifice of the Septimus /Part 1

Book 9 - Sacrifice of the Septimus /Part 2

Book 10 -Blood of the Infinity War

Book 11 -Happy Ever Afterlife /Part 1

Book 12 -Happy Ever Afterlife / Part 2

Transfusion Saga

What happens when an ordinary human girl comes face to face with the cruel Vampire King who dismissed her seven years ago?

Transfusion - Book 1

Venom of God - Book 2

Blood of Kings - Book 3

Rise of Ashes - Book 4

Map of Sorrows - Book 5

Tree of Souls - Book 6

Kingdoms of Hell – Book 7

Eyes of Crimson - Book 8

Afterlife Chronicles: (Young Adult Series)

The Glass Dagger – Book 1

The Hells Ring – Book 2

Stephanie Hudson and Blake Hudson

The Devil in Me

OTHER WORKS BY HUDSON INDIE INK

Paranormal Romance/Urban Fantasy

Sloane Murphy

Xen Randell

C. L. Monaghan

Sci-fi/Fantasy

Brandon Ellis

Devin Hanson

Crime/Action

Blake Hudson

Mike Gomes

Contemporary Romance

Gemma Weir

Elodie Colt

Ann B. Harrison

Ingram Content Group UK Ltd.
Milton Keynes UK
UKHW011258160523
421838UK00001B/173